A COAST-TO-COAST MICHIGAN MYSTERY

NORTHERN LIGHT

A NOVEL

DEB DAVIES

Livonia, Michigan

Edited by Chelsea Cambeis
Proofread by Hannah Ryder

NORTHERN LIGHT

Copyright © 2020 Deb Davies

Published by BHC Press

Library of Congress Control Number:
2019954386

ISBN: 978-1-64397-120-9 (Hardcover)
ISBN: 978-1-64397-121-6 (Softcover)
ISBN: 978-1-64397-122-3 (Ebook)

For information, write:
BHC Press
885 Penniman #5505
Plymouth, MI 48170

Visit the publisher:
www.bhcpress.com

To my family,
who have always encouraged me to write.

NORTHERN LIGHT

1

LOOKING FOR A NEW NORMAL

Claire and Laurel were sitting at a heart pine table, letting the day fade. The kitchen cupboards had, at some point in time, been painted lemon yellow, but the wood had been dented and touched up with lighter shades. White café curtains were pushed back from the two six-over-six windows facing the North Branch of the Au Sable. Sunlight lit the row of tall cedar trees that ran along the road to the east and turned a corner, shielding the garage that held what had been, for Claire's late husband George, a "driving around" car.

"Congratulations on your divorce," Claire said. "We should toast!" She poured out the last of the wine in the bottle, so bubbles wobbled and burst on the rim of Laurel's glass.

When Claire had transferred to ninth grade in Wyoming, a Grand Rapids suburb, Claire's would-be followers arrived in a gaggle, awed by Claire's physical attributes: blond hair, green eyes, heavy breasts, narrow waist, long legs. But that Claire wasn't who Claire was, or would be. She was still tree-climbing Claire, stone-skipping Claire, Claire who played street hockey with her brothers. Her brothers had let her be the goalie as a joke. Her nose had been broken in an hour, but she'd toughed her way through the taunts, split lips, and black eyes, and been their goalie in a number of games. Her mother was German and had read them Grimms' fairy tales; her Irish father adored *Beowulf* and crowed over the gore.

Arriving at her new school, Claire had sized up her admirers and decided to be practical. Win more flies with honey, her mother would say, and so Claire was kind to everyone. She relived the colossal relief she felt when she realized Laurel walked to school and back the same way she did. Laurel who was not popular, but was skeptical, honest, and, thank the Lord, smart.

A flood of good memories swept over her. Sharing a family vacation at a small Michigan beach. Swimming, running, swinging out on a rope swing tied to a tree on a hilltop, then letting go to land with a splash in deep water. Sitting up at night on a shed roof, looking at the stars, talking about plans for the future.

Laurel, even when she was that young, had wanted to be a teacher. After getting her Master's degree in English Education, she became an assistant professor at the same community college where David, her husband, taught literature. Claire had wanted to travel, and she and George had done that, never making it to Europe but touring Nova Scotia, New Orleans, and the Hawaiian Island of Kauai.

"What did we used to sing? 'Make new friends but keep the old'?"

"Who are you calling 'old'?" Laurel sounded rueful.

Claire looked at Laurel, whose thick, dark, short hair, now showing some white, looked part pixie cut, part hacked-off. Her arms and hips were thinner, and she had laugh lines around her eyes, but in her green rayon tank top, shorts, and amber framed glasses, she looked much the way she had when Claire had last seen her. Laurel, when she arrived, had looked at Claire, seeing places where her friend's once dark mahogany hair had faded to toasted marshmallow. Claire's pink, striped sundress revealed tops of breasts beginning to permanently freckle.

Neither woman had looked at the other for signs of age or mileage. Rather, each looked for reassurance time had not changed the connection that, since ninth grade, had made them instant friends.

"To you," Claire said.

"To us," Laurel responded, pulling her glasses down on her nose to look at Claire.

They clinked glasses. Laurel was sipping from a Waterford wine glass with a chipped rim, and Claire took a gulp of scotch from her own glass, big enough to be an iced tea tumbler.

"You made new friends here," Laurel said. "Which is a damn good thing, because I didn't get here when George died. I thought I would be here instantly, but David kept protesting he would turn over a new leaf, and Jen—our supposedly all-grown-up college graduate—fell completely, inexplicably apart. How could I divorce her father *now*? She wanted all three of us to go to counseling. She and I went. When David finally came, he tried to charm the counselor, who said I should dump him on his ass. So counseling helped, but the process took forever. By the time Jen took off with friends 'to heal,' as she put it, you had already gone through some of the shock of losing your husband within two years of moving to a new place. Be honest, Claire. We promised we would be. How awful do you feel? Do you hate me because I didn't come?"

"I'm mostly all right, I think. Of course I don't hate you. You called. You wrote. You know I've always kept your letters." Claire swiped tears from under her eyes. "Things could have been worse. George's death was peaceful. And you're right; we made friends here, so I had generous support. Maybe I ran on adrenaline, because now, I'm always tired. If I drink enough coffee or scotch, I can do odds and ends, but I don't seem to get anything done. I need to get my hair cut. Maybe colored. George would hate the way I look."

Laurel put down her glass, reached over, and not for the first time since she'd arrived, hugged Claire gently. "You will always be my beautiful best friend. You'll turn heads of lustful men when you're ninety-five."

"God, I hope not," Claire said.

The house was quiet. Both women took a deep breath and relaxed.

Claire's neighbors had welcomed Laurel and were gone, leaving leftover food they had brought: deviled eggs, hummus, fresh pita, a white china bowl of dark, sweet Michigan cherries. The remains of a New York style cheesecake still sat between them.

"Your friends here are interesting." Laurel waved a fork at Claire. "I think they were nice to me because they're worried about you living here by yourself. I have to say, I am flabbergasted to find you here, with or without George. I thought you two loved the condo in Grand Rapids and the life you had. Concerts and fundraisers and bookstores."

"Lots of single people live alone. I'm not on the yellow brick road here. You make my life sound like lions and tigers and bears."

"I was thinking thunderstorms and snow, and no power."

"I'll figure it out, Laurel. George lived in this area when he was younger, and moving here remained an ongoing dream for him. He liked working as a bank examiner when he was younger, but his job meant he traveled a lot. Expressways got busier, speed limits got higher, and his boss wanted his reports e-mailed the day before yesterday. He dreamed about retiring to a simpler life. We talked about Gaylord, which has class; Fairview, which has hills; and Oscoda, which has the beach on Lake Huron. Then he found this place, and the odd thing was that this exact same house had been his nana's—his grandparents'—home, up for sale after a different family moved out. They took his first offer. My gosh, Laurel, you should see your face!"

After a pause, Claire added, "Of course, if we'd known what was going to happen, we would have stayed in Grand Rapids. Oh, Laurel, don't cry. Do you want some more wine? There's more wine, more scotch, and more bourbon in the basement."

"I don't want more wine!" Laurel rubbed the back of her hand under her nose. "I want to have helped, Claire! We promised we would always help each other, no matter where life took us."

"We were kids, Laurel. We didn't know how tangled adult lives get. And you still can help. Look, isn't this sunset gorgeous?"

The sun had started to slide behind the oak trees on the far bank of the river, but was still reflecting off the water and pouring through the west windows. They couldn't see the river clearly. The bank nearest the kitchen was a tangle of raspberry creepers and tree-strangling nets of wild grapes draped over stunted cedars and tamaracks.

"I've already gone through mourning." Claire sounded determined. "I am not going to waste your visit doing it again. Even after he was sick, George never forgot how happy he was here, as a kid, catching his first trout in the river, eating wild blueberries, finding morels. The Campbells—that was their place to the south, before it burned—remember him first coming over when he was younger than four years old. Before he retired, we enjoyed planning what we'd do here: looking up repair options online, budgeting, watching *This Old House*."

Laurel could not picture George as a four-year-old boy. He'd loved good cars, expensive scotch, and good cigars. "Wild blueberries. Huh," she said.

"We didn't give up our lives when we moved here; we just changed them. Plus, once George retired, we weren't in his business friends' everyday lives. Friendships drift. People moved to live near their grandkids. Retired corporate friends moved to New Jersey or Gulf Shores. I may have more support than I did before we moved. This might have been an awful time to throw you a welcome party, Laurel, but the people we've gotten to know are welcoming, and they wanted to meet you. They seem drawn to this house."

"They're drawn to you." Laurel's tone was wry. "People always have been."

The flick of a cat door announced the arrival of a small black cat. Its hair was neither long nor short. It had small, owl-like ear tufts and a plume-shaped tail that stuck up like a bottle brush. Regarding Laurel with round gold eyes, it opened its mouth, revealing small, even white teeth and a curled red tongue, and made a noise that sounded like "mao."

"Yours?" Laurel asked.

"I think so," Claire said. "He has taken to sleeping near me. Pour him some cream, would you? You're closer to the refrigerator."

Laurel found a saucer and complied while the cat transferred his attention to her leather sandals, rolling on her feet and rubbing the side of his head against her ankles. He brought in outdoor smells of sun and clean dirt and pine needles and grass.

"You're a hit," Claire said. "He turned up on the patio a few days after George died."

"You know what most people would say."

"That it's George's spirit? I doubt it. George was lactose intolerant."

"Are you going to keep him?"

The cat eyed Laurel while she supplied another installment. From this angle, Laurel could see a little streak of white hair, like spilled cream, running down his throat and chest.

He stretched out one fur-pantalooned leg at a time and cleaned his paws before getting up, stomping over to the cat door, and butting it open with his head to let himself out on the porch.

"If he'll be a kept cat. I managed to get him in to Sanjay, my vet and a friend—you'll meet him—to be checked out and neutered. He didn't claw me, but he knocked a screen loose when I took him home and closed him in the house. So I had the cat door installed, and I give him a bowl of food twice a day. He likes me better now that he can come and go."

"What did the vet say?"

"Young, already neutered, with a chip that no one had ever bothered to register. Maybe someone left him. I don't know why he took to you so fast," Claire said.

"Recognized that I put up with bullshit?"

"Laurel, your David—"

"Not mine anymore."

"David," Claire continued, "couldn't keep his dick in his pants."

"Worse, he couldn't keep it out of my friends' private parts." Laurel tried to look determinedly amused and failed.

"Some friends those were," Claire said. "I hope your divorce attorney was not someone David slept with."

"I hired a lawyer from out of town," Laurel told her. "If David had been a teeny bit more discreet, we might have parted amicably. The last straw was when he and Beth Nelson—the woman who helped him input his grades—fell asleep together on the floor of his office and his officemate came in at 2:00 a.m. to work on assignments. His officemate tripped on them and dropped his computer on the arch of David's right foot, breaking four of the long bones." A quirky smile touched Laurel's face.

"You are smug," Claire said. "Good for you, Laurel!"

"You know what pisses me off," Laurel responded, "is my other friends—those who didn't succumb to David's charm—told me if I'd kept him under my thumb, I could have stopped his sampling, which definitely got worse as we got older. Oh, wait. I almost forgot the people who told me if I grew my hair out, got a boob job, and kept dying my hair different colors, he'd come back to me. People who cared about me said he would hump a catsup bottle. Even Beth dumped him."

"George thought David had an ego problem."

"A *what*? Was George losing his grip on reality?" She paused. "Sorry, Claire, I did think you'd tell George, but I never thought anyone could believe David lacked chutzpah. Still, that 'losing his grip' comment was an awful thing for me to say."

"George said there was a guy he worked with who, every time he got passed over for promotion, sued for a divorce and married someone younger. Not necessarily someone prettier than the woman he'd been living with, but someone who was easily impressed."

Laurel wrinkled her forehead. "George's theory might be right, especially for people who teach in colleges. Boy Genius earns his doctorate. He then has to wallow in office politics and chair committees before he gets tenure. But by then, B. G. sports a bald spot and is stuck behind a desk, supervising hotshot kids with new ideas and research. That definitely happened to David."

"That sounded sympathetic. Do you miss him?" Claire asked.

"I miss him," Laurel admitted. "And he always was crazy about Jen. I still picture him carrying her on his shoulders when she was a toddler and wanted to see over crowds. I miss him partly because he's in my memories of those years. I did shit work for him. Ironed his shirts and sent out his manuscripts. I miss him the way I miss my mother, some days. She and I were never Hallmark card close, but there are days when I find I'm talking to her about something no one else would remember. Her recipe, say, for spice cake with meringue topping."

"She gave me that recipe too," Claire said. "I've never made it, but I can share it with you. Heck, some day, when we feel better, we could even try to make it."

Both were quiet for a while, watching the sun slip below the trees. Laurel broke the silence.

"What do you call the cat?"

"Pearl," Claire said, "and I'm not changing it. Black Pearl, if we're being formal. I thought he was female. Scrape up the last of your cheesecake, and we'll get you unpacked." She reached down to get Laurel's gym bag and then winced, dropping it.

"I'm not packing any barbells or bricks, and not many books," Laurel said. "I know you used to heft crates around at the bookstore when you worked there. What hurts? Your knee? Your shoulder? How did you do it?"

"Crud," Claire said. "See that door to the right of the windows? How clean and shiny the floor is? I paid for that cleanliness, but I'm not telling you how until I freshen up my drink and get you settled in."

2

WHO'S WHO

"This was a dining room," Claire explained, leading Laurel through a small dim room lined with books. "George turned it into his library. You can come back and browse later."

They stepped into a long room, wood blinds drawn over a wall of west-facing windows. Claire pulled the cord on the blinds so Laurel could see more of the world. There were taller trees outside these windows—a few oak and hickory—also swathed by climbing vines, and when Claire pushed open the door to the overgrown flagstone patio, they could hear the river, gurgling and swooshing around fallen trees and stones. A little bleak, Laurel thought, neither wild nor domesticated, but "How beautiful!" was what she said.

Laurel could feel Claire's presence in the living room. In one corner, a black grand piano lurked, top down. She remembered Claire had taken lessons, at George's suggestion, but that Claire had said the only things she'd learned to play were "Londonderry Air" and "Loch Lomond." On the top of the piano, a blue ceramic bowl full of past-their-prime oranges perfumed the air with citrus and a hint of citrus mold, next to three of George's white T-shirts and one of Claire's recently shed, apricot-colored brassieres. Mismatched afghans and quilts slumped on the floor near the door wall. Books and magazines, ranging from Atul Gawande's *Being Mortal* to back issues of *Cosmopolitan* ranged across the couch.

George's taste was also obvious. The color scheme was brown and navy blue, dominated by a plaid couch and a cream-colored recliner, and blue throw pillows on rocking chairs. Oil paintings of ducks taking flight hung above the piano. *The Economist* magazines, also obviously George's, were piled in stacks beneath it.

"I'm still sorting through things." Claire sounded defensive.

"Homey," Laurel said. She sat down on the nubby beige carpet. "Let's just hang out for a while." She was trying to absorb the atmosphere of the room, in part familiar but also somehow foreign. Brown and blue weren't colors she associated with Claire. Aqua, maybe. Gold. Caribbean colors. What had it felt like, for Claire to walk into this room by herself, when so much in it reminded her of loss? When friends had crowded it barely an hour ago—laughing and eating, joking and drinking—the tone and conversation had felt casual, with many references to "up north," which in Michigan, meant anything north of the town of Clare. Now, Black Pearl, who had swaggered in after them and sprawled on the carpet, was the only spontaneous touch of life in the room.

"Claire, help me out," she said. "I can't remember all your friends. This wine is a lot better than anything I'm used to, and I've drunk a liter of it."

Claire plonked down in the recliner, looking pleased. "Prepare for a quiz," she said. "Ann Campbell."

"I know her," Laurel answered. "She brought New York-style cheesecake! She looked like the cheesecake—medium height, plump, gold-brown hair the color of cheesecake crust."

"Patsy Cluny."

"Wasn't that a big band singer?"

"No, numb nuts. You're thinking of Rosemary Clooney and Patsy Cline. My Patsy is Ann's friend, older than Ann. She has dyed, walnut-colored puffy hair and superpowers."

"Numb nuts is not gender appropriate. And Patsy can't have superpowers."

"Why not?" Claire frowned.

"Too old," Laurel said.

"You haven't been keeping up on super women," Claire said. "Patsy's stronger than you'd think. She and Ann haul heavy crates around a store. You'll see."

"The woman with the white Mohawk? Does she have superpowers?"

"Ah. That's Zoe Weathers." Claire shook her head. "Don't let the designer blue jeans and motorcycle jacket fool you. She's a retired doctor who inherited money and has a loud voice and a soft heart. Though, if she sees someone hurt an animal, she turns into Boadicea."

"No rings. Diamond stud earring, left ear. Is she gay? Divorced?"

"No. Zoe doesn't believe in marriage, but she does have a lover—my veterinarian. Sanjay Kaufmann. You'll know him when you see him. He's about five feet, eight inches tall, with curly black hair, a curly black beard, and muscles like a weight lifter. He couldn't be here tonight because he's delivering a foal.

"I hadn't thought about it before, but George and I attracted friends who are animal lovers. The guests who were wearing jeans and World Wildlife sweatshirts, Bill and Barbara Marsh, have a farm and take in animals that need care most people wouldn't provide. Or just animals that need care. I'm not sure about the donkeys, but they have expensive animals, mostly, like a llama with ingrown eyelashes. It went to a llama farm, once it had recovered. Ann and Patsy help with spare kittens. Maybe people here look after me because I'm some kind of stray."

"Didn't any of your Grand Rapids friends visit when you moved here?"

"Oh, sure. Some would come and stay for the weekend, sort of like in *Downton Abbey*, only not much illicit sex. That's part of the reason we did some modest remodeling."

"This door wall is new?"

"That was the most important change for me. Can you imagine this house, but without living room windows that faced the river? I guess a lot of farmhouses were built facing the road. The old door is still facing the front, but we don't use it. In fact, it's stuck shut. We redid plumbing and added a bedroom and bathroom on the northeast corner of the house. We replaced all the clapboard siding. Upstairs, we took down a wall between two of the small bedrooms, leaving a 'master,' which is an awful name for any room.

"Then George started sleeping more, even when friends came to visit. He lost some coordination in his right arm. He thought it might be Parkinson's, which would have been hard enough, but as you know, it was brain cancer. He didn't have pain, but more and more often, he couldn't think of a word or remember someone's name."

"I should have come," Laurel said for the tenth time.

"I don't think so." Claire patted Pearl and shook her head. "His private side, which did surface when he was stressed, took him over. It was hard to get him to even let me know what he was thinking, let alone what he was feeling. He wasn't a vain man, but people have boundaries. He wouldn't have thanked you or me, Laurel. Overnight guests were too much for him."

"Well, I'm here now. I can fetch, tote, help you sort through George's clothes. But if I'm crowding you, Claire, kick me out."

"I run out of energy for some things. I could use some help sorting the rest of George's clothes. He didn't bring much in the way of old clothes here, but I've been putting piles of brand-new T-shirts and shorts and wool socks on the bed in the small upstairs bedroom. I thought I'd send them to assisted living homes. Barbara Marsh took his coats to the homeless shelter. I keep opening drawers and finding handkerchiefs, tie clips, and receipts. But Laurel, I want you here to help me do something more important. I had done some of my grieving before George died. I'm trying to find my new normal. I need to blend who I've been and who I am now." She slid her wedding ring—a plain gold band—up and down on her finger. "I didn't wear this ring much when I was home. I was afraid I'd scratch it or lose it down the drain. If I don't wear it now, will people think I want to forget George?"

"Good friends wouldn't think that," Laurel said. "Got another example?"

"I remember I don't have to put the seat down before I sit on the toilet, for fear I'll get my fanny stuck because George left the seat up, but I still lie in bed some mornings thinking he'll bring me coffee."

Laurel stifled the thought that Claire could not, since her teens, have gotten her behind stuck in a toilet.

"Do I lock doors, now that I'm alone? We never used to."

"You could get an alarm system."

"I should," Claire decided. "That's a good thought. You're making me feel better already. It'll be just us women, so no toilet seats will be up, and some mornings I'll wake you up and bring you coffee. I want to talk and laugh and enjoy seeing you and Jen. I love it that your daughter calls me 'Aunt Claire.' She just finished her dissertation in anthro-linguistic something or other, isn't that right?"

Laurel felt troubled. "Mostly right. Turns out what I told her is true. There aren't a lot of full-time jobs in linguistic anthropology. She's thinking about doing the program at Parsons School of Design. Sorry, but about the toilet seats? She texted me this afternoon. She might bring a guy, if that's all right with you. Someone she met on a plane. I hated to text back 'no' just when I've sold the house where she grew up."

"My new normal is flexible," Claire said. "I can lower toilet seats. By the way, I mostly sleep in the recliner or on the couch. Or I travel from one to another, clutching pillows and a quilt. I don't use the bedroom upstairs. Too many memories. And the mattresses on the beds upstairs are hard, the way George liked them. But Jen and her friend should be able to deal with that, right?"

"Good memories?" Laurel asked cautiously. "That's not where George died, is it?"

"Absolutely not. He died in a leather camp chair on the patio, looking out at trees on the other side of the river. I went to get him ice chips, and when I came back, he had stopped breathing. The emergency responders called his doctor, who told them not to try to bring him back.

"I have extremely nice memories," Claire continued. "Some of the best are of him reading before he went to sleep at night, with his socks still on, his legs crossed, and his gold-rim bifocals down on his nose. Though there *were* activities that meant taking off the glasses and digging them out of bedclothes in the morning."

She got up, stretched, and beckoned Laurel to follow her down a small hall. "Right this way—I'm putting you in the bedroom just around the corner, where we added a bath. This is the room I took charge of, and I like the way it turned out."

The room they entered could have been as old as the rest of the house. There was no bedspread on the bed, but the white wool blanket had been turned back to show yellow-flowered sheets that matched the pillowcases. There was an old-fashioned cut lace scarf on the green-painted chest of drawers. An antique globed lamp, the interior of the globe painted with daisies, sat squarely in the middle of the scarf. The room smelled slightly of potpourri sachet. Cut lace curtains had been pulled back to show a sliver of a moon.

"Nice," Laurel said, dropping her gym bag on the bed.

Claire pushed open the door to a small bathroom that displayed a fiberglass, reproduction clawfoot tub, topped by a wooden rack that would hold candles or a drink, and keep a book upright.

"Towel racks are on the door, and there's this little closet for towels and toiletries. The door locks, if you want privacy."

"Where'd you find the old wood doors? This one must have been cut down."

"You know, I never asked the guys who put this in. I told them I wanted this room to blend in, and they went out of their way to please me," Claire said. "I don't think they charged me extra, and I never thanked them for it."

They sat side by side on the edge of the bed, the old box spring protesting. Claire's sundress hiked up, revealing ladders of purple, swollen flesh from her ankles to her knees.

"All right." Laurel frowned. "No more procrastinating. Tell me what happened to your legs. Were you in an accident?"

"This," Claire said ruefully, "is from the help I got, cleaning. It's actually a funny story, but ouch! It hurts a lot. Patsy Cluny, the friend of Ann Campbell, lives with Ann and in return, helps out in Ann's store and cleans for her sometimes. After George died, Ann sent her over to do some cleaning before the funeral luncheon. Patsy was *empowered*. She used this soap and vinegar concoction to get every vestige of grease off appliances and cupboard doors and trays that would hold the goodies Ann sent. We didn't have a lot of people here, just the people you met tonight, Sanjay, and Ann's daughter Tansy. The minister was a nice Episcopalian woman who said all the right things, even though George hadn't been to church in years. I ended up crying, which probably helped."

"Yes," Laurel agreed. "But your knees."

"I told Patsy not to use the vinegar and soap mix on the floors, because it's amazingly slippery—as slippery as oil. She said she wouldn't. But, she did. Patsy has this funny turn of phrase: 'And yet...' She'll say, 'It wasn't supposed to rain today, and yet...' Ann wasn't going to buy any more citrus soap, because it isn't really made in Michigan, and yet...'"

"Knees. Shins. Ankles."

"After I slid through the pool of soap and vinegar right in front of the basement stairs—that's where that door goes," she pointed— "I nearly fell straight down to the concrete floor below. I was so startled, I didn't even scream. I almost jerked my arm out of the socket grabbing the stair rail, and I somehow ended up flipped around, face-down, with my legs stuck through two different steps, and then I couldn't pull either leg out. I thought for a while I'd have to stay there forever. Patsy had gone off to clean a bathroom and didn't hear me yelling like a stuck pig. Well, I was stuck, you see."

"And yet?"

"And yet I didn't want to be found there in the morning by the funeral lunch bunch, so I wriggled my legs out inch by inch, working my way by walking down the stairs on my hands. And guess what Patsy said when I reminded her that I'd asked her to leave the dirty wax around the cellar door, rather than risk sending a guest careening to hell? 'And yet the floor was really dirty there, and it cleaned up good.'"

"And yet," Laurel said, "your legs look like kidney pudding."

"And yet," Claire observed, "my whole house is clean, for the first time since George became ill. You don't need to baby me too much, Laurel. I'm still physically tough. But I can use you as a touchstone, because sometimes I'm scared. I hate it when I can't see into the future!" she said, half laughing at herself.

"You? Claire, you're the strongest person I know."

"When I'm with people, I feel good. But sometimes, when I'm by myself, I feel exhausted. I don't want to get out of bed. I want to sleep, and sleep, and sleep."

"I'll make you take me exploring," Laurel promised. But at Claire mentioning sleep, she yawned, stretched, and then startled as the door creaked open and Pearl slipped into the room, looking stonily at them both.

"Do you remember that first time you were going to sleep over at my house?" Claire asked.

"Of course I do. The crucifixes scared the crap out of me, and I ran back home."

"Protestant wimp. And you're Italian," Claire said. "There aren't any crucifixes here. People say once a Catholic, always a Catholic at heart. The problem, for me, is the brain, saying 'endorse birth control, you bastards.'"

"The heart, though, makes sense to me. You have all that was left of the goddess. We Protestants got rid of Mary, along with the Lady's shrines. Some monks, you know, used to place statues of Mary next to those Lady shrines, which were often in a little hollow that offered running water, a beehive or two, and berry bushes, because those symbolized purity, healing, and fertility. As fewer of the old pagan places were kept up, they became symbols of the

Virgin Mary. But I used to envy the statue in your backyard. She looked so serene, so forgiving, with her hands held out. I used to pray to her, 'make my mom and dad stop fighting.'"

Pearl turned his back on them and stepped away, tail held straight up, signaling disdain. He might've liked Laurel during the day, but as evening settled about the house, guests were unwanted, and might, before the appointed three days, begin to stink like fish.

Laurel took a bath with apple-scented bubbles and fell asleep reading a Louise Penny mystery.

Claire dozed, as she had predicted, in the pillowy recliner. In the middle of the night, she woke with a dislocated, eerie feeling. Not as though she was being watched. Not as though she had heard something strange, though that certainly might have been true. She still wasn't used to owls, or whip-poor-wills, for that matter. She got up feeling as though she had awoken in the middle of a dream and could not quite recall it. Though she thought the dream had shown her a face peering through the west windows. Maybe she'd heard something inside the house. Maybe Laurel was awake.

She'd been sleeping in underpants and one of George's T-shirts, but pulled a long sweatshirt on over them before tiptoeing in to look at Laurel, who was sound asleep with the light on, her book and glasses next to her face. Claire made sure Laurel was covered, moved the book and glasses to the dresser, and turned off the light. Back in the living room, she opened the doors, determined to face down her unease. Fresh air flooded in, smelling of cedar and surprisingly cold. A single shooting star streaked above tree branches. The river's murmur was reassuring and hypnotic. She closed the doors reluctantly, found a blanket, and thought about getting one more drink, but then Pearl was swirling like silk about her ankles, herding her back into the recliner. She slid in over the armrest, and as the cat cuddled closer, Claire let herself be lulled asleep.

3

THE NEIGHBORHOOD

The next day dawned with a yellow-streaked sky. Laurel slept until 9:00 a.m., then wandered out to the kitchen to find Claire sitting at the table, adjusting reading glasses with purple frames while she looked through a stack of unopened envelopes. For breakfast, they dipped crisp ginger cookies into coffee swirled with clotted cream.

"Want some help with the paperwork?"

"Nope." Claire stretched and shoved correspondence into a folder. "We need to beat the shopping rush. A good selection of food disappears fast, and I want to treat you to good things. I've learned a lot about this area, if you have questions."

George's driving around car was a 1969 silver Bentley, which was more like a living room than a car. Claire sat up straight to drive, but Laurel, after admiring the burgundy leather seats, leaned back and luxuriated. Obviously, it had been a while since the seats had been conditioned, but Laurel could have sworn a new-car-leather scent vied with the outdoors.

Noon was glorious, scented with sweet fern. They left the car windows down, so gusts of wind swirled around them, hinting at rain later in the afternoon. As they headed toward Grayling, they drove through plantation red pines and jack pines, with an occasional clear cut area that looked stripped bare but was greening with poplar and shrubs.

They also passed Camp Grayling, a National Guard and Army Reserve base with fewer than its usual number of trainees, according to Claire. The base and the area around it, she explained, was being investigated for PFAS, chemicals the Air National Guard had used for years which are connected to liver and kidney damage.

"There's still so much open land here, people aren't always protective of what they've got," Claire said. "I'm a bleeding heart for every environmental cause, and most of my friends are, but caring is easier when you have money and time. People keep inventing new chemicals, and the next thing we know, we've got toxic paint stripper to take off lead paint."

"This area looks like it's struggling to find its new normal," Laurel noted.

"It's been doing just that since the end of the white pine era a hundred years ago. Someday this week, I'll taking you cruising near the Main Branch of the Au Sable, where there are a few remaining older homes and new homes designed by architects. In Grayling, though, you'll see some subsidized housing, which is fair enough. People need affordable places to live."

"What's *that?*" Laurel asked, as they passed impressive "*KEEP OUT*" signs. The river could just barely be seen, the water shining in flat, sheet-like panels.

"Closed trout farm," Claire said. "Closed for now, while the long range impact is studied. It used to be a tourist's hangout. Somewhere people took kids."

"Why aren't there more tourists? Isn't this where the Au Sable River Canoe Marathon starts?"

"That's earlier in the summer, my bookish friend. People turn up all along the river."

"Hey, Claire!" Laurel's jaw had dropped. "That house looks like it was built out of rubble."

"What's left over of big glacial rocks is more like it. Every year, snow topples some houses built on hillsides. Sometimes owners stack up what's left for foundations. Look at the hospital complex, though. It just keeps growing. The hospital offers cancer treatment and hospice care. I drove George here. They offer prenatal care and classes for parents. And believe me, doctors give a lot of Lyme disease shots."

"That's kind of cool. The elementary school next to the hospital complex."

"There's a little labyrinth in back, donated by the Dominican Sisters of Grand Rapids. George and I sat out there once. A raccoon came and ate our peanuts."

"Wow. A movie theater. The Rialto?"

"Yup. And there's a park the Au Sable runs through, in the middle of town, next to Spike's Keg 'O' Nails, which is the first place I ever saw offer poutine—French fries under white cheddar curds, all of it doused with beef gravy."

Laurel gagged. "Great, clogged arteries!"

"Don't look so horror-struck. It's probably no worse than doughnuts. And I like being able to shop in a town that isn't all chain stores. Outside of the main street, you can find usual town components—pharmacies, pizza shops, car dealerships—but the downtown area has some interesting places. There's the Paddle Hard Micro Brewery, for instance. And there are actually two 'Michigan' shops in town. I shop at Ann Campbell's place, because she's got fresh produce, but the other store, Tip'n the Mitten, has its own specialties. You can buy craft beer there, or Towne Club Pop. The owner stocks made-in-Michigan toys, books, and puzzles, and guidebooks and mystery books by Michigan authors."

"Thanks, guru of Grayling," Laurel said.

"Maybe I'll get a job with the Grayling Chamber of Commerce." Claire guided the Bentley into the one remaining main street parking place, leaving the truck driver behind them fuming. "This is," she said, "a humongous car to park."

"Look. They have lattes in the flower shop! Do you want coffee?"

"Be patient you must. Selling out Ann will be."

"You can be my tour guide. You may not be Yoda."

They headed across the street to Everything Michigan, where a truck was unloading fruit. A DeLorean was parked in front, the back seat already stacked high with bags of carrots, potatoes, and apples.

"Good Lord," Laurel said, as they walked out of bright sunshine. "There's a world here."

"Told you," Claire said smugly.

Patsy waved at them both. "Hi, Laurel. Good to see you again. Show her around, Claire. I've got to check this shipment of fruit."

Anyone wanting a picnic lunch or dinner could find their wishes here. Bushels of Summer Gold apples, the earliest to ripen. Loaves of crisp-crusted locally-made whole wheat, rye, and oat bread in their shades of toasty brown. Small, perfectly shaped orange carrots, green onions, radishes, and even celery, once grown commercially, but now only raised in small batches in Michigan. The produce section smelled of onion, dill, and rye.

"You need a map of Michigan in here," Laurel commented as they browsed.

Claire pointed to the map behind the counter, where hand-drawn pictures showed customers what they could find in each aisle of the store. These included butter-rich cheeses from nearby Amish farms, Koeze peanut butter from Grand Rapids, cherry preserves from the Leelanau Peninsula, and jars of white asparagus spears from fields near Ann Arbor. Jars of shining black turtle beans that, having thrived in Michigan, had been sent off to Mexico for packaging and returned to the "mitten state" for sale. Pizzas—a sign on the counter noted—could be made to order, and you could buy Vernors ginger ale that had originated in Detroit.

Salmon was the specialty, as a spread, fresh caught, or smoked. Where smoked trout usually filled shelves, a handwritten note signed with Ann's extravagantly looping initials warned about rising river temperatures and commended catch and release.

Everything Michigan wasn't short on sweets, either. Little cards identified various kinds of Mackinac Island fudge. Honey in the comb floated like whale baleen in the jar. Bottles of maple syrup glowed dark as amber, and maple leaf-shaped maple sugar candies reminded Laurel of her childhood. She could remember sitting in the back seat of her parents' car, on a family vacation, letting the sugar slowly dissolve on her tongue.

Jars of shimmering red thimbleberry jam from the Keweenaw Peninsula competed for attention with white paper bags of dried cherries. Next to these, a note in Ann's writing told customers the store would provide warm, fresh baked pies just out of the oven on request. Blueberries lurked plump inside overcoats of yogurt sweetened with beet sugar from fields near Marlette. Near the front of the store, cinnamon rolls with thick, white swirled frosting could be bought with local butter from the milk of contented cows. The store was redolent of baked goods, but amidst what could have been overwhelming sweetness hovered the scent of Baraga County lavender, making Laurel think of clean white sheets billowing in the wind.

Two aisles showcased offerings by local craftspeople. Hunks of driftwood sported obscene prices. Polished "lucky walking sticks" with spiraling indentations, like the internal spines of nautilus seashells, caught reflected light. Pressed wildflowers graced tasteful blank cards by local artists. A bench turned out to be a hand-carved cribbage board. The scent of citrus lotion led them to Ann, who was holding a creamy crocheted cape against the tanned female driver of the DeLorean. The driver was saying, "They don't use dyes? What if I want it in pink?"

Laurel bought lip balm for Jen. Claire bought a side of salmon big enough to be a bathmat, apples that glowed like sunshine, loaves of bread, and a wheel of aged white cheddar. She finished up by buying a peach pie. Their purchase came with free homemade caramels, bulging and rectangular in wax paper wraps.

Ann left the tanned customer, who was still fingering the cape, and walked toward them. "I'm surprised she doesn't want a cape labeled 'natural wool, no dyes' to come in purple." Ann wore a blue knit top and knee-length skirt, and green-and-white socks and tennis shoes. After she rang up their purchases, she looked at them and grinned.

"We all loved coming over last night," she said. "Laurel, we hope you'll fall under the charm of that house and stay a while. Besides the fact that it's about in the center of our circle of households, Claire always has the best parties. We think it's the river. Negative ions."

"How on earth did you build a clientele when you started this store?" Laurel asked. "You've got everything here but pot."

"We had that too," Ann said. "When my daughter Tansy worked here, before she went away to school, she used to buy and sell it."

Once outside the store, lugging packages, Laurel turned wide-eyed to Claire.

"She was kidding, right?"

"I'm not sure if Tansy sold it, but I know someone here bought it. Ann used to bring George joints."

They stopped at the house to put the salmon in Claire's refrigerator, and then drove out and did a neighborhood tour. Parts of the area were transitioning to residential housing, apparently without building codes. Doublewides that boasted statues of well-dressed geese rubbed shoulders with landscaped but largely unsold subdivisions lots. Other sections were still lush with orchards—mostly cherry, peach, and apple, leaves shining every color from bronze to green. They passed occasional fields of goldenrod and star thistle, and gently rolling hills with spruce and maple rising toward the north.

"Hey! That's Barbara," Claire exclaimed, breaking the silence. She gestured toward a white farmhouse with a long, curving drive. A small sign near the front fence read, "*Swallow Hill Farm.*"

"Bill and Barbara are the only two people I know who have done exactly what they wanted to do with their lives. They have the most amazing horses. Let's see what they're doing."

She turned into the drive and let the Bentley coast down the valley. Barbara—wearing one of Bill's T-shirts and a pair of stained overalls—was sitting near an extravagant splash of purple butterfly bush, dangling a grass stem over the kittens in her lap. A few feet away, lounging tummy-up, an orange and white tabby purred.

"How old?" Claire asked.

"I think six weeks. Aren't they darling? One wonders who Colby here has been consorting with, giving us two calico babies and one gray-and-white kitty. It's hard to imagine, but Colby was skinny, for a mama, when we took her in."

Laurel and Claire cast a quick glance at Colby, who now resembled a rotund wheel of cheese.

Laurel knelt by Barbara's lap, where the kittens mewled and skittered like yarn balls with wide yellow eyes and twitching tails.

"What are you going to do with them?" she asked, entranced.

"They're going to Everything Michigan. I think we'll keep Colby. She's fallen in love with Bill. He says her purr puts him to sleep."

One of the calico kittens climbed up Barbara's knee to make a break for adventure. Barbara raised her leg, and the kitten fell back, its tiny claws not quite getting through the thick overalls.

"I'd love to let Colby keep one of the kittens," Barbara said with regret. "But we just can't. We're always getting strays here. It was worse when we used to place the kittens ourselves. Seems like there's nothing like a sign that says 'free kittens' to encourage people to drop off cats." She gathered the kittens into her shirt and poured them into a small, plush carrier. Colby followed. "Want to see the horses? Bill is giving Ari a shower."

"I love to," Claire said.

"I'm glad you stopped by and brought Laurel. You haven't been around much."

Barbara led them through a large, high-roofed barn that smelled of clean mulch and straw and new manure. Industrial-sized fans were fixed to the ceiling in each of the stalls. Swallows flew between the rafters, and pigeons eyed them from rails.

"Hey, Orra," Claire said to a tall, square-shouldered woman sweeping out a goat pen and hip checking the goat aside.

"Hey, Claire," Orra said. She stopped and threw carrot pieces into the far corner of the pen. The goat, rolling his catlike eyes at them, trotted away from the gate and let Orra make her getaway.

She pulled off her gloves and held out a hand to Laurel.

"You must be Claire's houseguest," she said, her voice husky. She had a faded scar on one side of her face.

Claire made the introductions. "Next time, you come to my house and make Bill stay home and tend livestock."

"Nope," Orra said. "Don't like to be around a lot of people. You know that, Sugar. I like it here, where life is a teeny bit predictable."

"Pregnant goats?" Claire asked.

"Better than an asshole husband," Orra said.

"There's a lot of that going around," Laurel agreed.

They stopped to rub Braytoven the donkey's forehead. Bill the donkey hung back, less trusting, but Braytoven, who was warm from lying in the sun in the outside section of his pen and smelled of clean hay, pushed appreciatively against their stroking hands.

They caught up with Barbara, who had gone through a freshly swept horse pen and into an adjacent yard. The spraying water from Bill's hose fountained over Ari, a white Icelandic horse that would have been more at home in snow and ten-degree temperatures. The horse—small, compact, stocky, with a long, flowing tail and mane—positively basked in the cold water. Bill wielded a grooming brush with his other hand, working hair out of Ari's coat.

"You got his heart medicine?" he asked Barbara.

"In my pocket," Barbara said, fishing out half an apple that had been doctored to conceal a pill. She offered it to the horse, who spit it out. Bill swept it up and offered it again. This time the horse lipped it off his palm and thoughtfully crunched it.

"Hey, Laurel. Hey, Claire. Sorry to ignore you, but getting pills down Ari is a major pain. He figured out that we hid them in between graham crackers and in marshmallows. Now he won't touch those."

"I don't even think his pills taste bad," Barbara complained. "I tasted them myself."

They gave carrots to the other horses: Ace, a brown Gotland pony from Sweden; Rune, a blond Norwegian Fjord horse that shone platinum gold in the light; and Andy, an Arabian with a much more impressive show name.

Rune and Ari both had bad cases of founder and had to wear specially cast shoes to help support hooves that had sagged with girth and time. Weighted plastic bins yielded tufts of grass that had to be pulled out by a determined equine. "Better for their waist-lines," Barbara explained. "So, better for their feet. Speaking of waistlines," she added, "Want some cream cheese brownies? They're homemade."

"Guess not," Claire said. "We just stocked up at Everything Michigan. For gosh sakes, Barbara, when do you find time to bake?"

"I didn't say they were made in my home," Barbara raised one eyebrow. "You know we attend the Unitarian Universalist Church? We do a little trading and bartering and selling. One of the women has duck eggs and bakes fresh bread, which I think is as good as anything Ann Campbell ever has. Families take turns bringing food to eat after the service. Nothing fancy, usually. Chili or macaroni and cheese, and fruit, if anyone has fresh fruit. Crackers, processed cheese squares, carrot sticks, and cucumber slices. Rolls, often store-bought. We can pop them in the oven in the kitchen. Some kind of cookies. We try not to compete, and to have food that kids will like and older people can eat. If there's a lot of food left, there's no way to store it, so one of us will buy it. Voilà—brownies. I'd be glad to share. If I freeze them, Bill will eat them frozen."

"Chastening," Claire said when she and Laurel were on their way home. "Who knew horses had diets? For their feet, I mean? I knew horses could get swaybacked, and I know I'm not swaybacked, but I will say my last pair of sandals was a size wider than I used to buy."

"Less grass for you," Laurel exclaimed. "Good God, Swallow Hill Farm looks expensive to maintain. And that's not counting the surrey I saw, or the horse-drawn sleigh, or the track, or tack, or distemper shots, whatever."

"A simple life in the country. Not so simple, from what they say. Like a lot of farmers, they rent beehives for pollination. One year, a stray queen set up a colony in their chimney, and the next thing they knew, they had hundreds of pounds of honey and possessive bees inside a wall of their house. Last summer, they had wheat smut and had to buy grain from Indiana. And power is an ongoing problem when we get storms out here. They keep three generators—one for themselves and one for the horse barn, and a spare for the horse barn if the power stays out. Last Christmas, a field mouse-turned-house mouse—probably came hidden in a Christmas tree they'd cut—made a home in a desk drawer and ate their back tax receipts."

"Don't cats eat mice?" Laurel asked.

"It depends on the mice and the cats," Claire said. "Field mice are smarter than house mice."

"What will happen to the kittens?"

"Ann and Patsy will help find them good homes," Claire answered. "Kittens stay behind the counter most of the time, but they sometimes escape into the aisles. You wouldn't think people on vacation would adopt a kitten, but they do, if their kids fuss enough. Local people too. Ann hands out a free turkey roasting pan with clean kitty litter with every cat they place. We know at least one of the kittens born to stray cats at Swallow Hill Farm is living in Boise, Idaho, and one in Montpelier, Vermont."

"What if the people who ask seem like bad cat owners?"

"Sometimes Ann just tells people, 'I don't think you need a cat.'"

"She's pretty forthright."

"She can be, when she has opinions. We'd just started getting to know people when George was diagnosed. He wanted it kept quiet, but Ann figured it out when George started losing weight. He only tried chemo twice, and it didn't help, so he and the doctor agreed it wasn't a 'viable option.' During chemo, Ann came over with a couple of joints. She told George he was being selfish. That he wasn't anywhere near dying, and that I shouldn't have to be alone while he was sick.

"When Ann put it that way, he agreed people could be told. So Bill Marsh came by and swapped fishing stories, and Barbara would bring 'surprises' to entertain him, like a baby pig—now named Piglet—someone had dumped in their garden. A chicken with a white fluffy crest of feathers, named Olive, who would sit in his lap. Ann brought custards to help him keep pain pills down, because after a while, he'd cramp up at night."

"Where did she get the pot?" Laurel asked, fascinated.

"She says a kid in his teens stole some food and took off without paying, but left a plastic pouch near the cash register. Orra can roll cigarettes. Lots of people can. There's a veteran named Murphy who lives behind us, across the river and through the trees. We hardly ever see him, and when we do, he turns his back. But one night, I was sitting up late and saw him wading across the river. He left four hand-tied fishing flies next to George's camp chair, and then turned around and went back."

"Could George still fish then?"

"No. He'd never fished much after we first moved in. But Murphy used to give me the creeps, and that made us warm up to him."

The road was curving up a hill now, and fields had given way to maples and oaks. Laurel realized they hadn't passed a single car. The car's smooth movement and quiet hum was seductive. Laurel could feel the car drifting into another soft curve.

"Once, Jen brought a baby goat George bottle-fed—Laurel!"

Claire flung an arm out to keep her friend from sliding forward and braked to an abrupt halt in the middle of the turn, her car skewing at the sudden motion. Fifteen or so deer crossed in front of them, three splintering off from the main group to run along a ditch. One vaulted the hood of the car, seemingly without effort. They could see now that there were still a few deer in the trees on the left side of the road. One, confused, stood stock-still for a minute, staring at them with affronted innocence.

"I am so sorry." Claire pulled her arm back. "I should have been driving slower. Or been looking more carefully. Or both. There are often deer on this road. Sometimes, smushed deer."

Claire rubbed her shoulder. The affronted deer trotted across.

"I wasn't paying any attention either, Claire. Whew! Weren't they beautiful, though?"

They drove back in relative silence, each engrossed in thought. Laurel was thinking: I'm glad I signed my trust. If anything happens to me, Jen can avoid probate.

Claire was counting heartbeats, breathing deep, slowing her pulse.

I don't want to die, she realized. I thought I did, when George died. Maybe it helps to be outside. The world feels peaceful today.

But when they turned into the driveway and got out of the car, Pearl was hunched in a feral half-crouch in front of them, fur puffed out, gold eyes blazing, tufted ears back, lashing his tail. As Claire turned toward the kitchen door, the cat ran at her and slashed at her ankles. Claire sidestepped, and he pivoted in a sinuous half-circle to smack her feet again, this time drawing blood. He raised his hackles and produced a guttural yowl that made hair stand up on the back of Laurel's neck.

"Claire! Could that be rabies? Get away from him."

Claire backed away slowly, her eyes on the cat. "I don't think he can have rabies," she said. "He's had a rabies shot."

As she backed away, Pearl ran to her, mewing like a kitten, belly dragging on the driveway.

Claire knelt.

"Jesus! Don't do that." Laurel edged toward her. "He might have been poisoned."

"I don't care! It's not his fault, whatever it is." Claire swiped at blood trickling into her sandals.

Because she was kneeling, the sudden *crump!* from the inside of a kitchen window seemed even more loud and more startling. They looked up to see bird feet clutching the sill, and an oversized beak.

"*Khraaaaaaa!*" something proclaimed from inside the house.

Pearl had flipped over to again bar Claire from moving forward. His ears were again back. Frothy drool oozed from his mouth.

"I say," a man's voice exclaimed from the driveway behind them. "I think you have birds in your house."

There was a rental car from the airport and Laurel's daughter, Jennifer, looking like a taller, younger version of Laurel, accompanied by an unknown, tall, and unshaven man. Claire stood, steadying herself by putting a hand on Laurel's arm. Both registered that his five o'clock shadow was gray. He was too old for her.

"Jen!" Laurel hugged her close. "I've been looking forward to you coming. Though not like this."

Claire burst into tears. She didn't know what was worse: that something the size of a cormorant was inside her house, that she'd nearly killed her best friend by misjudging a road turn, or that she found the stranger attractive. Uncombed graying hair, horn-rimmed glasses, straight nose, square jaw, half of his raincoat collar turned up, half turned down. Until she fell in love with George, she'd liked men who looked a little rumpled.

"I think you have ravens," her guest said. "The young ones can get themselves in trouble this time of year."

Claire stared at him. "In trouble? Why are they in my *kitchen*?"

"I don't know." His tone was somber. "But let's get them out, shall we? Before they get hurt."

4

SALMON SKIN

"Charles is an ornithologist," Jen said. "Which is lucky right now."

"Passionate amateur," he corrected her. He handed Claire a large linen handkerchief—crumpled but clean. "Key?" he asked.

"It's not locked," she said.

He looked at her appraisingly. "Any other doors open? Not locked, that is?"

"The patio door," she said.

"Let's go that way, then," he said, sounding tired but determined. Pearl was sniffing his feet.

"Mom, Charles Blakely," Jen said. "Charles, this is Laurel Walker, my mother, and her friend, Claire Monroe. Mom, Claire, I met Charles on the plane. He was upset when some seagulls hit our engines, but mostly for the gulls. I changed seats, because the woman next to him seemed angry with him. I mean, who wanted to crash? But he had a point. The gulls were *dead*.

"I moved seats, and we talked about planes interfering with bird migration, and we somehow got to talking about sea eagles. I've always wanted to see them. It turned out we'd both been to the Museum of Anthropology at the University of British Columbia, which is an *incredible* place, Mom. I asked him if he thought designers exploit or give credence to First Nation art, and he said, mostly exploit."

"Jen, I love you," Claire said, "but I don't care if he's Jesus Christ in a raincoat. You're welcome here, Charles, but I want this bird, or birds, out of my house."

"I wouldn't be Jesus Christ," Charles said. "If I could, I would be Bakbakwalanooksiwae, Raven God of Reincarnation of the northwest American coast."

"You could help," Claire said, "instead of lecture. Whatever's in the house scares the crap out of my cat."

"I'm a bird guy, remember? I'm not any cat's buddy."

Charles worked his way around the edge of the foundation, followed by Jen, Laurel, and Claire, with Pearl trailing behind. They edged, on their tiptoes, past the kitchen and past the windows of the room filled with books. Wooden blinds hung lopsided, hemorrhaging rust-colored connecting cords.

Another raucous call. Another crash like clanging cymbals.

"Ravens won't hurt you," Charles said. "They're really smart birds, but I can't think how they got in here. Have you got a chimney guard? You should. Prevents against swallow nests and the odd robin."

Claire wanted to say, *Fuck the odd robin*, but didn't have the energy. "Not sure," she managed.

"I'll open the doors now," he told her. "You might want to duck, just a little. Be prepared for mess."

He slowly opened the patio doors and pushed back one of the wooden blinds at the same time, making a throaty chirring, muttering noise.

Absolutely nothing happened. It was as though stage curtains had opened only to reveal a deserted stage.

"Stay behind me," Charles said as he stepped through the door. "However your birds got in here, they didn't want to stay in here once they'd—once they'd—"

He stopped, and rubbed his forehead.

"Why," he asked, "would you leave food about like this? You might as well have left a garbage dump. Your whole house reeks of salmon. You're lucky you didn't get a bear." He had stepped into the room now, letting the others crowd in behind him, and looked at Claire, who had clearly disappointed him. Pearl shot them all a reproving glance and retired under a chair.

The bathmat-sized slab of salmon, reduced to shreds, was draped over the back of the couch like a Salvador Dalí afghan.

"What is that on the rug?" Jen asked.

"Black salmon skin," Laurel answered. "The gooshy part." She walked carefully through the room. Bird droppings sluiced down bookcases. Some of the whitish, greenish, yellowish deposits looked lumpy and solid, but other places seemed power washed with paint-thin guano.

"This is too bad," Charles said. "Raven excrement gets more watery when they're stressed. Your bird or birds gorged on salmon and then couldn't get out."

"You stupid man," Claire said. "Do you think I left salmon spread across my couch? Wanted to match a color for new drapes, maybe?"

"Aunt Claire," Jen said. "Why are you shouting at Charles? He's helping."

Laurel, with Charles and Jen following her, headed toward the kitchen. Claire picked her way toward the bedroom Laurel had slept in, wanting to splash her face with cold water, which had been her mother's all-purpose remedy. She heard Pearl give a small growling sound.

"Be right back, Pearl," she said as she kicked off the sandals. In the stillness that followed, she heard scrabbling, followed by frantic wing-flapping. It was coming from the bathroom. She flexed her toes and stood stock-still.

She knew that wildlife could and did invade bathrooms. When she was ten, she'd heard her mother screaming upstairs and the sound of a toilet seat lid being slammed hard, the way no one was supposed to slam it. Her father had come, wearing plumber's gloves, and scooped a wet squirrel from the toilet. It promptly bit through his gloves, and he dropped it. Then it raced through the house and up an upright piano, only to shatter a glass window shelf displaying antique cups. By then, Claire had managed to open the back door, and the squirrel sped out, looking damp and traumatized. If squirrels communicated, she'd wondered, what had he told his family about his evening at their house?

Her father explained it had doubtless fallen into the vent pipe that lets a toilet flush. He resisted Claire's mother's insistence that he see a doctor about the squirrel bite and then went off to smoke his pipe. Her mother had gone off to have a midday glass of sherry and later explained to her friends, "I thought it was a rat!" Claire, at that age, had hoped to catch the squirrel, dry it off, and cage it, eventually taming it and teaching it to do tricks. She remembered thinking that there must be other parents who wouldn't make such a fuss about the outdoors coming indoors.

And yet, she was now the age her parents had been then.

"Charles," she said, her voice calm as she backed away.

She heard nothing.

"Charles!" she repeated. "Charles, Charles, Charles, Charles, Charles!"

He appeared behind her, which blocked her exit from the bedroom.

"What are you fussing about?" he asked.

"Something," she said. "In the bathtub."

They edged around one another. She had a hard time getting her feet to move. He proceeded into the room so she could no longer see his face. He must've been approaching the tub.

"Oh good," she heard Charles say. "Nice, soft towels."

There were whole minutes of silence. Mom, she thought. If you're up there and can hear me, I apologize for calling you a coward.

The scrabbling resumed.

"There, there," Charles said.

A muffled, protesting *toc-toc-toc* broke off into high-pitched *clack-screech* protests.

"Come on," Charles said, his voice proud and avuncular. "You did all that by yourself? You're very strong. No, bite the towel. Of course I wouldn't hurt you."

A soft *prruk-prruk-prruk* came from the bathroom. The bird—she guessed—must've been tired.

"Come on," Charles said. "Let's find you a nice, safe, dark place to hide. How about the floor of this closet? I'll add more towels. How's that?" He turned to Claire. "I can't think how this injured bird got up to a kitchen window. Maybe it fluttered up to a trash basket, for a halfway point? I need to fix this wing. I need brandy, or cognac, an eye dropper, Q-tips, and Elmer's glue. And later on, get me some sticks."

5
THE COPS

Claire, Laurel, Jen, and Charles sat on the patio eating slices of cheddar cheese and apple. Claire was tippling scotch from a pink plastic cup. Pearl, who had recovered enough to hunt scattered salmon bits, now sat scrunched near their feet.

"How long?" Laurel asked again.

"God, Laurel, give it up. How would I know? All the desk sergeant would say was, 'Don't go back in the house. We'll get someone there when we can.'" Claire spit crumbles of cheddar from her mouth into the palm of her hand.

"Ugh. If you're giving that to Pearl and breaking off more cheese, wipe your hand on a napkin, would you? His whiskers smell like salmon."

"You're grumpier than I am. And my whole house smells like salmon."

"There's guano in my tub. Well, your tub," Laurel muttered.

"I'll clean it up for you when we go back in the house," Jen said. Her dark hair hung limp over one eye. She had been drafted to help Charles with his projects. "'Move that Q-tip four degrees. Don't smear the glue!'" she quoted him.

"I can't believe we couldn't get him out of my house," Claire said. "Raven—look it up. I bet it's the root of 'ravening.' There are stories that say ravens are ghosts or murdered souls! And yet, your Charles is not spooked or even swayed from his purpose by police advice! How did he know there wasn't a crazed killer with a cake knife upstairs? Or another penguin."

"Raven," Jen corrected.

"At least," Claire said, "Charles said George had first-rate cognac."

"I don't think he drank any. Well, maybe a swig," Jen said. "He put some in the eye dropper with a little water, and Oscar—"

"Oscar?"

"That's what he's calling the raven. Be glad he isn't calling it George."

"Jesus, Jen!" Laurel said.

"Oscar went limp, and then we glued the Q-tips on one of the 'fingers' of his hurt wing. Charles said Oscar most likely got clipped by a car when he and some buddies were munching roadkill."

"So we still don't know why Oscar was in my house," Claire said.

"That's true," Jen said. "We don't."

Pearl jumped on Claire's lap.

"Salmon breath," Claire said.

"Pearl was helping you," Laurel admitted. "That's why he clawed your ankles. He was keeping you away from the house."

"Tonight," Claire said, "we should cuddle him and lick his ears. He likes that."

"He would! He's male," Laurel responded.

"Female cats like it too. It reminds them of their mothers."

Laurel raised her eyebrows, but didn't say anything.

Charles had constructed a nest in the back seat of the rental car, though he would have preferred the Bentley. The mass of sticks and twigs, lined with fur from an old pair of George's gloves, had been set into a bigger, wooden box that had once held a croquet set. He ambled back from checking on Oscar.

"Still groggy," he reported with satisfaction. "He should settle in as the sun goes down and be out for the night."

The sun had disappeared behind the tree line and a bank of purple clouds before a lone police cruiser pulled slowly into the drive. Jen and Charles had retreated into quiet conversation. Laurel dozed in her chair. Claire's head was cradled in her arms, her face hidden, Pearl sitting in her lap with a look that said, "I told you so."

She straightened up when the cruiser parked beside the Bentley. A burly, gray-haired man and a short woman with carrot red hair hooked behind her ears walked toward them. Both looked comfortable in their uniforms despite the heat. Claire was familiar with the man's gait. She felt momentary guilt. She hadn't done anything to provoke the slight crush Arnie had on her. A *crush*—could a word be more adolescent? Was there a dignified word for attraction between adults?

She shooed Pearl out of her lap and walked forward to greet him, aiming for her everyday tone.

"Arnie? I thought you would have been home by now, watching a movie and eating take-out Chinese."

"Hi, Claire. I had to come figure out what got you out of the house."

Laurel stretched and groaned, her back protesting. The groan, actually, was pure irritation. She'd wanted to welcome Jen and apologize that her daughter's reception had turned into a complete cock-up, but Jen had brought Charles and seemed more interested in him than in her, or in Claire's trashed house. Now they had to deal with Mutt and Jeff.

"We're like that Hitchcock movie," Claire said. "Fewer birds. More bird shit."

"I think someone *put* a bird in the house. Charles says Claire has a chimney guard," Jen volunteered.

"You are?" Arnie asked.

"This is Laurel Walker and her daughter Jen. Laurel and I have been friends since we were ratty little kids. She came yesterday, and Jen joined her today, both hoping to stay and help me sort through some of George's things."

"Detective Robideu," Arnie's partner offered before Claire could introduce him using his first name.

"Detective Robideu." Claire nodded, acknowledging his formal title. "This is Jen's friend, Charles. She met him on her plane from San Diego."

"Last name?" Robideu asked.

"Blakely," Charles told him. "I have a place—a cabin—south-east of here, outside Luzerne. Jen and I were seated together on the plane, and she offered to share a rental car and get me the rest of the way home, if I'd stop by here first."

"Identification." Arnie was civil.

Charles pulled a cloth wallet that looked as though it had been through a trash compactor out of a rear pocket and opened it, producing a driver's license.

"Looks OK for now. This," Arnie said, nodding toward his female companion, "is Detective Elaine Santana, who'll be helping me with your salmon infestation."

Laurel's jaw clenched. "Excuse me, sir. Do you think, because you and Claire know one another, that you can joke? Why haven't you checked to make sure there's no one in her house?"

Arnie took off his hat and scratched his head.

"No, ma'am. What happened here, at Claire's house, is not funny at all. I joked because I'm relieved. We've got some gang going about in this area trashing houses—not taking anything, just messing things up. We think it's kids who don't have enough parental supervision. Sooner or later, they're going to have a fatal run-in with someone—a homeowner, police, or a neighborhood vigilante—which is not what we want for anyone."

"Why didn't I know about this?" Claire asked.

"Watch the news much?" Santana asked.

"Not really." Claire answered. "Damn, Arnie, this 'detective' thing is distracting."

Robideu said something inaudible under his breath, directed at Santana. The two looked at each other. Elaine shrugged.

"We had two other break-ins last night," he continued. "There are differences. The other houses were empty. Whoever got in broke a window or popped a lock. The other places, no salmon, no bird shit. Dog shit everywhere. TV smashed at one house, an heirloom clock at the other. Could just be high spirits. It's hard to patrol areas where houses are built on big lots, especially after summer people have left."

He leveled a look at Laurel. "There is no sign of an intruder or obvious sign of forced entry. Claire, you said in your call that someone put a bird in your house as a prank, but they didn't break a window or damage a screen. You don't lock up?"

"We've never had to. Honestly, Arnie, how many people around here lock up when they leave the house?" Claire asked.

"More than used to." Detective Santana directed a flat look at her.

"Sorry I snapped," Laurel said. "Claire did say she'd get an alarm system."

"Our department is stretched thin," Robideu admitted. "I know Claire because George worked on civic projects. He and Claire had some parties. Fundraisers, really. I don't think that prior acquaintance will prejudice me in this situation, but if at any time, you have concerns, let me know and I'll get someone else on the case."

"I'd like to have you here," Claire said. "You knew George, and I know he liked you. You won't think I'm a gutless wonder if I cry when there's not much wrong. I told Laurel I was working on a 'new normal,' whatever that means. But this—well, it isn't what I had in mind."

"You can call me Santana," his partner said.

"We're going to go look at your salmon," he said. "But after we've done a quick look to make sure there aren't any bodies in the closets, none of you can be here. We'll check the premises by daylight tomorrow morning, have a second team check for finger-prints, and at least try the tracking dogs. You all go to the closest motel. Call or text to let us know where you are. You're insured, yes? When you check in—or maybe even on the way to the motel—call or text and get your insurance agent out here. Once you've checked in, don't go anywhere. Claire said the bird was 'contained.' Do you need us to bring it out to you?"

"Uh, no. It's in the rental car."

Arnie's face remained impassive. "Good place for it. I hate rental car agencies. Tonight, check on the bird, but don't haunt the parking lot."

Charles nodded and stood up. "Can we go in and get our things?"

"You can't go in tonight," Santana said. "But we'll gather up things for you. Prescription drugs, underwear—we've seen it all before."

"Thank you. What do I do about Pearl? My cat," Claire asked.

"We should take her—er, him—with us," Charles said. "Don't leave him here. Awful people hurt pets to get at their owners. Some motels will take cats, or we can sneak him in."

"He's right," Santana said. "Take her with you."

Take her with "us," Claire thought. Hours ago, Charles had not been part of their little group. And not a cat person. But then, she had also said "my cat." A day ago, Pearl wasn't anyone's cat. If they were in a Disney movie, he could have captured Oscar and dragged him out the cat door. What Pearl had done, as best he could, was keep Claire out of the house until she had help.

Their traveling possessions ended up including the protesting cat and a broiler pan filled with kitty litter.

"Can we take the apples?" Charles asked. "They've been in Claire's car all day."

"No." Robideu's tone was abrupt and dismissive. Then, as if an afterthought, he rubbed his chin and added, "You're traveling with Jen. Do you two share a room?"

"I've been wondering about that," Laurel said.

Charles rubbed his chin stubble.

"We have shared a room," Jen said. "But we're not—we don't—it's platonic."

"I'm too old for her," Charles said. "We shared a room at the Doherty Hotel in Clare. They were booked with a convention, so that one room was all they had." His voice was dry as a Gibson without vermouth.

"We slept in separate beds," Jen said, shooting Laurel a venomous look.

"You are *way* too old for her," Laurel said, in what was definitely a warning. "Plus, you now have Oscar."

"Oscar. A partner?" Arnie asked.

"Bird," Charles corrected.

"Maybe Oscar is good partner for you." Laurel looked at Charles.

"Mom," Jen said, "don't be horrid to Charles. He helped Claire. And not everyone is like Dad."

"WHAT DO YOU think of Charles Blakely?" Santana asked as the Bentley and the rental car backed down the driveway.

"I looked him up on Google while you were getting Claire and Laurel's clothes. He was a post-doctoral student at Columbia. No one seems to know why he quit, but he's published a book on birds and some academic papers. Speaks at conferences to get people interested in bird migration routes. Here's why I think he's OK: he waves the fee when he's speaking at predominantly minority colleges. He's sort of an odd duck, with that piece of shit wallet and an Ivy League accent, but he was still with Jen in the rental car when the bird was discovered in Claire's house. What did he call that bird? Oven?"

"Oscar," Santana said.

"There is something off about this case." Robideu had an absent-minded look that Santana knew meant he was worried. "The whole setup is different. The place is occupied, and occupied by someone who's alone most of the time. Even once her friend comes, neither looks capable of self-defense. If there was a reason to choose them, who goes after people with a raven? Seems more like a scare tactic than anything."

"From what I know, sir, that raven was a chancy intimidation tactic. Whoever did it assumed that bird would go for zillion-dollar salmon, and that once it chowed down, it would produce some damage. Ravens aren't as guano-prone as crows when they're stressed, but no wild bird wants to be shut up in a house. I've seen ravens around here, sometimes flocks of young birds, but they can fill up on roadkill. Lots of deer crossing the road this time of year."

"Knock it off with the 'sir,' would you, Elaine? I've known you since you were eleven years old. What do you know about ravens?"

"My oldest brother Michael did a wilderness stint. He came back hooked. He says ravens are almost human-smart, but not always smart enough to avoid trucks and cars. Getting sideswiped by a cyclist could have broken that wing. Or an eagle could have done it."

"And another driver stops and says, 'I'll scoop this bird up with the shovel I just happen to have in the back of my car'? And then, since our perp doesn't want to keep it, he finds an unlocked domicile, checks out the refrigerator to see what will make a big mess, and pushes Nevermore into Claire's house?"

"Maybe we should be asking what kind of geek would use a raven to harass people."

Robideu tamped down the feeling, like acid reflux, rising in his chest. He had a soft spot for Claire, and George and his wife had been a couple who had invested in the area. He'd appreciated George's support for school millages, and Claire seemed to be the type, once planted, to put down generous roots. They were both people he respected. Someone hadn't waited long after George's death to pester his widow.

"You OK, Arnie? Ulcers acting up?"

Santana took his measure. They'd backed each other up, through thick and thin, for a long time, and he could usually tell when she had cramps, and she could tell when he had headache.

"Yeah, hell, I'm fine." He pulled out his Glock as he approached Claire's house.

6

IN THE NIGHT

At the motel, Jen curled around Charles. Both were still fully clothed, and the polyester bedspreads they were sandwiched between, which smelled faintly of laundry detergent, were cold.

"Want to snuggle?" Jen said.

"You're too young," Charles said. "And you want to feel me up to spite your mother."

"I hate you," Jen said.

"That sounds safe," Charles replied, and turned away from her.

LAUREL AND CLAIRE sat up in their double beds, passing the flask full of cognac Arnie had provided.

"Do you think he's sexy?" Laurel asked.

"Charles? A little."

Laurel moved over to Claire's bed and reached for the flask. "What?" she asked. "Who?"

"Charles," Claire said.

"Actually, I meant Arnie Robideu. I didn't like him at first, but he seems decent and concerned. I'm asking because he's got a thing for you."

"Laurel, that's your imagination." Claire replied, wanting to protect Arnie's dignity. How had Laurel picked that up so fast? There was no way Arnie would hit on a friend's wife. Or a woman grieving for a man who had been a friend of his. She reached for the flask.

"I still miss George," she added. "He was like Arnie. A good guy. A decent man." She took a deep drink. "I went around with an artsy crowd in college. Everyone slept with everyone, and I did too. I was in a hurry to lose my virginity. I felt like it defined me, and I was sick of it.

"Then George and I met at an art exhibit, and we went out for coffee, and next we went out for wine, and the time after that, for a drive before a lavish dinner. He was nine years older than I was, finished with college, starting out in business. He wanted to settle down and marry someone who was 'educated, pretty, a social asset, and a good kisser,' and he'd decided that someone was me." She tipped back the flask again.

"You had boyfriends hanging off you, Claire. How did he wade through them?"

"He caught me at a time when I'd decided to put sex on hold. I was growing up, and I could see some of my boyfriends had been jerks. One of them actually told me his mother loved to pick up his socks! Like she had a halo I could aspire to inherit. I was serious about taking some time off, and George said he would wait for me, and if I didn't decide on him, we could still be friends." Claire shoved the cognac at Laurel, who sipped from the flask.

"You believed that?" Laurel asked.

"In retrospect, he was pretty confident. He did wait for me. He waited almost a year, in fact. He took me to museum exhibits I couldn't afford without him. I'd taken art classes and could give him some background. One day, when he'd said he would pick me up after work, he didn't come because there had been a problem with wire transcripts. He couldn't call me because I was outside waiting for him. First, I was worried, and then I was angry, and then I was worried again, and by the time his car swung up to the curb, I'd learned some things about myself. Is there anything left of the cognac?"

"So, sex?"

"Not right away. Nothing that night but a hug. After that, he started easing toward intimacy. He'd pet my hair, kiss my ear lobes, nuzzle my thighs, but he was careful not to push me too fast, as though I were inexperienced. Though I'd told him I was, if anything, the opposite. I—I think he seduced me. He never seemed like the younger guys—all 'let's do this in a hurry.' It was as though George had all the time in the world."

Claire was one breath away from tears. Laurel shifted so she was on her side, curled around the slab-hard motel pillows, and facing Claire, and passed the cognac back to her.

"You had a courtship," Laurel told her. "I'm jealous."

"I did. And I don't know how I go on from here."

The two were silent a minute, and Laurel thought Claire had gone to sleep.

"It wasn't at all like that with David and me," Laurel said. "He was my first. You know I didn't get asked out much in high school, or even in college. Then David came along, a frat boy who wanted me. I'd never even enjoyed being French kissed before, but once we started making love, David could make me come seven ways from Sunday; it didn't really matter what he did! Later, after we were married, I started to worry. Maybe I wasn't special at all. Just easy."

"Laurel, I'll swear David was proud of you. He glowed when he was with you."

"David was proud of being married to a smart woman. He liked being married to a thin woman, someone who could find a sale dress—size six—and flaunt it at parties. And I will say, he loved being a father. After we had Jen, I don't think he cheated for a year."

"That long, huh?"

"His wanderlust didn't bother me so much at first. There were guys at the office who would have jumped my bones, but I thought David would slow down as we got older. After all, my own dad had 'business trips.' Before he left, my mom would hide little notes in his suitcase. 'I love you, baby. I miss you. Hurry home.' But he and my mother depended on each other as they got older, and I thought it was worth letting David sow some, uh, semen. I assumed he would grow out of it. Now I just wish I could be sure that for at least one sweaty minute, he cared for me."

"I never would have guessed about your dad's 'business trips.' He was funny, your dad. I used to wish my family was like yours. Your dad had this understated Cary Grant charm. He could talk to anyone, from bartenders to barristers. Your mom could mix any cocktail and dance any dance step."

Laurel found herself wincing a bit when she thought about her parents and their country club charm. She had *so* not been the daughter they'd expected. Slender as a wraith, late to "bloom." She'd never had a best friend until Claire moved in—Claire, the pretty Catholic girl who had working-class parents. They walked home together on Claire's first day of school and found in each other a certain snarkiness and toughness. Claire had dismissed boys who lusted over her by saying, "It's because I hit puberty early. Big whoop."

"At least you aren't flat as an ironing board," Laurel had told her.

"You're elegant," Claire answered. "If you parted your hair on the side and didn't always wear glasses—you could take them off when you don't have to see the chalkboard—and you unbuttoned the top buttons on these Peter Pan-collared blouses and maybe added a hair scarf..." She'd pulled the scarf out of her own hair and tied it around Laurel's head so Laurel's bangs fluffed out. It made Laurel's head feel sweaty, but when she ran home and examined herself in a mirror, she did feel glamorous.

As time passed, she became a tolerated member of the "in" crowd. She never decided if her popularity had bloomed because she had grown into her features, or because Claire always included her in any class activity and made it clear she wouldn't participate if Laurel wasn't invited. Laurel had loved being at Claire's house. Her father worked overtime, and her mother was warm and accepting. Claire, her five brothers, and her sister hung out, watched television programs together, deflated each other's egos, and told raunchy jokes. Claire loved being at Laurel's, because, as she'd once said, "Your house has real art on the walls. Not just dime store prints."

"Your parents had class," Claire muttered, picking at the motel bedspread. "How could they not be in love?"

"You never saw them throwing plates at each other. Then—it would have been when we were in high school—I think my mom had a miscarriage. She tried to hide it from me, but there were bloody—I mean really bloody—sheets in the back of her closet. I found them when she asked me to get her slippers. Dad wasn't home, and he didn't come home until a week later, because he was staying with a woman friend. Then, there was a long, brittle spell when none of his charm was charming and Mom mixed stronger drinks and got drunk at their parties."

"But they stayed together," Claire said stubbornly. "Just like my parents did. But then, my parents are Catholic. Bread and butter, those two. But they're doing all right. They bought in with one of my sisters on a condominium in Florida. Mom watches the grandkids; Dad drives his golf cart to the grocery store."

"My parents' relationship got better when my dad lost his job," Laurel said. "They moved into a smaller house, downshifted to one rattle-trap car, and spent more time together. After Dad's first stroke, he was never really articulate, but he teared up when anyone mentioned my mother. He knew she was dead."

"Would you get involved with someone again?" Claire asked her.

"Physically? Maybe. Emotionally? I'll never risk that again. What about you? Not now, I mean, but sometime in the future."

"Not for a long time, that's for sure. First, I want to figure out who I am."

She let her hand slide down toward her pubic bone, to see if there was the slightest tingle, a ghost-like chime of the sex she and George had shared. Her fingers touched Pearl's warm, softly purring shape. Far from being a pain, the cat had eaten dry cat food, used a litter tray, and was giving himself a thorough and satisfying bath. Pearl, at least, had adjusted to his new normal.

"Do you think your parents loved each other?" she asked Laurel.
"I don't have a clue. Do yours?"

"What does that mean, anyway?" Claire asked. "Love, as people get older?"

She rolled up like a hedgehog, taking Laurel's covers. Laurel pulled her pillowcase off her pillow to cover her own shoulders and scooched closer to Claire, glad for her warmth.

"WE'RE NOT FINDING a damn thing except glove prints and sloppy boot prints," Arnie told Elaine. "After the crew is in tomorrow, Claire will need a cleaning service. Hell, she needs a new rug. And that sofa is stripped down to the frame on one side. Her insurance agent had better get here to take pictures. Who would have thought one lousy bird could make such a mess?"

They'd covered the house twice, including the cellar, and now camped outside. The wind was coming from the west and smelled of white pine and fir.

Elaine reached up to rub Arnie's shoulders. She had a girlfriend at home, but she'd grown up with five brothers who, from the time they were kids, hid concerns by tensing muscles and clenching teeth.

"Look at the constellations," she told him. "It's hard to see the patterns. If we concentrate, we'll figure this out."

7

SOMEONE IS PISSED AT CLAIRE

Arnie let the motel sojourners back into the house in the morning, and though Black Pearl was obviously glad to be back, he resented being confined and pawed resentfully at the now locked cat door flap. The six of them sat around the pine kitchen table with mugs of weak coffee and stick-to-the-fingers glazed doughnuts Arnie had picked up.

"We didn't find much," Arnie repeated. "No fingerprints around the patio doors, which is where I am supposing our perp gained entry. There are some smudges that, by the way they're positioned, make me think the door wasn't even closed all the way when the jokester arrived." His voice could not have sounded more disapproving if he learned Claire was opening a house of ill repute.

"There were footprints we believe were made by oversized boots that sloped at the heels and probably are down a sewer in Gaylord by now. What we think are big, smudgy glove prints—the same that were on the outside door—show someone opened the refrigerator, pushed food around, and hauled the salmon out."

"I'm glad they didn't take the cheddar," Claire said.

Jen said, "I don't think they want comments on food, Aunt Claire."

Arnie continued, "We didn't find any hint of disturbances inside the house, food and bird aside, or fingerprints, except from people we all know here, and no sign of anything taken, based on Claire's list."

"You never took my fingerprints," Charles said.

"Your prints were all over the bathtub," Elaine pointed out. "And why would someone who writes about birds go around shoving them into houses?"

"Ah," Charles said.

"So no, we don't know much. It seems like someone played a mean prank. God knows why."

"It can't be that easy to just scoop up a raven," Claire protested.

"They can be addlepated in their first year," Charles said. "The bird could have gotten hit by a car—the side mirror, say—or attacked by an eagle that couldn't quite carry it off. No pun intended."

Elaine favored him with a "you shithead" look.

"I still don't like it," Arnie said. "Doors are to be closed. Doors are to be locked. Alarm system installed. Are you listening?"

"So if we lock the doors behind us, we can leave," Charles said.

Arnie glared at him, and Elaine ran a hand through her hair in exasperation.

"That is to say, I can leave."

"Yes," Arnie said. "Please do. You're taking the bird?"

"You think I'm giving you the bird!" Charles exclaimed. The rest of the group looked at him, looked at each other, and decided he was clueless but not truly offensive.

"How is Oscar?" Laurel asked.

"Doing well, but he needs continued care," Charles said. "Groggy."

"We want to know where you will be, in case we need to find you." Arnie glowered.

"Jen is going to drive me home," Charles explained. "I want to get Oscar someplace where he can recuperate."

Jen seemed to surprise him by refusing. "If we can think of another way to get you there, I'd rather not go," she said. "See, I've come up with a wonderful idea—something I can do for you, Aunt Claire, but it would help me too. Could you drive Charles to his cabin?"

"Me?" Claire's face was a blank. No one had asked her to do a favor for them since George died. In fact, now that she thought about it, everyone had been treating her as if she were as fragile as a small moth caught in the web of a big spider. Before she married George, she'd taken trips on her own. She'd learned new skills, taken risks. Moving had been a risk, and she'd done it for George without a second thought.

"I'd like to freshen up your house," Jen said. "And not just with air freshener."

"Jen!" Laurel sent her a look that said, *How could you?*

"A makeover," Jen explained seriously. "Nothing drastic, but the sofa needs some help…recovering? The blinds need work too. Then it might be nice to tint the paint to complement those changes. And I could do those things. I am applying to interior design schools. I've always had a good sense of color and the way it changes in light. Outdoor light, I mean, not just indoor light."

No response. She looked at Claire, determined to get through her pitch.

"I helped a friend pick out colors for a New York apartment, from which—if you were on just the right angle—you could see the Hudson. The right paint and one expensive Calder rip-off mobile, and everyone's eyes were drawn to the Hudson instead of the building next door. She took pictures, but now I can't get in touch with her." Jen faltered. She had worshipped Claire from afar for years, but now her own life was changing. She knew interior designers needed moxie to succeed.

"If you spruced it up for me, you could get some shots for a portfolio," Claire said.

"Claire, that's sweet." Laurel looked mildly horrified. "But how do you know you'll like what Jen comes up with?" Jen rolled her eyes at her mother.

"I've seen Jen's drawings since she was a little girl." Claire's voice was brisk. "She's right about those new paints that are supposed to coordinate with or play up vistas of trees, a barn, or whatever. I read an article about it in *This Old House* magazine. I sure don't want to do anything decorative just now, but the color scheme does make this house seem like *George's Little House in the Big Woods*. If Jen wants to experiment, I'll pay for what she does and enjoy the results."

"We could talk about your ideas," Jen suggested.

"You have carte blanche, Jen," Claire said. "Is that all right with you, Arnie, if I drive Charles back to Luzerne?"

Arnie and Elaine looked at each other. Elaine knew that Arnie had a schoolboy fixation on Claire, but neither of them had seen Claire so animated since George died. Charles did check out as a legitimate, if odd, writer. And if anything went wrong at the house, Claire would be safely out of the way.

"Get your stuff," Arnie said.

It took no time for Claire and Charles to pack. She grabbed a sweater, and Charles rifled the refrigerator for Oscar's sustenance. They drove off in the rental car, leaving the Bentley for Laurel. Arnie scratched his head and stared after them.

Laurel got a cup of tea and talked to Jen, who did seem to have good ideas that wouldn't cost too much. She took several deep breaths and headed out on her daughter's instructions toward Everything Michigan.

Ann had suggested she and Patsy do some touch-up painting, and that offer had been the start of Jen's design. My whiz kid, Laurel thought.

Tansy brought tuna fish sandwiches—rye bread, but nothing special—that had been left over from the assisted living center where she was an administrator. Ann had an infinitesimal bit of lettuce protruding from the corner of her mouth. Tuna was not something she sold at her own store, and as such, was a treat, as were the pineapple squares and piña coladas that accompanied their lunch. After she took a sandwich to Patsy, who was tending the counter, Tansy sat sipping iced tea and apologized for hurrying.

"I got a call this morning from a prospective client. We're meeting at Best to Be. I know the name is a little corny, but I wasn't responsible for the name of the place. We do offer a good range of health care services. People who are independent can rent an apartment and keep their own car. They can opt in or out of a morning and evening check-in to make sure they are fine. We have a small urgent care center, if someone is ill or hurt but is recovering, and an adjacent facility offering care for people who need extensive help. It's a good place. Usually."

"Usually?" Laurel asked.

"There can be sad times," Tansy said. "Some people check their parents in and never come see them. That's why sometimes, patients run out of pajamas or underwear. But there are times when people are just funny."

Laurel looked at her skeptically.

"One winter, even backup generators went out, and the refrigerators didn't work. We used a smaller than usual dining room to get food to people who, because of physical problems, might've needed extra help eating, and told the staff to give out cookies after dinner instead of offering ice cream. We wanted to keep the freezers closed. But one aid ignored us and gave one man an ice cream bar. Pretty soon, we had a crowd of white-haired people thumping their walkers, shouting, 'He got a nutty bar! We want nutty bars! We want nutty bars too!' We couldn't outshout them, and two of our diners got into a fight about who had the right of way. Residents were lurching out of wheelchairs to take sides and throw silverware. One woman smacked another with a plate and said, 'That's because you always interrupt me!'"

"What happened?" Laurel was goggle-eyed.

"I lit a match under a sprinkler head, and people left the room, many of them helping each other. One man using a wheelchair remained in the room until it emptied, out of chivalry, I thought. He confided that he hadn't had so much fun in years."

Laurel tried to think how to word her question. "Were those people mentally OK?"

"Oh, sure," Tansy said. "Anyone who wasn't 'all there' got food trays in their rooms that night, so they would feel more at home. The nutty bar rioters? I think they were just being human."

My parents died years ago, Laurel thought. If they hadn't, would they have led nutty bar riots?

"So." Tansy became businesslike. "Back to decorating questions. I could pick up a couple of porch chairs if you think Claire would want them. Deck chairs would be nice on her patio, and one of our clients is leaving a ground-floor apartment. Her husband was the gardener, and now she wants a place on the second floor that has a better view."

Laurel didn't know what she had expected of Tansy, but she had not anticipated short brown hair and lipstick complementing a white tunic over beige linen pants. In tan leather flats, Tansy was the same height as her mother, who wore medium-height cork-heeled sandals and a Beatrix Potter apron over a yellow cap-sleeved dress. Ann had a pencil tucked behind one ear.

"I hope the couch Zoe wants to give us isn't too big and blocky," Ann said, patting crumbs from her mouth. "That big piano and a big couch? What will that look like, Laurel?"

"OK, I guess." Laurel was thinking: Zoe? Zoe Weathers? She sipped thoughtfully at her piña colada, narrowing her eyes, pretending to try to visualize Jen's work. Actually, she had no idea what that combination would look like.

"Patsy says the floors will polish up," Ann continued. "Jen hired a local company that refinishes old wood. Some women from the Unitarian Universalist Church have signed up to clean the windows all through the house. They're taking contributions for a new boiler."

"Does Zoe need help getting the couch here?" Laurel asked. "Elaine Santana says one of her brothers has a trucking service."

"Let me know what you think about the chairs, Mom. If we don't want them, the woman will sell them to someone else. They're Adirondack chairs, and the backs were cut to Michigan's mitten shape."

Tansy checked the time on her cell phone and rose to shake hands with Laurel. "I should get back," she said. "I'm glad I got to meet you. Love you, Mom." She daubed the small piece of lettuce off the corner of Ann's mouth, and gave her a quick kiss, leaving Laurel a bit jealous, because, while she and Jen were on most of the same wavelengths, they weren't physically demonstrative.

"Check your lipstick, sweetie. Better text Jen and ask about the chairs," Ann called after her daughter. "This, I think, is Jen's parade." She stood and stretched, one hand rubbing the small of her back. "What do you think Claire will do once the house looks better? You know her better than anyone here."

"I don't have a clue," Laurel said. "Having some color in that room couldn't hurt. Maybe having some changes will make it feel as though the house is really hers, and she can do what she wants with it. I know she still has the condo in Grand Rapids. She could rent this place in the summers if she wants."

"I need a massage," Ann said, watching Tansy leave the room. Some of the cheer radiating from the yellow dress had left her. "I am not," she said, "an afternoon woman. I was when I was younger. I used to love the way flowers would smell—so intense. Lavender grows wild in fields around here. I've read that we don't adjust to heat as well when we get older. And customers get grouchier by the hour. They all think they should be to Sault Ste. Marie by nightfall."

Laurel grinned. "Especially if they're from either coast."

"Yup. New Yorkers are the worst. They think the Midwest is a bridge they cross to get to California."

"Can't you take a nap, or just rest your back when Patsy's working?"

A smile touched Ann's lips. "Patsy would be glad to run the store for me, if I asked her. She's my loyal helper and strong as a horse. And yet…"

"Where did you find Patsy?" Laurel asked.

"She was my husband's nanny," Ann told her. "She did the laundry for his parents. Not usually housekeeping, because she scrubs silver with steel wool. Cleaning the way she does is good for the store. By the way, I'm sorry Claire got hurt when Patsy helped her. I did tell Patsy not to clean pine furniture with Comet, but I didn't think to tell her not to leave dish soap and solvent on the floor."

"How the heck old is Patsy?"

"Maybe seventy?" Ann looked vague. "After Monty died of pancreatic cancer, she stayed on with me. He left me enough money to start this shop. It was smaller then. And Patsy was a godsend. She'd help with Tansy, who was just a baby. We could put Tansy right in the store, in a bouncy chair or a playpen, and paint, stock shelves, whatever."

"Will Tansy take over the store from you, someday, do you think?"

"Hell she will," Ann snapped. "Tansy has a good job where she is. She's got a retirement plan, and there are places where she could work that have stock options. I started this store so I could see her succeed. When I get too old to haul my ass around this business, I'm selling it, and I'll sit back and watch it go bust. You've got to know the community to run this kind of store. We're swamped most of the summer months, but even in the winter, with heating bills, we break even. We have book signings and craft and cooking demonstrations. But it's got to be the right kind of books and the right projects.

"There are trade-offs. I buy those spiral lucky walking sticks from Murphy, Claire's neighbor. He doesn't buy anything from me, but other veterans hear about it and tell their friends about me. The Marshes are good people, and I like to help them, but finding homes for their kittens also guarantees that when they stock up for winter, they'll come here.

"Everybody thinks they'd like to own a little store in the country. Like if I can run this store, running it must be a snap." She drew a breath and smiled at Laurel. "Sorry," she said. "It's something I get peeved about, especially when couples from Chicago come by and say, 'Isn't this the quaintest place? I've always wanted to own a little store.' But it's like owning a bar. It's hard work."

After she left the store, Laurel thought about Ann's frustration and found she could empathize. Many of her students were between jobs or struggling to achieve credentials that would help them survive the future. For many, completing college classes made significant differences in their lives, but underprepared students needed individualized attention. Recently she heard more people say teachers are overpaid and lazy. The thought of going back to the world of "teach more people more, and have them learn it by yesterday" made her feel she might be too old for her job.

Rain clouds were forming in the west when Laurel drove back to Claire's. Then fat raindrops spattered on the Bentley's windshield. Her thoughts turned to Claire and her drive with Charles to Luzerne. When she pulled up to the house, she barely noticed another car that should have been familiar to her.

When she walked into the kitchen, rain dripping down her neck, she recognized David's voice. He was sitting at the table with Jen and Arnie, holding a glass of cider.

"David," she said, feeling the world shift around her.

"Laurel." He stood up, favoring his right foot, and touched a hand to her cheek.

His brown eyes, behind bifocals, looked kind as always. His mouth quirked in a not quite smile. Laurel thought she registered something like regret.

"I needed to see you. And Jen," he added.

Laurel looked at Jen, whose expression was tired. She bit her lip, looking a bit like she'd just sucked on a lemon slice. Next, she looked at Arnie, who, she guessed, was not happy to know Claire was driving Charles and Oscar home. His mouth and eyebrows looked like horizontal lines sketched in with a stick of artist's charcoal. Somehow, she didn't think he was buying David's angst.

"Laurel, you look good. Look good, baby. Whew. That tan looks good on you."

"Thanks, David. What brings you here?"

"I wanted to see Jen, and you, of course. Here's the thing I thought you both should know. I've been dating Bethanie Belknap. I'm not sure if you'd remember her, but we are getting serious."

Laurel sighed.

"So, I was wondering. You still have that ring that was my mom's, right? The antique diamond we had reset?"

"Uh. Yeah. I do. It was the most important gift I've ever received."

"It can't mean much to you now, Laurel. Because I was thinking, Bethanie might like a token of our new start. We're probably getting married." He shifted his weight from his left foot to his right and back again, then sat, a bit clumsily, back in his chair.

Arnie's eyebrows flatlined. He knew by now that David was Laurel's ex. Laurel still looked gobsmacked at seeing her ex-husband. Jen watched her father at work with a sad expression. He said nothing, because it wasn't any of his business. He could think, however, and he thought, *What a horse's ass!*

A slow flush of anger rose up Laurel's body, rising from somewhere between her breasts, up her throat, and into her face—almost like the flush of sexual arousal. She didn't know why she felt demeaned. She hadn't worn the ring to the office, but she had worn it to conferences and parties—places where people were more likely to take you seriously if you looked financially secure. She and David had gone together to pick out the updated setting for the princess cut diamond. She could still smell David's aftershave, feel his arm around her waist. So was it the ring she cared about, or the life she'd lived with David? The life that had included their earliest sexual endeavors and the sweet, mutually agreed upon liaisons that had produced Jen?

She drew a deep breath. "How could I say no to that request?"

"Thanks, hon. Bethanie would love a little something to show off. And to tell the truth, I'm going to be strapped on taxes, now that Jen's out of school and I can't claim her as my dependent. And there are the house payments. Us splitting up, huh, old girl? A good thing for you, maybe, but it set me back."

Arnie stood up. "Mr. Walker, you have to whine somewhere else. I need to you to leave now. Unless, Jen, you want some time with your father? I want Laurel's thoughts on a case."

"You're offensive, do you know that?" David glared at Arnie. "And how could Laurel help? She teaches basic literacy."

"I teach other classes too," Laurel protested.

Both men ignored her.

Arnie's mouth looked as though he'd swallowed raw nettles. "The fact that Laurel is not from this community reduces some bias. She's a disciplined thinker and from what I know of her, judiciously fair."

"I think you're overestimating her," David said, "but I do have to get back soon. Raining, you know." He slicked back his hair. "Jen, you and Laurel are always welcome to stop and meet Bethanie."

Jen sucked on her teeth before asking, "Hey, Dad? How old is she?"

"She's thirty-eight, darling." He looked contemptuously at Arnie.

"About halfway between Mom's age and mine."

David nodded, seeming pleased Jen had worked this out. "It's a beautiful age for women. She deserves a gorgeous ring. Give Claire my best wishes," he added. "I guess things aren't going well here in Bumfuck, Egypt."

"You're making progress," Jen said. "Aren't you, Arnie?"

Arnie didn't reply, swept back into a memory of being unable to breathe, held facedown in the mud. He'd turned into a muscled teenager but had been chronically ill as a child, and he had come to hate bullies, which was one reason he'd gone to work for the police. Physical bullying, making fun of people, kicking dogs in the street— any and all of it made his blood pressure rise. Laurel could probably defend herself more eloquently than he could, but it was clear she was trying to keep the peace for Jen's sake.

He, on the other hand, wanted to kick David in the butt.

"That's odd," David said. "It seems to me that someone is pissed at Claire and being quite up front about it." He fished in his jacket.

"I picked this up off the driveway. Didn't want Laurel or anyone else to run over it, and then I was so happy to see Jen, I forgot I'd nabbed it. I don't know what you're dealing with, Arnie, but it's my unbiased opinion that this is a clue."

He held out a laminated piece of printer paper.

In black marker, in the center of the paper, the words were written in a broad printed scrawl that angled downward:

Widow Woman
Witch
Cunt
GET OUT

8

OSCAR AND THE BEAKLESS BEINGS

"I don't get it," Claire said to Charles. The rental car was not as comfortable as the Bentley, but took the slight curves of the road well enough. She could barely see the water of the Main Branch. "Why is your cabin on a creek instead of on a river?"

Charles seemed more relaxed now that he was driving home. "Inheritance, mostly. My dad inherited a piece of property he didn't want from his father, and my younger sister, Mary, didn't want it either. So the cabin was literally free, if I wanted it. Well, taxes. Fifteen hundred a year, about, and there's some upkeep. But I can live cheaply there. In the winter, I often travel. And it's free in another sense, too. Rivers are part of the riparian rights system of law, which came from English common law. You can't impede people from traveling on navigable water that their property borders. That's even true for my part of Big Creek, so I can access the entire stream, and when you see my place, you'll realize I only see a few diehard fishermen."

"Privacy, then. You're a misanthrope. You like canoe races."

"No, not exactly. I can stand the Au Sable River Canoe Marathon. It's probably the premiere canoe race in the world. What I don't like are people who tube the rivers linked together, shouting 'chug, chug, chug,' and throw empty beer cans into stands of cattails. I want to see otters, not some drunk, half-naked girl standing up in a canoe, waving a plastic gin bottle, and pretending to 'fall' in shallow water. Then, some muscle-bound lout dives in to 'assist' her, scaring the fish as he does. If anyone is going to be concupiscent on an island in front of my house, it had damn well better be me!"

"No argument," Claire said. Her posture had almost impercep-
tibly softened, but Oscar noticed it.

Oscar, like all ravens, was curious. Curiosity might kill the cat,
but it had made ravens successful on almost every continent, where
they ate food that would choke a goat. When the car started moving,
he'd popped his head out of his stick nest in the wayback and foot-
beaked his way to the top of the back seat. There, he assessed his
situation. The moving box he shared with the beakless beings was
made of material much harder than his nest box had been, and for
all the two beakless ones had pale, grasping appendages, they had
not gathered enough sticks and twigs.

One of the beakless beings was being raucous. Probably male.

"Sorry," Charles said. "I'm not good at conversation. I'll go a
week without talking to anyone and be perfectly content. But then,
when I'm with someone sensible, I talk on and on."

"Don't worry about it," Claire assured him. "I like people with
convictions. You don't see Laurel being sweet all the time."

"That's true. Jen can hold her own in conversations. We've had
some good discussions about anthropology. She and I are both pro
Neanderthal."

"Uh, what?"

"Pro Neanderthal. They were human beings. The evidence—
burials with flowers, that rock circle, handprints, so much more. We
carry their DNA. They may have had rudimentary speech."

"Oh. I have read that. I guess I'm pro Neanderthal too." She
rubbed the corners of her eyes.

The larger beakless being was male, Oscar concluded, and the
female was responding, not turning her back, as she would have if
she wanted no part of him.

The hard box raced along. He could feel the sense of motion
and even some sense of their direction. The moving box compen-
sated for his companions being wingless, and they could, he
supposed, see dead things and stop if they were hungry, but there

was no swooping, soaring, or gliding, and very little chance to find newborn squirrels or late summer eggs.

"I gave Oscar deviled eggs and some berries, and there are carrot sticks and mozzarella cheese sticks for us," Charles offered. "Our food is in the glove box. Let me know if you want some. I got stuck in a cave once in a two-day November blizzard. I ate spruce cambium, the layer under the bark, which is high in sugar. Since then, I always travel with at least a little sustenance."

"What were you doing in a cave? And yes, I'll get us cheese sticks. You know we could have taken any of the food I had at the house."

"I like caves, actually, though not for spelunking. There are bats in the caves in Dickinson County."

Actually, the large beakless being was not entirely beakless. He had a good-sized outcropping on his face, but like mammals and other lesser beings, he stuffed his food in a hole below. The protuberance, Oscar assumed, was sexual adornment meant to attract females.

"I didn't think of taking your food." He took a proffered cheese stick. "God, these are tasteless," Charles muttered. "The cheddar would have been better."

"Mmmm," Claire said. It was a passive, reassuring noise.

Oscar tut-tutted and preened cautiously, not liking the encumbrance on his wing. He'd almost made a grab at the cheese stick but was afraid he would overbalance. At least food didn't seem to be a problem. There were blackberries and two strange-tasting eggs next to his nest. He wondered if the bird that had lain the eggs had been eating pepper plants.

When he'd first awakened, feeling groggy but rested, he wondered if he'd been feeding on fermenting cherries, but had quickly discarded the thought. Peering at his wing, he had seen it was pinioned with small, straight sticks and a membranous coating that kept it positioned. Now, he pecked one of the sticks, tasting it. Jarring the wing still hurt. Soaring could wait for a while. He'd seen birds with injured wings, and if no weasels trapped them on the ground, and they had food and water and the use of their feet, they healed.

Boxes were not, however, ideal for raven hygiene. He, for one, was fastidious about droppings on his feet.

He foot-beaked carefully over to the female. She made an eerie whooshing noise, but remained still as a woodcock with babies. Using the female for footholds, he worked his way up the firm perch where she rested her head. She moved to let him claim the headrest, which was the correct behavior since he, as a male, was dominant.

Rain was starting, making it hard to see outside. He clacked his beak and went to sleep.

9

CREEK WATER AND SAND

By the time they got to the cabin, a drenching rain was falling, and the night had become surprisingly cold. Charles had gotten Oscar settled in a freshly papered and food-stocked box in the cabin's loft, started a fire in the soapstone stove, and gone back to help Claire in. She was sound asleep and had barely registered him tucking her into bed, piling quilts over her, and throwing his belongings on the futon where he slept. She woke up in the morning when he went out and found he had left coffee waiting for her, and the small but recently remodeled bathroom was still warm from his shower. He'd left her a note, a scrawl that read, "*Oscar ate canned corned beef hash! It's going to be hot today, so don't add wood to the fire.*"

She had a cup of coffee and watched out the back windows as Charles appeared with a ladder, a cordless drill, and a reciprocating saw. He disappeared up the ladder. Could Oscar use a bird door?

She stepped outside when she heard a truck pull up in front of the cabin. A large man set a package down on a tree stump.

"Saw your lights," he rumbled, running his fingers through his beard. "Thought Charles could use these." He peered at Claire, who was conservatively clothed in shorts and a T-shirt, then turned without waiting for her to answer and climbed back into the truck and left.

Charles came down the ladder to inspect the package. "Breakfast! Fresh eggs and a trout!"

"Who was that man who looked like a black bear?" she asked.

"There aren't many of us on this branch of the creek," he told her, "so we look in on each other and make sure we're at least hobbling and have coffee, canned milk, the basics. That was Ed who just now brought the hens' eggs. He raises chickens. The eggs will be great for Oscar. The filleted brown trout—now, that wasn't a good thing to do. The streams and rivers are heating up; catch and release gives the brown trout that are left more of a chance. But what's done is done. Come back in for a minute, and I'll fry this fish up, while it's still right out of the water. I'll remind Ed later he's not supposed to bring me jigged frogs or trotline trout."

The trout, fried in bacon grease, was delicious. The smell of freshly brewed coffee and bacon and the trout made her feel at home.

"Building a birdhouse?"

"That wouldn't help. But in a couple of days, that wing will be healed enough to let Oscar climb out into that scrawny apple tree and get back in when he wants."

"Then what? You have a hole in your house?"

"I've been thinking. Summers are hotter than they used to be, at least in June and July. I'm making my raven exit the size to accommodate an air conditioner—a small one, once Oscar's gone. Right now, he's chewing up the apple branches I gave him. They've got some kind of fungus on them that he likes."

Charles went outside again, armed with a metal framing square and a tape measure. Claire went out barefoot to explore the creek. She stuck her toes in the icy water and promptly pulled them out again.

She hadn't gone down to the river in front of her house for months. The bottom was sandy, but the water—about five feet deep—was clogged with detritus from old maple trees that storms had brought down. Once George stopped fishing, keeping the pool cleared hadn't been a priority. Heavy, waterlogged branches made the bottom treacherous for walking; others had jammed together on sandbars like oversized pickup sticks.

Here, the creek was broad and mostly shallow. Sun-splashed water rushed around small islands, some the size of footstools, some the size of double beds. Some of the islands had clumps of white-tipped wheat grass. Tamarack trees clumped together along the bank, and white-cupped flowers with green veins grew on the bank. Upstream, there was a darker, shaded area that led back into a tangle of stream and swamp. Behind her, she could hear the noise of Charles's saw.

She gritted her teeth and went back to the creek, finding a place where it was easy to step in. The bones in her feet ached at first, but as she moved gingerly from sandy underwater bits to sunny sand spits, she got used to the water flowing around her ankles. She bent over to pick a caddisfly larva, house and all, out of the water. It seemed that, some time ago, a bead bracelet had broken, and the caddisfly had enterprisingly added red and purple glass beads to its house. She placed the larva—not much bigger than a fishfly—back in the water, wishing it luck in its brief life. Though maybe that brief life wouldn't be brief to a caddisfly.

She waded upstream and back for the better part of an hour before she heard the splash of feet in the stream and turned to see Charles. He was standing close enough that she could feel his body heat and smell his sweat mixed with the scent of the pine-stoked fire. He was wearing cut off shorts and a faded gray shirt, one sleeve streaked with bird shit.

"Did you see the otter?" he asked her.

"I didn't think to look," she said. "I saw a heron, though."

He stopped a foot away from her, looking like a deer by a salt lick, not sure whether to move forward or to turn and bolt.

On impulse, she cupped her hands full of water and splashed him. He bent and brought one hand skimming across the water, drenching her hair and making her own T-shirt and shorts cling. After a few more minutes of deluging each other, he threw up his hands.

"I give! No fair. I'm going to lose my glasses in the creek any minute. You people who see things without glasses cheat."

Claire caught her breath, her skin on fire with cold and exhilaration. How long had it been since she'd felt exuberant?

"Cataract surgery," she said. "I recommend it. That is, I guess you have an ophthalmologist?"

"I have an ophthalmologist," he said. "He said I'm not ready. For cataract surgery."

Claire was suddenly aware her nipples showed through her T-shirt. Rubbing her own arms, she felt duck bumps. She was getting cold feet.

They looked at each other.

"Let's go get toweled off. You're shivering," he said.

The coffee's strength was cut by condensed evaporated milk and lumps of brown sugar. They sat side by side by the futon near the fireplace. Inside the stove's glass door, embers still glowed with last night's heat.

"I'd stoke this up for you, but the day's getting warmer."

"I know," she said. "If a fire doesn't draw, you just end up with smoke." She pushed her hair back self-consciously. "I look a mess," she said.

He pulled back from her, surprised. "You look fine. More important, you're curious and kind and funny. That's an attractive combination. I'm not making a pass."

"Oh," she said.

"Jen told me about you," he said. "How when she was little, you'd get down under the kitchen table and scribble-draw with her."

She took a deep breath. "You probably know more about me than I know about you. Mind you, I've never heard of a serial killer, or even a serial masher, who built bird nests."

"Don't be too quick, my dear, to assume people are harmless." His tone was joking, but his eyes were somber. "Jen says Laurel—except with her dad—is a skeptic's skeptic, but that you trust too easily."

"I shouldn't trust you?" She tried to turn the conversation to a lighter level.

"If you and I see each other again, Arnie will check me out from gold fillings to toenail parings.

After he's done that might be better timing."

"It might be," she said, pulling off her shirt.

He sighed and slid down to kiss one, then the other nipple that now stood erect like berries on her breasts. She moved her hand to cup his penis through his shorts. He gasped but moved her hand away. "Move to the futon?" he asked. "It's still warm from the fire."

She ran her tongue down the side of his sweaty neck as he lifted her by pressing his weight up against her. In a moment, they were both naked on the quilts. He pressed his penis against her thighs, wet with arousal. The hot, nudging pressure moved against her clitoris.

For one brief second, she thought, oh Laurel, what am I doing? But her body carried her forward, overriding her qualms.

He waited until she arched her back, drawing in her breath, then slid inside her, thrusting and pulling back, thrusting and pulling back, until he collapsed with a guttural exclamation. She felt his penis slip out of her, small now and limp. His left hand reached to stroke her hair back from her forehead.

She moved his hand so he would touch one of her eyelids. She hoped he had enough experience to know why she had teared up with release. It had been close to two years since George had aroused her senses, and she hadn't been sure her sexual responses still worked.

What did she really know about Charles? He could be fickle and have perfected a way of luring women in. Maybe she was only one of a string of women who had succumbed to the "I'm just an amateur, ma'am" brand of charm.

How he would get the quilt clean? Would he anchor it in the stream and hang it to dry on the apple tree branches, or simply leave the residue of their sex? Had she made love on a quilt already crusted with cum?

"I hope that was all right," he said. "That it didn't feel like a betrayal."

She gave a sigh that came all the way up from her diaphragm, like the sigh she gave to show a doctor that her lungs were clear.

"It didn't feel like a betrayal," she said. "In some ways, it felt like a confession. People assume I'm the good-as-gold wife, the woman who looked after her husband and never stopped loving him. And it's true, and it's not true. There were times near the end when I just kept doing what I could. I was the only one George wanted near him, but he didn't want me to touch him, unless I had to. Sometimes, even then, he got angry and pushed me away. When that happened, especially after I'd just brought him a bed pan and changed his pajamas, I wanted to run away from the stranger he had become. Do you have anything to drink?"

"Courvoisier," he said, and climbed out of bed, retrieving his shorts in the process, then slid back in to join her once he'd handed her the drink.

The brandy, even in its plain, somewhat scratched glass tumbler, shone pure as gold. The color wasn't that different from that of the white cedar planks that made up the cabin walls. There was a small desk overflowing with books, notebooks, and papers in the kitchen, and bookshelves on every wall except one that held the window facing the creek.

She swirled the brandy, inhaling the faint scent of grapes that bloomed over the glass. She took a swallow, and warmth flowed from her toes to her hair roots.

"I've been meaning to ask you," she said. "Why do you have Lawrence Durrell's *Bitter Lemons*? Shouldn't you have all the Gerald Durrell books instead?"

"They're under the bed you slept in last night. I thought you were the dancer and Laurel was the brainy type."

"I like that." Claire sat up. "I read. Or I used to. And Laurel dances. Some. At least she used to."

"I have Lawrence Durrell because he's a marvelous writer. So is Gerald, but Larry's writing is often darker, more political. Fits with how I see the world."

She sat up straight, having just taken in a huge, mouth-burning swallow of brandy.

"Why don't we go out and get something to eat?" he asked.

"I had that nice trout," she said.

"That nice small trout," he responded. "And I gave you most of it."

"Where are we going?" She tugged on her clothes, rubber-legged with sexual lassitude.

"There's a bar near here—Ma Deeter's. It was built right about at the end of second-growth white pine logging. It burned to the ground and was rebuilt, but the sign has stayed the same—*This Is God's Country. Please Don't Drive Thru Town Like Hell.*"

10

BLOODY MARYS AT MA DEETER'S

The room smelled of secondhand smoke that clung to the clothes of people sitting near them, while beer battered fish, jalapeno fortified chili, hot dogs, and French fries competed for dominance.

"Luzerne—spelled with a Z, not a C the way it is in Switzerland—has seen better days," Charles admitted. "But a lot of my history is here. Besides Deeter's, which is pretty well known in Michigan, the town has a post office, a small IGA, and a good hardware store. Everything else changes over the years."

Before they left the cabin, Claire had called Laurel on her cell phone while Charles checked on Oscar.

"I slept with him," she'd said to Laurel, sotto voce.

"Why on *earth* would you do that?" Laurel, who was out of books, had been perusing George's book collection.

"I don't know," Claire said, expecting Laurel's help.

"Well, figure it out," Laurel responded. "Find out what it is about Charles that made you slide off the celibacy wagon. If you can't analyze the past, you're doomed to repeat it."

"Callous," Claire had accused. "This isn't a quiz on motivation."

"Sorry," Laurel said. "There are books all around me, and I can't find anything to read."

At the restaurant, Charles kept talking, but so much had changed so abruptly in her life, she couldn't focus.

"I hate four wheelers," he said. "Good thing riders usually stay on the trails."

"Or else what? You'd blast 'em with a shotgun?"

"There was a wiseass kid who chased Ed's dog with a snowmobile. It was a good dog, but it was so scared it had no idea what to do. We watched it dig under the branches of a snow-covered pine. While it was digging, a bobcat loped out from the back of the pine tree and took shelter in the woods. Ed's dog stayed there, cowering while the snowmobile missed it by inches. Ed and me, we thought of stringing piano wire at throat height."

"I can see you in prison, building birdhouses."

"With some luck, they wouldn't have found the snowmobile or the body. There are secrets in the swamps here. Can I have that pickle, if you're not going to eat it?"

Ma Deeter's rebuild after the fire had resulted in compromises. The pine table where Charles and Claire sat was covered with protective plastic. "I miss the pool tables that were here when I was a kid," he added. There were a few families sitting near them, and one couple groomed to the gills on a date, but most of the clientele sported graying or bleached hair. One rowdy group had their attention fixed on a televised Tigers game. One man at the bar was so drunk, he made sitting on a bar stool look like riding a mechanical bull.

Claire ordered a second Bloody Mary with four olives and a pickle, and a chicken club sandwich. Charles had a three-inch-thick Reuben and coffee.

"You shouldn't drive home tonight," he said. "You drink like a fish."

"Tactful, aren't you?"

"Not what I'm known for."

"Did you ever used to drink, Charles?"

"Some. I never had a great head for it. My grandfather was always disappointed. He drank Wild Turkey bourbon and thought a gentleman—self-made or not—should be able to hold his liquor. But it didn't stop him leaving me a bequest."

Claire chewed an ice cube. Charles, looking moody, caught the eye of their waitress.

"Jeanne, put a shot of Jameson in this for me."

"Irish coffee," she said. "You've got it, Charles." She swiveled away, looking comfortable in a blue Ma Deeter's T-shirt, jeans, and tennis shoes.

"Oh, hell," he said. "If it's called Irish coffee, it's going to come in a glass cup. Why can't they put the booze in a coffee mug, the way it ought to be served?"

"I thought you weren't drinking tonight."

"I decided to try for Dutch courage," he said. "I may want a rematch in sexual grappling, and fear I am outclassed."

"So," she said dubiously, "tell me more about yourself."

The Irish coffee, with whipped cream floating on top, was served in a glass cup. Claire held up her half-filled glass, suggesting a third could be brought at Jeanne's convenience.

"Plus, I feel I should explain myself. This is an awfully good Reuben. Stacks of corned beef. Good Thousand Island dressing."

"Helpful to know," Claire said.

"It's hard to know where to start."

"Pick a place. Any place," she suggested. "I've been a lot of things in my life, and no one ever judged me. At least, not that I know of. Tell me about your grandfather."

"Right," he said. "When you get back to the cabin, look above the bed where you slept. There's a leather hanging, pretty time-worn, that I framed in glass. The words burned into it read 'Maintiens le Droit.'

"My grandfather was tall. Spare. A good-looking man who golfed his age or better into his nineties. Strong facial features, craggy nose and jaw. He was born in England, but according to a family rumor, had been sent to Canada after having compromised a girl. That was easy to do then, without legal birth control. Lambskin condoms are still popular, but they aren't always effective. His family had money; they would have sent the girl to France to have the child. They sent him away and made his scant inheritance conditional on his not returning to the continent.

"He was a member of the Royal Canadian Mounted Police, which is where 'Maintiens le Droit' came from. Then, when he had a family, he went to work for a lumber company, when no one thought second-growth white pine could disappear. When the old forests were gone, the value of land bottomed out, but he bought property when everyone else was selling. He had a home and property on the Main Branch for a while, near Lake Margrethe, but he sold almost everything when prices went up."

"Why do you think he kept the cabin?" Claire asked.

"I don't know," Charles admitted. "Maybe it reminded him of his days in the Canadian Mounted Police."

"Can't you just call him a Mounty?"

"Not properly, no. He was, in spite of his faux pas with the girl in England, a man concerned with maintaining the right as best he could. When he was in Canada, he had to go track down a man who'd killed someone in a bar fight. He found the man, who'd fled drunk into a snowstorm. My grandfather, who wasn't armed, found him in his tent, lifted the tent flap, and said, 'Joe, it's time to come home.'"

"What happened?"

"Joe and my grandfather walked back to town." Charles took a sip of his drink. "My own father had no interest in staying in the north. He took his share of my grandfather's money to Indiana, where he started a chain of restaurants. My sister Mary, who I was close to as a child, took over his original restaurant, so Dad left her his money when he died a few years ago. Mary offered to share her inheritance with me, but nowadays, restaurant chains are risks, and her husband's a little iffy. I like to know she's got money in a bank. In another state."

"No other women in the family of interest?" Claire asked.

"My grandmother died in childbirth when my father was born. My own mother, who I remember as elfin and charming, parted with my father when I left for Columbia. She accompanied me there, dropped me off, made sure my trunks were taken in, and moved to Italy with a widower she met on the train. We got a few postcards from her, in her inimitable handwriting, saying she loved us all, but that we should remember 'pure passion' doesn't often arise in midlife."

"That sounds incredibly unfeeling and mean," Claire said.

"My father never discussed it. I'm not sure how much he missed her. Her leaving was harder on Mary than me. Mother had always wanted to be a socialite. She and I didn't have much in common."

"But you're all right, financially?" Claire asked. "If you weren't, would Mary help you?" George had not left her filthy rich, but her attorney said their portfolio would keep her comfortable, even if medical insurance went through the roof.

"I'm all right. I have enough to do what I want to do."

"What do you want to do?" Claire fidgeted. She'd tried to get Charles talking, but so far, she had no idea why she was sitting here, at this restaurant, asking for the story of his life. Her chicken sandwich was good, as were the salad and sweet potato fries, but the sand caught in her underpants—she thought she'd powdered adequately—was making her edgy. She tugged at the elastic that rimmed her conservative panties.

When her third drink came, she concentrated. She could almost meditate by sucking her drink through the straw and then blowing a stream of bubbles down around the olives. The pickle complicated the effort. She handed it to Charles, but he put it down and looked at her.

"I've only wanted to do one thing in my life, besides loving a woman I loved long before I met you. I would have liked to go on doing that. I want a life that lets me keep learning. I did publish my dissertation when I graduated Columbia, and that was released as a book—*Feather Findings*—documenting pesticide evidence in generations of birds that have nested, or still nest, in the same or nearby sites. Clever title, I think. Sounds cheerful. That book is how I can make Ed, and other homeboys up here, leave me alone. 'Professor's workin', let 'um concentrate,' they say. It's also how I can justify a meal out, gas for the truck Ed and I share, and the occasional haircut."

He looked over his glasses at her. His frames were crooked, riding up on one side of his face. He also had Thousand Island dressing smeared on one lens. She thought about reaching across the table and straightening his glasses and wiping the salad dressing off, but thought about the phrase he'd used—*a woman I loved*. She reached down and readjusted the fit of her shorts.

"They'd resent you if they knew you didn't need to make money?"

"They wouldn't resent me, but they would be different. I like hearing their stories. Stories they wouldn't share as easily if they thought I didn't need to work. They talk about winters they remember when snow came up to the windows of two-story houses, and of tunneling from house to barn. Logging small, hilly properties with horses. Not getting friendly with men who beat tourists to death."

"Wait," Claire said. "Who what?"

"'Crushed a guy's skull,'" Charles said. "Think clan loyalties. There aren't many jobs here, and some of the people who stay are like the infamous Cornish pirates who lured ships onto the rocks with lights and beat survivors to death. I've heard it said that not everyone who comes from 'down below' surfaces again."

Claire checked the level of Charles's Irish coffee. Not that much gone. "So, you love this place, with its dog-chasing, off-road vehicles and chop shop cutthroats?"

"I do love this place. I virtually went into hiding here, during one part of my life. I realized I slowed down here. Thought more. Listened better. Remembered better. And most of the people here— most of the off-road riders, too—you could trust with your life.

"But anger builds when land gets played out. Can't fish it, farm it, or mine it. There are logging companies here, but they don't need the number of people they used to. They've got machines that move through forests like Transformers. The machine cuts off a tree at the base and picks it up easy as a man plucks a toothpick out of a toothpick glass. People could move where jobs are, and some do, of course, but it's hard to move Grandpa and Grandma in the back of a Toyota. People from down below buy land and build summer houses three or four times as big as an ordinary house. Folks who've lived here three generations get bitter. And if you're going to strip a truck, who better to help than your cousin? It's not just here. It happens all over the world."

"What was the land here originally? Ojibwa?"

"Their villages were more in southwest Michigan. Ojibwa and Ottawa—*Odawa*, they'd say—did have villages near here, but they moved around more, fishing and harvesting wild crops."

"Mister Authority," she said. "You do remind me of George. Sometimes talking to him was like reading the center column of *The Wall Street Journal*."

"I'll take that as a compliment," he said. "Though I bet George's knowledge was organized in columns."

"I bet you hate malls."

"I shop in small stores when I can. There's been talk about a Costco store in Grayling that's at least, for the most, part employee-owned. Leelanau Books, in Leland, has a great selection of new books, and First Edition too, in Moran, is a terrific used bookstore."

"So, what the hell were you doing in San Diego?"

"Remember what I said about the love of my life?"

"I need another drink."

Charles waved for the server again, and Jeanne came over.

"Another Irish coffee and another Bloody Mary?"

"You will have had four Bloody Marys," Charles marveled. "You could drink Bluto, from *Popeye*, right under the table."

"The love of your life? Is she the woman in the picture on the bedside table?"

He gave her a long look. "Let's get the bill with this round of drinks," he said. "We may be having an actual conversation. I want to be able to remember what we said."

Claire looked abashed. "I do too, actually. I think, Charles, I'm going to remember everything you've said."

They drank their last drinks in relative silence, eavesdropping on other people in the bar. A group of older people, mostly gray-haired and in motorcycle clothes, was discussing the pipeline under the Straits of Mackinac, where Lake Michigan and Lake Huron join.

When the bill came, Charles insisted on paying.

"You fed me trout," Claire said.

"You drove. And I want to over-tip."

"You buttering up Jeanne?"

"She's got a kid with an immune system disorder. Jeanne's husband's insured, but her working here helps them pay for medicine not covered."

Claire stopped at the restroom on her way to the car. She checked her hair in the mirror while she was washing her hands, and thought briefly about brushing it out, which she always would have done with George. This is ridiculous, she thought. This is Charles.

Then she brushed her hair.

"Want to drive around and talk?" Charles asked, and Claire did.

11

AFFAIRS AND REVELATIONS

Charles drove west, past the cut-in for the cabin, and after a brief time on M-72, turned northwest between red pines and onto a sandy logging road.

"Lane Delaney," he said. "We were lovers through our graduate work at Columbia. She was a serious musician then, and now plays cello in the London Symphony Orchestra. I saw her play, twice, when I was in England, and when I had articles published, she sent me congratulatory notes. We broke up because she wanted kids and I didn't. Kids are fascinating, smart, alien beings, but they grow up to be people, and there are already too many people in the world.

"Her daughter, Simone, is geneticist who graduated from Oxford. I didn't go to her graduation ceremony, though I've since seen her name in publications that call for reduced use of fossil fuels. Lane's son, James, just graduated from Scripps Institution of Oceanography in San Diego. He's researching whether planted corals could clean flooded subways as sea levels rise. I think Lane wanted me to meet him to prove her kids will help the environment. Maybe as a way of saying I could have been the father of those kids."

"Was that depressing?" Claire asked. "Did it make you jealous?"

"No. Their father is a brilliant mathematician. If she and I had had children, our kids might have been twits."

She thought of the photo on the bedside table. "I doubt it. Maybe *I'm* jealous. Lane has a flat stomach and has produced two children who are geniuses, whereas I have no children but do have a squishy gut."

"You don't understand your own attraction," Charles responded. "If you don't believe me, ask Santana. Arnie has a crush on you. We meet you, and *pow!* We're smitten." Charles sighed. "Lane is beautiful, like a juvenile heron. All legs, all angles. Age doesn't matter. If you're a man or a woman, to this day, she takes your breath away. And she could belch in a way that somehow sounds like a bittern.

"You're more like a mourning dove, Claire. It's a bird people think is ordinary. Most people don't know a mourning dove can take off straight up at close to eighty miles an hour. They mate for life and are pretty much monogamous."

"A pigeon," she said. "Lane's a heron, and I'm a pigeon?"

"Mourning doves' feathers are buff-colored, but with an undertone of rose."

"Huh. What kind of bird are you like, Charles?"

"Not sure. I could be a bittern," he said. "Tall, streaky, long-necked marsh bird. Secretive. Points its bill skyward and blends in with the reeds. Perfect camouflage. Only, they're a bit inflexible; if in an open field, they still stick their heads up." He looked rueful.

"There can't have been only one woman all these years," she challenged him.

"There was a woman who I thought loved me. There was a girl who thought she loved me once."

The car bumped down a hill. The road looked more like a two-track now, and jack pines too crooked to cut scraped the car's sides.

"The first is a better story," he said. "After Lane left Columbia, I was in my forties, and I lived with a writer. I'm not telling you her name. She does romance fiction. You've seen her face in beach reading suggestions in magazines.

"She was different from Lane, who still doesn't know she's beautiful in her fifties. My inamorata had her eyebrows tattooed on, and eyeliner inked in as well. She looked like Elizabeth Taylor. And she loved me! Unbelievable. We met at a conference on Great Lakes dune erosion. She was setting a novel there. I moved into a house she was renting. Near Honor. Used to be a lighthouse in the area."

"I know the town. Back to Elizabeth Taylor," Claire said. She rolled down her window, and the air that blew in smelled like broken balsam branches.

The car scraped through a sand pit. Wheels spun and then caught. Rain was beginning to drip from the trees.

"Her house looked like that catalog. *Hump's.*"

"*Gump's.*"

"She had this sculpture of a panther on her breakfast bar. Beautiful, long-backed, snarling thing. I was in awe of it."

"Oh, Charles. You didn't break it?" Claire asked.

"We lived together for two years. I wore a tie when she told me to. Got expensive haircuts. We went on book tours together. She'd be sure *Feather Findings* was on display."

The car lurched over a log. Good rental car, Claire thought.

"What happened?" she asked him. "The two of you, both writers, you using aftershave lotion. That doesn't sound so bad."

"I was always careful of that panther," Charles said. "It was glassy black. Wildcats are splotchy."

Claire knew that, but stayed quiet.

"We'd just gotten back from a book tour. Her last book wasn't selling as well as the one before it, though she'd sold twenty copies, mostly to women, including to one nice transgendered woman who had liked the sex scenes. I'd sold four copies, all at our last stop at a bookstore in Ann Arbor. Ecology was starting to be 'in.' We were back home, sitting down to Zingerman's chile cheddar bread, toasted with cream cheese, and I'd fixed coffee. I was bringing food in on a tray. I'd done it before. No problem. This time, though, my eye caught on the sheen the hanging LED lights cast on the panther's haunches, and I spilled the whole pot of coffee onto her computer."

The car jolted and bumped over a series of small logs.

"And?" Claire asked.

"She turned into a harpy! She said she had a new manuscript started and she hadn't backed it up on her time machine, and I was ruining her career, was a boor at sex, and a lot of other unfounded things. She started throwing coffee cups at me. One hit my ear and bounced off and hit the panther, which fell on the marble counter and broke in half. Well, Maybe in thirds. She said she hoped I'd die from elephantiasis. I took the chile cheese bread—after all, I'd bought it—and my computer, and I left and never went back, not for my ties or my pointy-toed shoes. I drove here and didn't leave Luzerne for a year."

Claire leaned against his shoulder, which was much more difficult to do now than it had been in the days of bench seats.

"The woman who thought she loved you?"

"Too young," he said. "I met Nora at a conference. By then, I was in my late forties and had published some articles, and she was seventeen."

"Like Jen," Claire said.

"Not at all like Jen. Jen is a college graduate and a mature woman, with a brain. I never touched Nora, who had the brains of a soggy tea bag, but she just kept finding me. Her father threatened to shoot me. I have been careful, since then, to stay clear of women who are younger than I am."

"So," Claire said after a pause. "We should get back to the cabin."

"The one time Nora drove here, I walked down the creek and stayed with Ed for a few days. That's why he gave you the stink eye, but then he saw that you were older."

"Charles," she said, "Let's go back. I have to pee."

"Should I stop the car for you?" he asked. "This road used to be a logging road. We've been driving in a circle. We're almost home."

Walking from the car to the cabin, they could hear the rush of the creek. She used the bathroom and doused her crotch with a handful of water, dried off, and used talcum powder—Gold Bond, not Johnson's. Charles used the bathroom next.

"I thought you'd pee outside," she said.

"I don't mark my territory."

She picked up on his conversational tone as he checked on Oscar. The raven *prrrted* back.

"Yes," he said. "This time, I brought you real corned beef. And some peppers from my salad, and new papers."

Claire stripped off all her clothes but her lace-edged black underpants. Of course Ed had seen she was older. She was older.

"I still may harbor sand," she warned Charles when he returned and washed his hands fastidiously.

"I can deal with that," Charles said. "Anyone who loves this creek gets used to some sand in their teeth."

"Good God, shut up and come here," she said.

Afterward, she lay with her head cradled on his arm.

"Charles? You awake?"

"Languorous."

"You would have been a good father. Look how conscientious you are with Oscar."

"You and George didn't? Or couldn't have children?"

They could hear the creek through open, screened windows. "No, we didn't. There was a time when I wanted kids," she said. "My sister, Jan, had heartbreakingly beautiful children: tousled curls, long eyelashes, eyes so dark brown they looked black. Their hair smelled clean, like my mother's sheets when she dried them in the sun. When one of her children relaxed in my arms, I thought I'd died and gone to heaven, and was holding an angel. Her third child was autistic. Jan spent her life finding school systems that would work with autistic children, and every moment she spent has been worth it. But George had taken care of a younger sister, and since he was on the road a lot, and I'd be alone, he didn't think I realized what I would be signing up for. He didn't want for us to turn into burned out, cranky parents.

"He wanted to be able to travel, which we did, and to just take care of me. I thought he might change his mind, but then we got caught up in the life we were living. And it was, you know, a very good life. I miss him."

"I miss Lane," he said.

"Did you two sleep together in San Diego?"

"Of course not. I like her and her children. Even her husband is tolerable, though I can't say I like him. There are moments you shouldn't seize, though I am glad we seized this one."

"I was going to wait a year, before I slept with anyone."

"Mourning doves are monogamous, but if they lose a mate, most mate again."

"Are you offering?" she asked.

"God no," he answered. "We hardly know each other."

"I do like you, Charles."

"I should hope so. Actually, I'm honored."

"Part of what I like about you is knowing you don't need me. Taking care of sick people is really hard. When you're done, especially if you've lost someone, you feel guilty and depressed and like a zombie. Like you might clutch on to someone and be so needy, you'll gut them."

"I don't think you can gut me," he said. "Though if we got more acrobatic, I might get leg cramps."

They fell asleep in a tangle of limbs. After half an hour, he woke. It had been years, decades, since he'd smoked, but a cigarette sounded good now.

As he looked down at her, he pictured hunters shooting mourning doves.

12

BOLT

The stallion reared, towering above Elaine Santana, who fell back, hitting her hip on the two-foot-tall stump of a slender birch. The plate-sized hooves floundered over her head as the animal pivoted away, its rank, hot sweat stink filling the air. She looked up at it as it turned away. Its nostrils flared, flanks dripping, chest heaving with labored breath. Then it was gone, crashing through the underbrush.

Elaine swore, cursing her own paralysis that had left her in its path. She'd heard the blue jay, then the brush breaking around the horse, yet she'd stood there, hand on her Glock, and damn near been run down.

The stallion was heading downhill, to the river in front of Claire's. She forced herself up, found her cell, and hit Arnie's one-digit number. Then she fell back, her hip throbbing with sudden, sharp pain.

Robideu made it out the patio doors at the same moment the big white horse broke through the clumps of alders and, like a trained Lipizzaner stallion, leapt over the deepest part of the river. It struggled part of the way up the opposite bank and suddenly stopped, legs spread wide, head down, gouts of saliva pouring from its mouth. With its coat darkened to gray by sweat, it looked like a Remington bronze, only no Cherokee straddled the collapsing horse. Murphy, the Vietnam vet, stood near his cabin looking down at it, wearing out-in-the-knees jeans and braces, a rifle braced against his bare shoulder.

"Goddamn, don't shoot," Arnie said. "Murphy. That horse's owner will sue the shit out of you. She'll come over there and scalp you first. You've seen her—white-haired woman looks like God with a Mohawk. Goddamn, Murphy. Just don't shoot. Don't shoot."

Murphy spat a wad of tobacco and lowered the rifle, muzzle up, butt resting on the ground.

"I could shoot your ear off," he said, voice conversational. "I coulda shot an ear off that horse. Wanna see me bang a bullet off that chimney?"

"Hell no. Jesus Christ. Why would you shoot at a standing still target, you goddamn fool? Somebody must've spooked it. Too old to race, but the last I knew, it still stands to stud."

"Good some of us can. You call the owner? Must be worried, if she saw her horse take off like that."

"She's coming. Zoe Weathers. Dr. Weathers if you meet her."

"*Dr.* Weathers. Right. I gotta tell you, Robideu. I'm sick of disturbance. First, the old man dies. That was fair enough, but since then, I'm thinking someone's stalking around my house at night. I won't stand for it, you hear me? You think I'm not armed, now?" he said, dropping his rifle to his feet. "I got a knife. I got killer hands."

Zoe Weathers called Sanjay Kaufmann even before she drove to Claire's. When she arrived, she left her car running in the driveway and the driver's side door open, and half swam, half lunged across the roiling stream. She eased up to the horse, which snaked its head up, walleyed with panic. Its lips curled back over its teeth. She slowed her own breath and movements, muttering sweet nothings, until she could press the horse's massive head against her chest, letting it catch the scent of her body. She stroked him, tears trickling down her face. Then she walked Whitsuntide Whirlwind—Whit— across the river, downstream where it was shallower. When they were back near the house in a shady area, she found a hose connection and began hosing him down with huge, splashing arcs of water, moving the hose back and forth.

Laurel and Jen, who had been sitting at the kitchen table, looking at paint colors on Jen's computer, had at first been frozen in place for fear they might spook Whit. Once he was under Zoe's control, they both came out, wide-eyed and wobbly-legged, to help. Laurel followed Zoe's instructions, scraping away the lather of rank sweat as Zoe sprayed on more water. Jen filled a pail of water from the kitchen tap and then got rubbing alcohol and extra pails, and dragged bags of ice from Zoe's car. She filled the pails with a one-to-three mixture of rubbing alcohol and water, then added ice. She didn't hear Murphy until he appeared at her shoulder, carrying the pail of drinking water to Whit. When he returned, he wordlessly started lugging pails with the alcohol, water, and ice mixture, and heaved them up and over the big horse.

Whit lowered his head to the water.

"He's drinking," Zoe yelled.

"Why wouldn't he drink?" Jen asked the sweaty, scrawny Murphy. "He's so hot he's steaming."

"Some horses—when they get run ragged—don't drink," Murphy said. "They don't even know they're thirsty, but they got systems punking out. They don't drink, they die. They drink too much, they die."

Jen looked at him, horrified.

"Fill buckets," he said.

By the time Sanjay arrived, the big horse was bobbing his head up and down while Zoe ran water down his back. She rubbed behind his ears. Whit pressed his nose against her, leaning forward, as though Zoe supported his weight, which she would have done, if she could have supported him by herself. He might've been a stallion standing to stud, but Whit was also her baby—her heart that beat outside her body.

"Looks like you got a good start," Kaufmann said. He was preternaturally calm. He had not gone to one of the top veterinary colleges, but since he was a kid, he'd been able to put animals at ease. He had absorbed his Jewish father and his Hindu mother's respect for life, regardless of religion or external packaging. Now, he set both hands on the horse and probed gently, checking external temperature, heartbeat, and gut sounds. Whitsuntide Whirlwind not only belonged to his beloved, but was—because of the horse's mild disposition—a favorite of his. He doctored Whit, boarded Whit when Zoe had to leave him, and his brother shoed Whit. Sanjay Kaufmann had known Whit since he was a colt.

"What you been doing, you old fool? Got yourself in a sticky wicket?"

"Idiot," Zoe said affectionately. "You're not British."

Whit half leaned against Sanjay, soaking him with water and sweaty lather. "Racist," Sanjay accused Zoe. "I have colonial brethren."

"A cobra and mongoose are cousins."

They led Whit to Sanjay's carrier and up the ramp. Zoe stopped to pull her car out of the way and turn off the ignition.

"IV fluid?" Zoe asked.

"Don't teach me my business," he told her. "If you keep bossing me, asking me questions, I'm going to charge you extra."

"You use a 0.9 percent normal saline with potassium and calcium?"

"Yeah. Come off it, Zoe! We've looked at the same research. You'll see the serum chemistry panels and the blood count results as soon as I get them. And yes, I'll keep monitoring the gut."

"My good big boy," she said to Whit, then hiked herself sideways, weight on one hip, into the horse box with him.

"Where do you think you're going to sleep when we get to the clinic?" Sanjay asked. He knew better than to suggest Whit would stomp her.

"You'll find me a place to sleep, and dry clothes," Zoe said.

Murphy watched them drive away. "That's a strong woman," he said.

Jen was fatigued and hung her head. Murphy's socks had sagged into his boots. The haft of a sheath knife protruded from one gray wool sock.

"You didn't see me here," he said. Then he was gone.

Jen went back to the house to take a shower. Laurel texted Arnie, and Arnie texted Dannie Christie, Elaine Santana's lover. Once Dannie got to the emergency room, Arnie headed back. They'd do an X-ray, in spite of Elaine's protests, and send her home with medication. No point in hanging around when he couldn't help.

He walked around Zoe's property, narrowing his search down to the area where Whit had been tethered. There was a three-sided building in which Whit could take shelter when it rained. The inside walls had obviously been organized to hold tack and give her room to groom Whit inside the shelter if need be. The day had been so beautiful, she'd let him graze a section of grass that was ignoring the season, soaking up sunshine to bulk up roots.

Arnie found what he suspected he'd find. Someone had used insect-like drones to panic the stallion. He looked at them with loathing, knowing these miniature machines would hurt more people and make his job more complex. He wanted to gather the drones up and, when they had their perpetrator, shove them up the creep's ass. Gritting his teeth, he gloved up and followed proper protocol to collect plastic and metal bits; on the box, he noted the date, time, and place he found them. He shook his head hard, for a minute imagining he heard and felt the vibrations of the spider-legged dragonfly gadgets buzzing at his own ears. Elaine Santana was going to be livid. And Zoe Weathers would flay someone alive.

I want backup, he thought.

ELAINE SANTANA GINGERLY lowered her naked self into the pink-enameled bathtub full of ice. No one but a masochist could like this process, but it would keep bruising and inflammation down. As it was, she took the offered codeine tablets with gratitude.

Dannie lit a sandalwood candle, leaned over the tub, and crooned an off-key version of "Dink's Song."

"I got a woman not so tall/Moves her body like a cannonball."

"Not funny." Elaine groaned. "I need more ice."

CLAIRE AND CHARLES had slept in the next morning and for brunch, eaten cream cheese on graham crackers. "Staples," Charles had explained. "I don't want you driving and drowsing." After they'd given each other an awkward, coffee-flavored kiss, she drove home.

By the time she got back, Laurel and Jen had showered and eaten. Jen was upstairs texting, and Laurel was curled up on the couch, waiting for her. Claire looked for Bloody Mary mix, couldn't find it, and poured a scotch. They sat at the kitchen table, with Black Pearl curled on Claire's feet. Laurel told her about Whit's thunderous run and subsequent salvation.

"My trip was quieter." Claire looked at the ice in her glass, not at Laurel. "I learned that alders have cork in their stems, so they're buoyant during spring flooding and hold stream banks in place. Would you have guessed Charles thinks of himself as a bittern?"

Laurel looked at Claire as though expecting a scarlet letter to bloom on her friend's chest.

"Poor Arnie," Laurel said.

13

WHO HATES YOU

When Arnie arrived that evening, he studied Claire for a long minute, tightening his lips as though he didn't like what he saw. He pulled out a chair and joined them at the kitchen table, sitting at an angle so he could read Claire's face.

"Is Jen asleep?" he asked.

"I don't think so," Laurel answered. She was wearing an old pair of George's flannel pajamas, which were too big for her. She looked like a kid wearing her father's clothes, but she also looked thin-lipped and mulish, prepared to defend Claire if she saw the need.

"Good. Get her down here."

Jen arrived wearing shorts and an old white T-shirt that hung down to her knees. "I wasn't asleep," she said. "I was texting, but I want to know what happened to Elaine."

"Would you please make coffee?" It was not a request. This was official Arnie—a harder, colder version of the man Claire had met before.

"Elaine got shaken up and bruised." His tone was brusque and emotionless. "Deep muscle bruising that'll take time to heal. But she would have been killed if that horse had hit her square on. And no friggin' doubt somebody messed with that horse. We found bug-sized drones where Whit was pastured. He broke his tether—pulled it out from a stable wall. Lucky part of the wall didn't swing at the end of the tether, or we'd have had a ton of stallion pulling a death flail. As it was, Whit could have killed whoever was out there. And if Murphy had shot at Whit and missed, which I don't think would have happened, God knows who could have been hurt. So now we sit down and start figuring out this mess."

Claire sat with her feet tucked under the hem of a green caftan and her hands, which no longer sported jewelry, clasped in her lap.

"We assumed, Claire, that you have been the target of a malicious prank. Now, we have a new, much more significant assumption. Someone wants to scare you or hurt you. You're in danger, and by extension, so are your friends. They could be targeted simply to hurt you. You're grounded—as in, you don't leave these grounds without permission. Laurel and Jennifer stay here with you. You're not safe outside your home. For example, it's easy for someone to cause a car wreck by shooting out a windshield. You can't leave until we're done with this investigation."

Laurel looked over her glasses at him.

"I wouldn't leave, but I don't like having Jen here."

"I'm an adult, Mom. Plane flights? Backpacking? I'm probably more at risk riding in a car than I am sitting here."

Arnie made a noncommittal noise. "I am sorry, Laurel. Even if the person or persons who panicked Whit wasn't aiming to harm a human being, the behavior has escalated. I'll be here as often as I can, but I've also called for backup until Elaine is better. Bertram Allarbee doesn't say much, but he's quick on his feet and can stay awake for thirty-six hours—not reading, not doing crossword puzzles, just sitting there."

"How is Whit?" Jen asked.

"You helped get him cooled down until Sanjay could start an IV. If Whit wasn't still improving, I'd have heard from Zoe by now, loud and clear."

"Murphy helped too," Jen said. "Can we thank him?"

"Thank him, hell. Can we hire him?" Claire tossed her hair back over her shoulders.

Laurel put both hands on the table, as though she was at a teaching conference and trying to keep her temper in check.

"Take this seriously," Arnie warned.

"I don't want to take it seriously," Claire said, her voice uneven. Her brain had stopped working when Arnie had said her friends were at risk. The only thought trickling through her mental block was that Bertram Allarbee was an odd, Charlie Brown kind of name. Who would want to be babysat by a Bertram, anyway?

"Claire," Arnie said. "Have you been drinking?"

"Hardly at all," she said.

Laurel shook her head and said, "Claire, you've had most of a bottle of wine."

"Claire doesn't drink wine," Jen said.

"The hard stuff was in the basement," Claire explained, and looked away.

"Fuck this," Arnie said. He reached inside his shirt, where he had squirreled away the laminated message. He gently took Claire's chin with his right hand, so she couldn't move her head away, then used his left to bring the threat in front of her face.

Laurel and Jen had seen it before, but the plastic edges looked more yellowed, the whole of the threat more murderous.

Still holding the message by one corner, he dropped his right hand to her shoulder. She paled under her sunburn and slowly turned to face him. He rotated with her, so she still faced the block letters:

Widow Woman

Witch

Cunt

GET OUT

"David found this in the driveway," Arnie said. "He was here when you were with Charles."

"Charles and Oscar," Claire said.

Laurel put her hand to her forehead and groaned.

"I don't care if you were with the Pope and he appointed you honorary virgin." Arnie shoved the laminated message under her nose.

"Who is this, Claire? What widow?"

"Stop bullying me, Arnie! All right, it's for me. Why didn't you tell me right away?"

"Things have been a little busy."

"Can I have a drink?" she asked.

"Get her something, would you Jen? Pour her a short, straight one."

Jen retrieved a bottle from the basement. She put Maker's Mark in a coffee cup, which meant Arnie couldn't see how much she had poured. He uncurled Claire's fingers, took the cup from her hand, and grunted approval.

Laurel expected Claire to knock it back, but she took a small sip through pursed lips and reached her hand to the message, now flat on the table between them.

"May I touch it? What's happening would seem more real, if I could touch it."

He pushed it toward her, and she held it in a slightly shaking hand.

"We drove this to the state police post, and they found the same things we did—smeared prints of a glove, big prints. Doesn't prove anything. They made computer duplicates, but we need to keep it."

She ran her fingers lightly over the laminate. It felt crackly and slick, like the surface of an old bus seat.

"I'm certainly a widow." She sipped the whiskey again. "I'm not a witch, though. It's a brainless insult, witch history aside."

"If you had occult powers," Jen said, "you could tell who sent this."

Arnie looked at Jen thoughtfully. Jen took a pull at the bottle of bourbon.

"If we don't get anywhere," he said, "we could try a psychic."

Jen, her mouth full of bourbon, spat some out on the table while tilting the bottle so it puddled on the floor. She wiped the table clean with the hem of her shirt.

"Tell me you don't believe in poltergeists," she said.

"Jen," Laurel said, knowing she sounded like her own mother. "Change your T-shirt, please. There's one on the piano. You reek."

Jen ignored her and took another swallow of bourbon, staring at Arnie as though he had sprouted a second head.

"I don't believe in ectoplasm and séances," he said. "But there have been cases where a psychic brought closure to an inquest."

"An inquest! Oh great!" Laurel said. "This isn't a murder."

"It isn't now," Arnie responded. "I don't believe in forensic psychics. That doesn't mean I wouldn't try one. No one believed in fingerprints at first."

"You'd have to get Oscar back," Jen said. "For the psychic."

"If he hasn't flown the coop," Laurel said, then looked ashamed of herself.

"I'm not a cunt," Claire said. "That's just a cheap insult people use when they don't like a woman. Or, occasionally, a man."

Laurel looked at Arnie. "I think a man would use that word to hurt someone. That's what linguists would say. Maybe, a man who hates women would use that."

"Could be." Arnie scribbled in his notebook. "We're going to have to rethink everything, from the idea that the raven was a prank to what kind of person would write this and would hide behind the way it's written."

Jen got up and moved to the refrigerator. "We might as well finish up some of the food." She got out hummus, pita, slightly dry cheddar, and the last dark cherries. The few cherries left had dark spots on them.

"Thanks," Arnie said, making a sandwich by folding pita around a hunk of cheese. "I haven't eaten in a while. Elaine keeps me on track."

Claire picked through the cherries, discarding most of them. She was facing Arnie, and her caftan fell forward, revealing the tops of her sunburned breasts.

"Pull your dress up, Claire." His voice was flat. "You're distracting."

"It's a caftan," she said as she rose halfway and pulled up the green silk.

"And?" Laurel asked.

Arnie ignored them both.

"Who hates you?" he asked Claire.

She startled and sat up straight.

"No one?" she said. "Or someone does. But no one I can think of."

"We checked with everyone who has employed you. You have a checkered past, but we only found one woman who strongly dislikes you. Called you thoughtless and selfish."

"Mrs. Pilcher, I bet," Claire said. "I thought I'd love working in that kids' store. She sold gorgeous puppets! But after five o'clock, the kids' parents were usually yuppies waiting for restaurants to open. Mom and Dad would hang around an hour, then go off and spend $200 getting smashed over sushi, without buying so much as a wooden puzzle toy for their whiney, hungry kids."

"She said you were abrupt with customers. Coffee was also mentioned. She said you never made a new pot."

"Oh darn." Claire took a slow, large sip from her cup.

"No spurned lovers?" Arnie asked, looking straight at her.

"No, Arnie. I was married."

"You were," he said. "That doesn't stop lovers, or spurning."

"You can fend off propositions. You just keep mentioning your spouse. I would say, 'George likes sunsets. George likes golf. George likes bowling.'"

"Bowling? George bowled?" Laurel said.

"It's the technique," Claire said.

Arnie awarded her a grudging smile. "It's a good technique. It says, 'I love my husband,' instead of 'You repulsive scumbag.' Actually, you're adroit at staying on people's good side. Let's leave the hate list for now. Anyone who would want this house? This property?"

"I can't think why," Claire said. "George wanted this house, in part, for the memories it held. I'd guess his grandparents grew vegetables here once, so there might be some decent soil. Way in the back to the south there are buildings that have collapsed or are collapsing. Tool shed with the roof gone. Thingy to catch rainwater for use in the barn," she said.

"Cistern," Laurel said.

"What?"

"The thing to catch water. A cistern."

"It's broken in on one side," Claire said. "But Arnie, you know this."

"This house has a great location on the river," Arnie said. "Quiet. Peaceful. But you must have put more money into adding the door wall and new bathroom plumbing than you could get out of this place. Did you get an appraisal before and after you tackled the money pit?"

"We wanted the house. What we did with it was for us. Neither of us cooked much, so we didn't redo the kitchen then, though the logical time would have been when we put new plumbing in. We hadn't decided whether or not we wanted to add an addition. That would have meant the kitchen would be the center of the house, and we'd have another bath and bedroom, and big closets, on the first floor. Which might have made sense, if George had lived twenty more years."

"Appraisal?" Arnie plowed on.

"George got two appraisals," Claire said. "We paid $146,000. Based on selling prices for properties comparable to what we have now, both came in between $166,000 and $186,000. That is, if I'm willing to wait for a buyer."

"That seems low," Laurel said.

"Sandstone and cement basement. The sandstone is installed the right way, stacked horizontally, so rain doesn't get in cracks and cause it to split, but some people expect so much from basements.

Pool tables, built-in bars, humungous hot tubs. The attic ceiling is so low, there's no storage. From the first floor—from the road, for that matter—you can't see the bend in the river, where it deepens and could be a swimming hole. Besides, a lot of kids want to be on a lake, where they can Jet-Ski. And George and I didn't add a garage or workshop where a family could store 'toys.'

"Not everyone is going to want to live in or near Grayling. There is not much night life here for young adults. Generally speaking, there is a hiatus between high school kids, itchy to move on, and those now grown people nostalgic for a quieter way of life and wanting to move back."

"That's true of most small communities in Michigan, isn't it?" Laurel asked. "We drove by new houses when we were riding around that first day." The day she'd arrived seemed like a long time ago.

Claire continued, "There are other reasons some buyers wouldn't want this house. You can't have a washing machine this close to the river. Everyone does a little lingerie, but you could get in trouble running family-sized loads of wash. To find a dry cleaner, you have to go into Grayling. For first-run movies, into Gaylord. There used to be a hotel in Lovells that had dining and dancing, but it's been closed and gone through an estate sale. There are two museums in a groomed little park—one historical and one that's the founding site of Trout Unlimited, but no one's going to want this house because of them.

"Insurance is expensive. Lightening starts wildfires. We've had two tornadoes. In winter, it's easy to be snowed in, or snowed out."

"You and George wanted it," Laurel said. "Someone would want it. Someone would want it if they were like you and George."

Claire, Jen, and Arnie looked at her somberly.

"Someone's going to fall in love with this bit of river the way we did," Claire agreed. "But no one would want to scare me out for a profit."

"Anyone else bid on the house when you bought it?"

"Nope. Nada. Not one other bid."

"Mineral rights?" Arnie asked.

"No oil, no copper, no silver."

"What about a real estate development?" Jen asked. She tipped back the bottle again and passed it to Laurel, who absentmindedly swigged from it and passed it to Claire.

"I doubt it," Arnie said. "The riverbank is protected. All of it. That means you can't make changes within two hundred feet from the water. There are some other properties on the river that would cost more to buy, but less to develop.

"The other problem with that theory is there are two developments on rivers near here. The best locations sold early, and there are still waterfront lots, but neither development is full. That's one of the problems we have when kids trash houses. There may not be a house built on either side of their target, so there are no neighbors looking out. Or, with summer people, who knows who's home?"

"Couldn't a developer hire someone to check out property?" Jen asked. "Give some buyer a price break to wave a flashlight around?"

"Hard to find anyone reliable to do it. The economy isn't exactly booming here, but anyone who is willing to work hard and in good health has found a job. Even if the job takes a commute. Would you want to insure an over-the-hill construction worker to climb around snow-covered swamp lots in winter time?"

"A woman might be better," Jen said.

"Some are," Arnie agreed with her.

"A dog," Laurel said. "Those people ought to get a dog."

"That," Arnie agreed, "is a good idea. But you'd have to think things out. Electric fence? Not with a river. Fenced yard? Limits the protection you get. And don't forget, perpetrators can put a dog down."

Claire looked crestfallen.

"I thought you were saying I ought to get a dog. But I don't want to get a dog poisoned. As far as that goes, should I worry about Pearl?"

All of them looked stricken.

"Yeah," Arnie said. "Keep him in."

"Pearl is going to *hate* this," Claire said.

"Change of topic," Laurel suggested. "Any of Claire's neighbors have a record? Is someone vicious lurking in the neighborhood?"

14

THE POTLUCK CLUB

"Zoe Weathers has one conviction for a felony," Arnie told them. "She used a riding crop to beat a man who was drowning a sack of puppies right in Grayling's Au Sable Park. The puppies were the ugliest mutts I've ever seen, but once Sanjay treated them, they went to good homes; in fact, two went to the judge who presided over the case. He gave Zoe probation and told the lug who got beat, 'We don't do that here. You may not have noticed, but Grayling is getting civilized. You give Ms. Weathers any trouble, in court or out of it, and I'll have you arrested for spitting on the sidewalk.'"

"Did he spit on the sidewalk? I mean, habitually?" Laurel asked.

"He would have been known to if I testified," Arnie said.

Laurel looked more cheerful. "That was a good story," she said. "Was it true?"

"Actually," Arnie said, "I don't lie."

"But you would have lied about the man spitting on the sidewalk," Laurel pointed out.

"I don't lie to, or about, people who deserve the truth. And that's almost everyone. Even most people who've committed crimes."

Laurel pushed back her chair and got Arnie fresh coffee. "What about Sanjay?" she asked. "Maybe he secretly hates Zoe Weathers and wanted to see her horse die."

Jen looked supremely skeptical. "He helped us save Whit," she said. "Honestly, Mother. You can't cast aspersions around."

"I like him," Laurel defended herself. "But lovers—married or not—are always suspect, right? Maybe he wanted to get into Zoe's good graces. Maybe he has gambling debts he needed to pay off. The money Zoe owed him for Whit's care after those drones spooked him must have been astronomical. Besides, he has a hairy back. I distrust men with hairy backs."

Arnie turned sideways to give Laurel a quizzical look.

"Mother!" Jen exploded. "That's just *prejudice.*"

"I know. But I can't help it. Something about him spooks me. He kowtows to Zoe."

Arnie intervened. "I think Sanjay's an OK guy," he said. "I've seen Zoe help him out."

"Got an example?" Claire asked, curious.

"This spring, I got a call from the woman who manages the Dairy Swirl Delite in Mio, saying there were coyotes hanging about the Shrine, which is pretty close to the Dairy Swirl."

Laurel and Jen both looked blank.

"Our Lady of the Woods Catholic Shrine Grotto," Arnie explained, an ambivalent look on his face. "The Shrine is this mountain of cut limestone. All grottos and niches are filled with statues and, ah, relics of saints. There's no fence around it, but you can't, in theory, get into the grottos at night."

Laurel made a wrist-rotating get-on-with-it gesture. "What does that have to do with Sanjay and Zoe?" she asked.

"So, it takes me twenty minutes to get to the Shrine," Arnie continued. "I'm guessing Zoe has a police scanner, because by the time I pull up in the parking lot, her Mercedes is already there. She's rummaging in the back seat of her car and completely ignores me. Sanjay is pounding up the slope, and I can now see a black lamb tethered to a statue of whozit—Joseph, I mean. I can see the lamb, squirming and kicking, and I can see three young, I think male, coyotes doing the coyote slink, closer and closer to what to them looks like dinner."

"Oh no!" Jen said. "I hope you shot those coyotes!"

"I don't," Arnie said, "have anything against coyotes, per se. We make it easy for them to hang out with us, leaving food out for them: garbage, pet feces—"

"Gross!" Jen responded.

"Coyotes can eat things that would gag a seagull," Arnie said. "And these particular half-grown coyotes are too close to town, too close to schools, and too close to the Dairy Swirl Delite. I get out of the car, slam the door, and take out my sidearm. The coyote nearest me turns, raises its ruff to look more like a big old wolf, and growls, because unlike wolves, coyotes aren't all that impressed with us. I take a firing stance, and the next thing I know, there are packages—parcels—sailing in all around me. The coyote looks horrified, and I fire into the air, and there I am, standing in a rain of braunschweiger."

"Oh, Arnie, what the hell," Claire protested.

"Zoe is throwing food. Sanjay is still charging toward the shrine, heading for the lamb, but he's strafing the hillside with liver sausage. I'm yelling, 'Get down!' so I can get a shot off, but neither of them pays any attention to me. The coyote closest to me has what must be a pound of braunschweiger in its jaws. Its lips are curled back over salivating teeth, and the two other coyotes have bloody butcher packages in their mouths. Zoe throws down a flashbang, which are, of course, illegal. When my vision clears, the coyotes are half a mile away, Zoe's got the lamb tucked into her camel hair coat, and Sanjay's reached behind a rock where the lamb was tethered, and collared a gangly teenager who obviously planned to film *The Silence of the Lamb*."

"Is the lamb all right?" Claire asked.

"The lamb is fine," Arnie reassured her.

"You arrested the little fuckhead?" Laurel looked nauseated.

"No charge would have held up," Arnie said. "He hadn't done anything. He could have used a dozen excuses."

Jen looked green around the mouth. "Arnie, that was an awful story."

Arnie shrugged. "But around here, how many people are going to worry about one lamb? Or the coyotes he was setting up?"

"Sanjay did." Laurel nodded slowly. "Zoe did."

"The kid got off scot-free?" Claire asked, sounding incredulous.

Arnie said, "It's possible that Sanjay kicked him in the nuts hard enough to put his gonads where adenoids belong. Then he took the shit-caked, trembling lamb from Zoe and got in her Mercedes, holding it on his lap."

"Wait a minute," Claire said. "There's a black sheep at the Marshes'. It hangs out with Bill the donkey."

Arnie shrugged. "I did talk to the boy's father, who said he'd get the boy into counseling. He said his son had been dared by older kids."

"All right," Laurel said, throwing up her hands. "Sanjay is an OK guy."

"That brings us to the Marshes," Arnie continued. "They have no records of any kind between them. They're a problem because everyone swears they're angels, and we don't believe in angels. However, we haven't been able to disprove that theory yet."

"I'm glad the lamb was all right," Claire said.

"You eat lamb," Laurel pointed out.

"Only at Easter." Claire was defensive. "Ann finds me a butcher that she says is humane."

"On to Ann Campbell, then," Arnie directed. "Maybe you know, when she was young and a real looker, she married a rich old fart named Montgomery Montgomery. Montgomery Montgomery drank himself to death. Maybe she helped him drink himself to death. They could go through bottles of booze at a local tavern faster than a blue racer cuts your path. But he loved her, and she made him happy. Far as I know, you can't force anyone to develop liver cancer.

"He left her the money she used for the store, and she's done well with it. She's got that half-log house uphill from the store—probably cost $400,000—and a view over pine woods to the east, and maple forests to the west. Everyone thought Tansy would move in with her someday. Patsy lives there, cleans for her, house-sits if Ann takes a trip. Patsy's not the brightest star in the sky, but she wouldn't hurt anyone. Not deliberately, that is. Claire, you've still got bruises?"

"Who'd you hear that story from?"

"Ann. Who else? As for Tansy, she was a wild kid when she was younger. But since she went away to school and got that job as an administrator at Best to Be, butter wouldn't melt in her mouth. What kind of a name is that for an assisted living place? Best to Be. What does it even mean?"

"'Grow old along with me! The best is yet to be,'" Laurel quoted. "Look forward to old age, Arnie."

"Balls," Arnie said. "Who wrote that? Tennyson? I think I read that in high school."

"Browning," Laurel told him.

"Browning, Tennyson. Balls," Arnie repeated. "Whoever wrote that must have had money. We can do more now than we used to, but my father ended up in a wheelchair with my mom taking care of him. Please, shoot me if that happens."

Claire, out of habit, crossed herself.

"What about Murphy?" Laurel asked.

Jen looked troubled. "He helped with Zoe's horse when Elaine got hurt," she said. "But that's when I saw he has a knife in his boot."

"He's got a Purple Heart from the Afghan war. He drove a tank that hit a mine. Survived by a freak chance. Dragged out half of a friend who'd caught some major shrapnel. I don't think he is looking for trouble," Arnie said.

"Jesus, Arnie, don't sugarcoat it," Laurel said.

Claire stared out the window. "I don't know, Laurel. Maybe if you die like that—really dead, really fast—you don't feel it. Pow. Shock sets in. Doesn't that happen, Arnie?"

"Yeah," he said. "It happens. Your nervous system goes out before your brain knows you're dead."

Laurel got up and hiked up her pajamas. "Bathroom," she said. "Are we winding this up?"

"Yeah," Arnie said again. "When I get philosophic, it is definitely time to wind it up. Don't forget, when you get up, Bertram Allarbee will be here. Maybe earlier. You'll know him when you see him. He's like a tall, brick-shaped Boy Scout." He yawned.

Claire yawned and finished her bourbon. "G'night, Arn. I'm glad you're staying. I'm going to bed. Or to recliner."

When the house had settled for the night, Arnie sat awake, his Glock out on the table, waiting for Bertram Allarbee to show up, which he did in about an hour.

Allarbee looked exhausted.

"Carousing?" Arnie said.

"No, sir. I don't sleep much. Never have," Bertram said.

"I knew there was a reason I asked for you."

The two went over Arnie's notes, including Claire's laminated missive and a quick sketch of the house—bathrooms, bedrooms, windows, and exits.

"Take a flashlight with you. Look around. Don't trip on the recliner. I'll wait up until you're back from casing the place. There's food. Eat what you find."

Allarbee made it around the house quietly for a man who was, except for a penlight, moving in the dark. He spent extra time on the second floor.

When he got back to the kitchen, he said, "Sir, there's a skinny sugar maple growing up against the house. Reaches a second story window."

"Good point. Cut it down tomorrow, Bertram," Arnie said. He stretched his arms out on the table and laid his head on one arm.

"Homeowner may bitch, sir. Sir?"

Allarbee waited a minute. At first, there was no answer, then a wavering snore.

"Consider it cut down," Allarbee said. He pulled his service weapon out of his pocket, surveyed the tray of leftovers, and sat down to wait.

15

YOU HAVE TO BE LUCKY

Charles, who had gotten Claire's e-mail, arrived not long after Arnie had fallen asleep and immediately fell afoul of Bertram Allarbee. "I'm Charles," he said, as though that explained everything.

Allarbee did what he did best. He remained silent and stolid.

"Claire must have told you. It took me some time to get the truck and ask Ed to stay with Oscar."

Bertram Allarbee handcuffed Charles to the steering wheel of his truck.

"Wake Claire up," Arnie said groggily. "Don't, for God's sake, tell her Charles is here. See if she's expecting him."

Allarbee found Claire in the process of getting dressed, which should have been more embarrassing than it was.

"Terrible sounding truck," she said, pulling a sweater over her head. "I might as well get up. I think Charles is here."

Arnie uncuffed Charles. "Let her go back to sleep," he said, his voice curt.

"I'm not going to jump her in a reclining chair."

If Arnie had any doubts about Claire and Charles's situation, that statement cleared them up.

Charles, realizing he'd committed the biggest faux pas of his life, skulked into the room lined with books and fell asleep on the floor.

The next day, while working in the basement with Claire, Charles knew he should confess his blunder, but she wanted to catch him up on the detecting. Her description of the laminated warning destroyed any conversational plans he'd had. He tried giving her a reassuring hug, but she didn't seem reassured, so he just listened. He grimaced at her descriptions of Whit's misadventure, and at the story of Sanjay and the coyotes. Predators, he thought. Can't live with them, can't live without them, which brought him to a question.

"Claire, do you have any idea how Pearl gets out? I saw him out on the patio this morning. Allarbee risk-proofed this house so tight a red ant couldn't get in, and I know he boarded up the cat door." After a minute, he added, "Thank Arnie for sharing the notes he collected. Who attacks an old horse? Who knew Murphy had a cutlass in his boot?"

"It wasn't a cutlass," Claire corrected him, as he had intended. "And I don't know how Pearl is getting out. I think he hates kitty litter."

"It's smelly, that's for sure. I think Oscar is about ready to vacate the coop, which will mean less crawling around the loft cleaning up."

"Ed can take care of him?"

"Well, yeah. Ed can't crawl around cleaning the loft up, but he's looked after hurt birds and small mammals for me before. I check on his chickens, remember?"

Claire didn't answer Charles. Long ago, there had been a washing machine there—maybe a wringer washer, she guessed. She thought traces of George's family's life had disappeared, but the faint smell of Lux soap flakes kept company with the smell of cigars George had smoked there. When the weather was inclement, he'd hunched down in one of two old, cracked brown leather armchairs. An empty can of Scrubbing Bubbles bathroom cleaner and a pile of damp sponges and paper towels testified that Patsy had scrubbed the old splay-legged Ping-Pong table. Cartons of wine, scotch, and bourbon had been pushed back under the stairs.

Even an old handcrafted oak cabinet had not escaped cleaning. It sat against the opposite wall, the door slightly open, revealing a fly rod. The front of the cupboard looked bleached, scrubbed lighter than the sides. The box of hand-tied flies lay tipped over on the floor, the feathers that had adorned some lures eaten by mice.

"Oscar good. Kitty litter bad," Charles tried.

He set another beer case filled with comic books onto the table for Claire to go through. The table quaked but stabilized. His job—sorting out George's meager coin collection—was something he could do, owing to a brief infatuation with odd forms of currency. He sat on the floor, back against an armchair, piling up small stacks of nickels and dimes. The task was boring, but useful, and he wanted to be useful.

George's comic book collection, left over from his teens and stored in plastic bags, left Claire feeling emotionally off balance. Grisly faces from *Tales from the Crypt* stared at her. The Crypt Keeper had a neat center part and shoulder-length white hair. Wizened, nearly fleshless skeletons lurching from graves made her thankful George had been cremated. Who knew her urbane husband had been a teenager once? Had that teenager pictured a wife who would cheat on him after his death? She would not—*would not*—allow any of these stumblebum bone piles into her dreams.

She and Charles were equally dusty and tired. At least the basement was cooler than the rest of the house. Previous comic books examined included frayed issues of *Archie*, *Captain America*, and *Superman*, but had not yielded an *Action Comics* Number One. George's collection of coins—mostly Indian Head pennies and V nickels—had not yielded a 1909 S VDB.

Pearl had slept in Claire's lap the night before, purring and stretching, then kneading her with front paws and the tips of his claws. Charles had slept on the floor in the room with George's books, and at one point, Pearl had inspected him, sniffing him carefully. He had given Charles a measuring look when Charles put cream down in the morning, as though to say, "I trust you got rid of that bird."

Claire had an uneasy feeling that Arnie had conscripted Laurel so she and Charles would spend time together. As a result, they had headed for the basement feeling coals of fire on their heads. Claire had known it was inevitable that she would hurt Arnie, but that didn't make the process of hurting him easier.

Pearl rubbed against her ankles. Claire glanced down and saw he had a dead shrew in his mouth.

"Back, are you? Charles is right," she said. "We should know how you get in and out." She forestalled conjecture by using a Kleenex to accept Pearl's offering and then handing it to Charles. "Ick," she said. "Teensy weensy intestines are still intestines. And please, Charles, don't tell me about shrews or shrew guts."

He fell into his role of court jester. "The Romans thought you could tell the future from animal intestines. Haruspication."

"Don't tell me about haruspication, either."

LAUREL, WHO DID not believe in haruspication, had no way to predict her future. She stood in Arnie's living room, which consisted of practical, dark brown upholstered furniture, a black-and-brown carpet, drawn black drapes, and a surprisingly large television screen. He was already heading for the kitchen to get his laptop computer. Although he'd reviewed the case notes with everyone in the morning, department discipline, not to mention his own good sense, dictated information and theories be typed up and saved. Besides, he'd promised Elaine he'd e-mail her a copy.

Trying to work on Claire's computer hadn't gotten him anywhere. All three women's computers were Macs. He was used to department PCs.

Laurel called after him, "Thank you for my defense, with David."

He stopped and turned back toward her.

"Damn it," she said. "Why not tell Claire you love her?"

He stared at her, his face bleak.

"At least get your feelings out," she urged him.

"I don't want my feelings out," Arnie said. "I want them inside, where people can't see them. And I can't tell Claire I love her."

"Why the fuck not?"

"I'm married," he said.

She stared at him.

"I don't have affairs. They're too much trouble. And Claire couldn't be an affair, not for me."

She still stared. Her bones felt locked in place.

"My boy, Sawyer, is ten. He has insurance through his school, but my wife, Neddie, uses my health insurance. When Sawyer was younger, he came to stay with me every summer, but now he's in a gifted program in Ann Arbor that runs in trimesters."

Arnie nodded toward an end table. "There's his picture." Sawyer was a thin, tall boy, with no-rim glasses, curly hair, and a shade of dark color to his face. "Neddie's family is from Bogotá, Colombia. Her dad works at the cancer clinic in Grayling. Her mother's a dental assistant. My family lived next door to them when we were growing up."

He lowered himself into a square brown chair. "You want to sit down?" he asked.

She sat down in a chair across from him.

He sat staring at his hands, picking at calluses on his gun hand.

"The girl next door, from Bogotá," Laurel said.

"Yeah. It's a beautiful place. Neddie took Sawyer there for his tenth birthday. He's a neat kid. Very smart, open to new stuff. If he'd grown up here, he'd find it's not easy, being a cop's kid."

He looked away. "There's another thing. I wasn't a good reader when I went to school here. My parents worked their butts off. My mom was a nurse who worked second shift; my dad was a cop. They were good parents. They really were. When I was sick, they made me chicken soup from scratch. But I was sick a lot, when I was a kid. When I got to second grade, I knew I was behind, but it didn't seem to matter. I started growing into a tough, coordinated kid teachers liked. They patted me on the head, passed me along from grade to grade—an average student everyone knew would grow up to be a jock. I could figure out answers to most stuff from class discussion, but by high school, I was starting to sweat the harder stuff.

"Neddie's two years older than I am. I asked her to tutor me. I couldn't pay her, so summers, I helped her dad put in a garden, and in winter, I shoveled their walk and drive. She read to me; I read short things back to her, and pretty soon, we were reading more, talking more together. That's how we got, uh, intimate. That's how she got pregnant."

"She got pregnant from reading?"

"Yeah," he said. He looked up at her, seeming relieved, as though he had confessed a fatal flaw. "I doubt that 'you win, and we'll ignore these test scores' thing would happen these days. But it left me feeling funny about the school system. I wanted to be liked for what I wanted to be, what I could be. And Neddie—she's pale-skinned, but she is Colombian. I understood when she thought Sawyer would thrive in Ann Arbor, and she didn't want him to grow up hearing the comments she had heard here: "Oh, Neddie dear, you know we think of you as white.""

Laurel tried to think how she would have felt if Jen, when she was younger, had left with David.

"How old was Sawyer when they moved to Ann Arbor?"

"They moved when he started third grade. By the way, Claire knows I'm still married. Everyone who lives around here knows, except for you and Charles and Jen."

"Oh. You still garden?" she asked.

"Yeah," he said. "It's relaxing. Peas don't snap like people do."

"You've seen people snap?"

"Oh yeah," he said again. "Cold coffee sets some guys off."

"Why do you stay with your job, then?" Laurel asked him.

"I like problem solving. Why do you teach?"

"Problem solving, I guess. Solving problems with students who've always had problems with words."

"Why do you think that happens?" he asked. He was quiet, but obviously had a personal interest in the question.

"Lots of reasons. Some students do have physical problems. Or they were sick, or shy, when other kids forged ahead, and that messed up how they think of themselves. Some are more visually connected, rather than gaining understanding through text, but the smarts are there. Others never had anyone listen to them."

"I like that phrase—visual connections," Arnie said. "Kirtland Community College has a course in literacy that includes film studies. Shows films at the Rialto on Monday nights. You don't have to be a student to see the movies, though parents have to sign off if kids are under eighteen. You ought to come."

"You think I need to be more well-rounded?"

"I've been wanting to ask. Why are you so thin?"

"That's rude!"

"Cops work with school kids. We start in elementary schools, talking about problems they face—not just drugs and drinking. Image problems. Getting beat up. Cyber bullying. Laurel, you look like a beanpole that's been on a cleansing fast."

She stood up, angry, and then slumped back in her chair. "David, my ex. He likes beanpoles. And when you're not used to eating much, you don't just pig food in."

"That's ridiculous," he said flatly. "People ought to be able to enjoy what they're eating. What would you do if your daughter lost weight to make her dad proud?"

Laurel changed the subject. "Why did you and Neddie separate?"

"It's none of your business," he said. And then, surprising her, he added, "Neddie found she didn't want to be a cop's wife. Sometimes, the people we love when we're twenty aren't the people we can live with when we are older."

"When did you two separate?" Laurel asked.

"The important issue was the school system, so Neddie looked around until she found the program she wanted, and then found a job doing tech stuff for an Ann Arbor firm. Grayling to Ann Arbor is only a three-hour commute. But two years ago," he said, "we stopped visiting so often."

"What happened?"

"Changes. Sawyer plays soccer. He's on a chess team. I try to get there to see him, but now that he's got a schedule, my life can't always fit with his."

"Does she have a lover?" Laurel shook her head. "Oh hell, Arnie. I'm sorry I asked that."

"Neddie sees someone. He goes to Sawyer's games when I can't."

"But you don't see a woman you like."

"I don't like that many people." He seemed to be receding from the conversation. The muscle that flexed just above his jaw let her know she'd gotten into territory that still was raw and personal.

Laurel thought frantically. What did she know about Arnie?

"When I first saw you at Claire's house, Claire said she thought you'd be home, watching a movie. What's your favorite?"

He concentrated. "*Strictly Ballroom* is my favorite. Newer stuff: *Get Out.*"

Interesting that he liked a movie where the precinct police are idiots.

"I didn't like *La La Land*," he added. "Pretty colors, but the whole thing seemed fake. Maybe that was the point."

"I'd forgotten *Strictly Ballroom*," she said. "I loved that movie."

"You want to see what else I've got? I stream some movies, but my collection's in the, uh, bedroom. More room for shelving, and I keep my movie collection pretty much private. You see what books someone reads or what movies they watch, and you know who they are. Sometimes, that's not so good—for a cop."

The bedroom, like the living room, was square, but was predominantly white. A navy blue polyester bedspread was drawn up neatly over white sheets under two identically sized pillows. Dacron stuffing, Laurel guessed. Against one wall, on the far side of the bed, was a large mahogany chest of drawers. There was a faint smell of woodsy aftershave, but not one thing on the dresser. The other wall shelves were lined with a colorful array of videos; larger shelves held boxes labeled in neat block letters. Her first impression was: very John Wayne. A guy's room.

She read labels. "Sci-fi. Drama. Action. Comedy."

"I used to have more kids' movies," he said. "I still have a few, but Sawyer's taste outpaced me. We both like Groot."

"I watched the first *Guardians of the Galaxy* with Jen," she said. She walked across the room, skirting around the bed, and flipped the top on the box labeled "*Drama.*"

"What's your favorite Shakespeare movie?" she asked.

"*Richard III* set in fascist 1930s Europe. Ian McKellen. That scene at the end, when the car breaks down."

"'A horse! A horse!'" Laurel said. "'My kingdom for a horse!'"

"I want to get something out of a drawer for you." Arnie's voice was tentative. "Not a gun. Not a condom."

"Jesus, Arnie. Why would I think you'd want to show me a gun or a condom?"

"You don't know how some cops think," he said.

She stepped back, and he sidled around her. She sat back on the bed, the polyester slippery and cold on the back of her legs.

"Let me explain this first," he said. "This isn't a gift. But if you'd like, I'd loan it to you for as long as it helps. I picked this up at a pawn shop. Did a favor for the owner, and he gave me a good price."

She looked at the small square box he held out to her. Then she looked up at him, looked down, and pried the lid off the box.

Inside, there was a ring sporting a large citrine in a faceted older cut. It caught the light coming through the window over the dresser, and directed it into a ceiling corner, like a flashlight beam.

"Your ex-husband is a horse's ass. That's an insult to horses' asses. He's coarse, and you aren't. He's slippery, and you're honest. You'll find someone better than he is, and it won't be hard. You deserve someone a lot better than he is. In the meantime, you're likely to see him, with Jen, at least, and I thought it might be interesting if you were wearing something new, something to make him think about what he lost."

Laurel handed him the box.

"No?" he said.

"Would you put it in the dresser again, for now? I think I might take it with me, if you're willing to trust me with it. Someone could kill everyone in Claire's house and strip the jewelry from our lifeless fingers."

"I won't let that happen," Arnie said. He put the ring box back in the drawer.

When he turned back, she'd turned down the bedclothes.

She patted the bed. "Come lie down," she said. "You have god-awful pillows."

"Laurel," he said apologetically. "I sounded like Steven Seagal, just now, didn't I?"

"Ah," she said. "The Refrigerator."

"You're supposed to be intellectual," he told her.

"There should be a little leeway for trash in everyone's life. Arnie, will you come to bed with me? I've never slept with anyone but David. I could use your help getting the taste of him out of my mouth."

Their fumbling lovemaking didn't last long. He peeled his clothes off, and they started out under the bedspread, but it soon landed on the floor. He pulled a sheet across them both. She pulled him toward her, hard, feeling his erection, and no sooner had he slid his penis into her than she arched her back and spasmed with a long, aching moan. He thrust into her—a few hard, quick, desperate thrusts—and collapsed on top of her. The sheets were wet with a thin, viscous puddle pooling beneath them.

At last, he said, "I must be squashing you. I think I weigh twice what you do."

"You lose weight. I'll gain weight. We'll fit together next time."

"I gotta think about Neddie and Sawyer."

"That's what's nice about you," Laurel said.

16

COLD CURRENT

Jen walked through Claire's house again, surveying the way her redecorating looked to people who stopped by. The gray paint in George's bookroom had been covered with soft ivory. Two Oriental rugs, found under a bed upstairs, brought blues and golds and crimson into the room. Charles stacked them when he slept there at night and spread them out in the morning.

In the celery-green living room, the gold pine floors reflected light now that the rug had been removed, and the furniture gave off a faint scent of lemon polish. The enormous leaf-green couch that Zoe had sent faced the unadorned piano.

Zoe had sent a note with the couch, which had been delivered by Dannie's brothers. "*Whit apologizes. Please, Claire, don't leave.*" Whit had sent Elaine certificates for massages. On both notes, Zoe had jotted a postscript, "*We will catch the son of a bitch. I've promised Whit.*"

Over the piano hung a wordless apology Whit had also sent: a one-of-a-kind artwork made by an anonymous quilter, who had captured the range of hues the Great Lakes displayed during sunlight, moonlight, halcyon evenings, and storms.

"The quilt should be in a museum," Jen had said. Charles went so far as to say that letting a bird destroy it would be sacrilege. Zoe, when Claire told her she couldn't accept the gesture, had waved a hand dismissively as if swatting away a fly. Claire's favorite recliner picked up a frothed-cream lake color in the quilt, and the rocking chairs and old quilts gave the room warmth.

Laurel's pride in Jennifer reached new levels. How had she doubted her own smart kid? Did David have any idea how talented Jen was, not just seeing ways to make the house more authentically Claire's, but motivating so many people to help?

Outside, the chairs Tansy had sent helped make the transition between home and wilderness. Between the chairs lay the kit for a fire pit, with a note from the woman who had sold Tansy the chairs.

"*We never used the fire pit,*" shaky writing confided. "*Turned out Best to Be wasn't insured for them. My children tell me they're fun for younger people. My Robert and I did s'mores over a gas stove burner. They turned out fine.*"

Barbara and Bill Marsh had bought pizza at All Things. They laid the offering out on the kitchen table on an old checked table-cloth. The cheese was thick and bubbly, the ham was lean prosciutto, the tomatoes were homegrown, and the scent of garlic warmed the room. The white china bowl held kidney bean salad full of crunchy celery, sweet onion, and red and green pepper, with fresh-grated horseradish in a glass dish on the side. Pears filled an old wooden bowl sitting next to a pewter pitcher brimming with iced tea.

"We have to get back to the farm," Barbara said. "If we do any redecorating, house or barn, I'll get in touch with you."

"I," Zoe said, snagging a piece of pizza, "will write a fantastic letter of recommendation for you."

"Thanks, Zoe," Jen said. "That might not help me get into a design school."

"I'm going to send it to millionaires I know."

Dannie and her brothers had chopped away brush that had invaded an old trail down to a swimming hole.

"What happens to fishing if people swim?" Claire had asked.

"Don't worry about it," Dannie had said. "Trout like to be under banks and bushes lining the water, so we won't touch alders or tama-racks. Alders hold banks in place. Tamaracks give shade in summer and sunlight in winter. I want to get rid of the raspberry canes that ripped up Elaine's legs before that horse plowed into her."

Their work gave anyone in the living room a view of the path Whit had traversed. The rotting stump Elaine had fallen against was gone. Trailing net-sized swatches of wild grape had been cleared from around small apple trees. Once branches from long dead trees had been dragged away, you could see the river, its sand bottom reflecting sunshine and an aura of peace.

Black Pearl sat in front of the patio doors, eyeing changes with disapproval. No one had consulted him about clearing the bramble tunnels that had never failed to yield chipmunks. Since he hadn't been able to stop Dannie's crew of workers, he marched away with his ears back and his tail straight up.

There was beer in the refrigerator, but nobody was drinking alcohol, not even Claire. The day kept getting hotter. By 2:00 p.m., the temperature hovered at ninety-six degrees. Laurel retired to the basement with her laptop to type up Arnie's notes. Charles sat at the far end of the driveway, sketching wild turkeys that were nesting in aspen trees.

Claire curled on the bed in the room Laurel had been using. At times, she talked to George, though they remained one-way conversations. In Claire's world, heaven was like a James Herriot village, including a set of houses with roses lining front yards and maybe some lavender and a few daisies near the brick front steps. The houses would face a winding street, and the opposite bank would slope to a slow-flowing river. Sturdy cast-iron benches would accommodate sturdy behinds. People would bring dogs to splash in the shallows, where there might be offended ducks, but no ever-pooping Canada geese or aggressive swans. One could simply sit on the front steps of a brick house and pat—say—a black cat.

She had never opened the door to his house. It seemed an intrusion. He had crossed into a world she couldn't enter, but she could still sit on the steps and talk to him, and he could hear her, because of course the windows were open.

She sat down on the steps.

"George," she prayed. "I'm happy here, dear. I desperately miss you a thousand times a day. I even miss the way sometimes, you'd come to bed and your hair would still smell like cigars."

There was no sound from the house.

"George? I had an affair. I think that's what you'd call it. It wasn't sleazy. I feel like I'm waking up. Is that wrong?"

The black cat climbed up next to her. It stretched out on the steps.

DANNIE AND HER lot went to check on Elaine and send Arnie back in their stead.

The house was quiet.

The afternoon crept on.

Arnie arrived, noted Charles, who was still sketching, and after a few baffled minutes, located Claire, who had fallen asleep. He helped himself to pizza. He found containers and put away the kidney bean salad, then sat in a rocking chair, drinking coffee in spite of the heat. He was working on computer notes when Jen passed him, opening the patio doors and heading down to the river.

"Hey," he said.

"Hey, Arnie. If it's OK with you, I'm checking this progress out. If Dannie can clear a way to the pool, I can at least swim."

"You got sunscreen?"

"I do. I reek of cocoa butter."

"Shouldn't swim alone," he told her.

"I'll be fine," she reassured him. "Dannie says when it's calm, you can see to the bottom of the pool." She knew he'd put away the kidney bean salad to save them all from salmonella.

"You want to swim?" she asked him. "I'm going in wearing shorts and this T-shirt. You could roll your pants up and get wet."

He pulled his wire-rimmed glasses off and rubbed the side of one hand against the bridge of his nose. He looked more relaxed than he had, but tense, too. Jen thought he was like a shirt that had been washed and hung out in wind and sunshine, but had then been bullied back on a hanger.

"I guess not, Jen," he said. "I should get these notes done. Laurel is helping. Thanks for the thought. Say, what's the best movie you've seen that takes place in or on the ocean?"

"I don't know," she said. "Not *Waterworld.*"

He checked the score of the Tigers game and went back to his work.

There it was—the touch of color Jen had noticed when she'd first glanced outdoors. She picked her way down the path, looking out for protruding tree roots. Once she was on level, if stony ground, she could see she'd been right. Someone's persimmon-colored scarf was caught on a willow branch that was still alive, although the tree itself had keeled over on the far bank years ago. The scarf looked like the one Claire had been wearing the day before. Well, hey, she thought. Anything for Aunt Claire.

The river's cold enveloped her as she stretched out and eased into the front crawl she'd swum in high school. Swimming into the river current was harder work than she'd expected. She struggled for forward motion, head turning just enough to keep herself aligned in the current. She reached a place where she could climb the silty bank, steady herself, and reach the scarf. I can still do this, she thought.

As she stretched out an arm, the rusting jaws of a trap clamped on her right foot, yanking her, gasping and flailing, under the surface of the river. Shock blocked part of the pain, but she couldn't gain the surface and make her way to the shallows with her foot in the trap. She pushed up with her left foot and felt the silt she'd dislodged cascade down, carrying her into deeper water. At first, she could see the sun and sky above her, even tree branches. Then blood oozed up around her, clouding her vision. She felt disoriented, nauseated, and suddenly, crampingly cold. Once, she'd been able to swim the length of a good-sized pool underwater, turn, and swim back. But that had been when she was in high school.

Don't inhale, she told herself. Count to one hundred.

She got as far as twenty before she breathed water in.

17

WATCH THE BIRDS

Black Pearl arrived at Arnie's chair in the kitchen. The cat, yowling in a deep, strangling tenor pitch, landed on his chest and smacked him across the face.

Arnie knocked the cat to the floor, but it spun toward his ankle and bit him hard, then launched itself at the patio doors. Arnie repeated Laurel's thought that the cat might be rabid, since rabid skunks at times roamed the neighborhood. Then, remembering Pearl's response to the raven, he touched the Glock at the back of his belt and started after Pearl, his jaw set. From the top of the hill where the house sat, he could see bits of someone thrashing in the water. Dark hair. An elbow. A shoulder. An ankle. Jen. Then she was gone.

Arnie never remembered getting down to the pool. What he did remember was trying to hold Jen up so that her head was above water, but he couldn't simultaneously support her limp body and unfasten what his groping fingers determined to be an animal trap. A big animal trap. Not a bear trap, thank God, but a big fucking heavy trap, one that was weighted or anchored in some way.

He lugged Jen, cold and unresponsive, to the shallows. He tried to prop her up. She collapsed, the sand-churned brown water licking up her neck. He pulled her up again, tugging on her. Red ooze stained the water. Every time he pulled her head above water, he was wrenching her spine, her hip, her mangled foot. Desperate, he let her lolling head slip below the surface and dove below to try to release the trap, but the roiled silt and blood forced him to repeat the dive three times, her body sliding toward deeper water each time he circled down. Arnie tried struggling with the trap itself, pulling on it with one hand, the other hand trying to pull his gun free to shoot at the anchoring chain. Then Murphy was beside him, one hand steadying the chain, the other supporting Jen's neck and head.

Arnie blew apart the chain that anchored the trap to a waterlogged tree trunk submerged at the bottom of the pool. He lifted the trap as though he held a poisonous snake. When he sprang the device, Jen's bleeding leg rose to the surface. He and Murphy dumped her seemingly lifeless body on the riverbank, where a few gold tamarack needles drifted down. A blue jay screamed from the trees.

Murphy tried to cushion Jen's blackened, swelling foot while Arnie turned her head, checked for leaf and mucus clogs, and started artificial resuscitation. When she began to gag, vomit, gasp, and breathe, Murphy spoke shakily.

"That trap?" he said. "I sold a trap like that to a junk store years ago. The store was in Lovells. It closed when the hotel closed."

Arnie spat twice before he spoke. "Thanks. So what was that shit you said when Zoe's horse bolted? 'I won't stand for it?' Given what's just happened, that sure could be taken as a threat."

"That's just what that was. Shit. I tried to sound tough. Didn't work, did it?" Before Murphy gimped back up the hill, he turned to Arnie, who had lifted Jen and was cradling her in his arms. "That trap. That was meant for George's widow. You know that, don't you? I take it back, Robideu. She's not to blame. But get this mess figured out, will you? Put those women in protective custody. Marry them, move them, something. I ain't got the heart to try to save lives again."

CLAIRE WOKE AFTER dreaming she was safe, sleeping in George's arms.

Charles woke with his head on pine needles. He'd brushed off a few ants before he realized he'd awakened to the sound of an ambulance siren. His legs were stiff from sleeping. He shambled toward the house.

The wail of the ambulance brought Laurel to the driveway, where she saw Jen, head lolling, face pallid, in Arnie's arms. She stumbled, looking at her daughter, and for a minute, the trees and people in her field of vision wavered.

The ambulance driver gestured for her to stay away. Arnie, having transferred Jen's dripping, limp weight to the men by the gurney, waved them off. They knew what they were going. He turned back to Laurel and after one look at her face, put a freezing cold arm, dripping with silt and water weed, around her waist and held her up.

Laurel turned to him. "Will you drive me to the hospital?" she asked. She could feel his hesitation.

"I need to be here."

Then Claire was by her side, easing Laurel away from Arnie so the two women clung to each other instead. Charles appeared.

"I have to go back to the river," Arnie said. "Get pictures of that trap, the way it was set. I'm calling support."

"What do you want me to do?" asked Charles.

Arnie's anger broke through the surface. He was angry at everyone now, though mostly at himself. He hadn't thought, after Elaine had been hurt, that there would be an immediate second injury, especially one worse than the first.

"I don't know, Charles. Why don't you go watch birds?"

After snapping photos at the bottom of the pool, Bertram Allarbee helped Arnie swing a plank across the river to the bank where the trap sat. Anything that had to be transported to help the investigation could be moved across the plank, for now. The chain anchoring the trap had been fed around the remaining branches of the old pine trunk that crossed the sand bottom of the pool. The branches stuck out like the stripped, slippery rib bones of a chicken carcass.

Allarbee sat on the bank, pulling on his trousers, then staggered to his feet, walked a few paces, and dry heaved. There was a scarf on a tree where he and Arnie had been working. Cheap cloth. Weird color, he thought. He wiped his mouth with it and stuffed it in a pocket.

Arnie had been staring across the pool, looking to see if Murphy's small house was visible.

"Sir?" Allarbee asked. "How often do you see something like this? Not like a car crash. I've seen crushed bones. I've seen motorcycle riders smeared into the highway. I'm not used to them, but I'm used to them. You know? They fit in my mind now. But this? This was *malice*."

Arnie turned back to the younger officer, whose eyes were squinting at him, puzzled. That was more than he'd heard Bertram Allarbee say since the boy had been hired.

He tried to answer, but ended up shrugging, patting the kid's shoulder, and walking away from him.

BLACK PEARL APPEARED in the driveway, sniffed at the puddles of blood and water, and rubbed against Charles, who sat on the grass at the edge of the drive. He'd been watching a hawk circle.

Charles reached down and scratched Pearl's head. Laurel and Claire had turned to each other in crisis. The others were investigating. He might have said something about decay time of pines in water, but he couldn't think why the information would have helped. Coffee, he thought. I'll make pots of coffee. He walked slowly back to the house, glancing back to be sure Pearl was following.

The kitchen was dark and quiet. He turned on lights, then found and set out towels. Something in his nature seemed to put people off when it came to asking for help. He caught a glimpse of his reflection in the window. When had he gotten older? Pearl looked quizzically at him.

"You did better than I did," he said. "I'll find your food."

There were still a few pieces of pizza. He peeled off the remaining prosciutto, chopped it into bits, and fed them to the cat. He stood for a minute, watching Pearl eat. Then he crooked his elbow and leaned against a kitchen cupboard, resting his head on the back of his forearm. He tried to remember how many turkeys he'd seen, but they flew up in his mind like orange, open-beaked Thanksgiving turkeys on greeting cards.

18

COLLECTED WORKS

"Pizza tastes a little off, don't you think?"

"Can't say I noticed," Charles said.

"Seems like it used to have more zing to it," Arnie said.

They were sitting in the kitchen, in the half dark. Arnie and Bertram had taken hot showers and rubbed down hard with towels. Arnie had gotten back into his uniform but told Bertram Allarbee to change into one of George's Black Watch plaid wool bathrobes. Then the boy—when had he started thinking of Allarbee as a boy?—had suddenly, unexpectedly fallen asleep in a rocking chair.

Pearl had climbed into his lap.

"Maybe he can't sleep in his uniform," Charles said.

"Maybe he misses his momma's titty," Arnie said.

"No shame in it," Charles said. "You want Elaine to come over? I know you don't put much faith in my staying power."

"You made coffee." Arnie thought Charles might apologize again for the turkey sketches.

"I want to look through George's books," Charles said. "Laurel says they're boring or something."

"What the crap are you looking for? You think he's got an old US treasury coupon bond hidden between book pages? Isn't that like something out of a Rex Stout plot?"

"No. I don't know why I want to look. But I lie there at night, looking up at those books, and think they should tell me something, but I'm missing whatever it is."

"I'll have Elaine come over," Arnie said. "When she gets here, we can both go listen to the books talk. Not till then."

Elaine let herself in and positioned a gel cushion on a kitchen chair.

"Don't say anything, Arnie," she said. "I'll kill you if you joke."

"Elaine, for God's sake, pile up all the pillows you need."

"Dannie didn't have any idea when she and her brothers cleared that path that Jen would get hurt."

"None of us did. None of us could have," Arnie said.

By then, Charles was already in the library. He'd found a card table and was spreading out a few of George's books so the copyright page showed on each.

"Some of these books might have belonged to George's parents," he said. "That's where we're getting the little bit of old book smell. Dickens, Kipling, Churchill. *The Collected Works of Justice Holmes.* I've just spread out the ones that are leaving me perplexed."

"What's the problem with these?" Arnie moved to the card table and peered down at the books.

"Cormac McCarthy," Charles said. "George has all of his books. *All the Pretty Horses* and *Blood Meridian* were good, but a lot of his stuff was crap. Steinbeck's *The Wayward Bus.* What was wrong with Steinbeck when he wrote that book? *Christine* in a dust jacket. One good book: *To Kill a Mockingbird,* ragged copy. A shitty copy of *Stalky & Co.* A first edition of *Little Dorrit.*"

"So? If you want me to feel like an ignoramus, you've got me. I've read a few of these. *To Kill a Mockingbird. All the Pretty Horses.* But I never even saw the movie *Christine.*"

"Well, there's a lot of Stephen King here, too, but it's not his best stuff. Larry McMurtry, but his later stuff. Nothing much by women."

"So? Would Laurel care about that?"

"I don't think George collected these books," Charles said.

"Claire said he did."

"I think he had a book scout. Look at this. There's no uniting theme through this collection. No time period, no single writer he loved enough to get all the guy's books. Not even an attempt to get the best book or books by favorite authors."

"So?"

"I don't know," Charles said. "But it's not what I expected. I thought George had more focus. Was more choosy."

"What makes you think he didn't focus?" Arnie asked. "I bet some of these books cost more than Bertram Allarbee makes in a year."

"And that's just it. These books would knock the socks off someone who doesn't read a lot, which I do, because sometimes, I'm snowed in. The average party guest would come in this room and say, 'Wow, George sure loves books.' And I think he wanted to hear that. I'm not saying he didn't read and love these books. I'm just saying, you can look at collections, even collections by birders, and most bookshelves show some quirks and obsessions. Everything say, by Willa Cather. *The Shakespeare Riots. Freddy Goes Camping*, or Little Lulu comic books. You walk away from browsing bookshelves like that, and you think, that guy has a sense of humor. Who knew? Or, I didn't think that woman would collect studies of nudes!"

"You're saying someone with a collection that contains oddities is into books, not adulation. These are make-an-impression books."

Damn, Charles thought. Arnie used *adulation* in a sentence. Correctly.

"Yeah," he said. "That's exactly what I mean."

Arnie said, "That's odd. I wonder why he, of all people, would want to make an impression. I just assumed he was born upper middle class. He went to the University of Michigan. Not a shabby school."

"No, it's not," Charles said.

"Where'd you go?" Arnie asked.

"Columbia."

"Not shabby either. I went to KVCC. Kalamazoo Valley Community College." He rubbed a hand up and across his five o'clock shadow.

"Arnie, I gotta tell you something," Charles said. "The smartest woman I knew lived on a farm as a child, quit school at fourteen to help her parents—which you could do then—then opened a grocery store and took care of kids and grandkids. She didn't follow international politics, but anything about snakes, birds, birch bark baskets, preserving food for winter using layers of fat, fish traps, copper mines…you get the idea."

"She was Indian?"

"No. No, she was just *interested*. I'll never know as much as she did."

"Huh," Arnie said. "My dad used to say, 'Everyone's smarter than hell about something and dumber than dog shit about something else.'"

19

PATIENT LOUNGE

Arnie's phone rang. Charles directed his attention to the books, but Arnie tipped the phone so Charles could hear. Claire's voice was faint, maybe because she was using her cell.

"Jen's knocked out with opiates and full of antibiotics. She's been checked by emergency room physicians and by orthopedic surgeons. Her whole foot went into the trap, which snapped her ankle in a clean break above the articulating bones."

Arnie gave Charles a thumbs-up with his free hand.

"They're waiting till they read the X-ray tomorrow before they have anything definite to say. There are punctures they'll have to deal with before they put on a cast, but right now, they're leaving those wounds open so stuff can drain."

"Fluid in the lungs?" Charles asked.

Arnie conveyed the question.

"Maybe some, but they're watching it. If it gets gunky, they can drain some out through her back. Sounds awful, but they said they numb the spot where the needle goes in and it's not painful or gruesome. Laurel is going to stay here, of course. Jen's in an intensive care room, so we can't stay with her." Claire's voice wavered.

"The patient lounge at the end of the hall is OK. I'll call tomorrow morning, if nothing changes. Someone should tell Dannie that if she and her brothers hadn't cleared a path to the river, I would have hired a work crew to do it. The fact that the path was cleared wasn't the problem; the problem was the bastard who set the trap that hurt Jen."

"Of course it wasn't Dannie's fault," Charles said.

"Yeah. Hell, we all feel guilty. I should have been making everyone stay in the house."

"That would have eliminated my inspired turkey sketches."

"Crimes around here are usually pretty simple, unless guys get into a fist fight that turns lethal in a bar. I can't anticipate what this perp is doing next. Claire should put in cameras. I can do that for her. She's not going to object after Jen was hurt. Seems like whoever hates her, or wants to hurt her and her friends, is getting more desperate."

"Oscar and the salmon were in her living room."

"Yeah. But whoever was there was in and out of her house in— what would you guess? Five minutes? Leaving that threatening note takes less than that. How long would it have taken to spook Zoe's horse? Whoever set this trap up left that trailing scarf. Now that I think about it, that person took a risk of being seen."

"Could you ask Elaine or Bertram Allarbee to go through every single book, hold them upside down, fan out pages, and see what falls out?"

"Good idea. And while I call a security company, you could do something. Check out the basement again. Pearl's driving me nuts with his weird little gifts. Check the attic; make sure squirrels haven't chewed a hole in the roof."

"There's no way Pearl can get in and out of the attic."

"Check the back of closets again. Make sure none of the ceiling panels open."

Charles said, "I'll do anything I can."

CLAIRE AND LAUREL sat on a hard, plastic-coated couch in the hospital lounge. The seating wasn't that comfortable, but a cart provided bottled water, coffee, tea, sweet rolls, rock-hard melon, and blueberry yogurt. Donations were requested. A pop machine bore a sign reading, "*Out of order. Check cafeteria hall.*" The room smelled of disinfectant and floral spray scent.

An elderly volunteer who looked like a raddled strawberry muffin went down to the hospital's cafeteria and got eggs and toast on a tray for a diabetic father whose daughter was in surgery for a broken sternum.

"Thanks," he said. "But I left my wallet in my jacket in the truck. I can't pay you."

"They didn't charge me for it," the woman said. "Any of you want cold water, there's a drinking fountain in the hall."

Laurel leaned against Claire's ample shoulder. She'd cried herself out after the woman surgeon had told her, "We're guardedly optimistic. I'd hug you, but then I'd have to prep again."

Claire was still drizzling. She leaned her head away from Laurel, so her tears made a damp splotch on her own shoulder. Thank heavens the toast and egg man had agreed with them, and the television news—which could not be turned off—at least had the sound turned down. The room was quiet. Fluorescent lights, with their mosquito-in-the-ear keening, had been turned off. Instead, three lamps with identical blue, Chinese urn-shaped bases lit the room, throwing splotches of light on the ceiling. The clock on the wall had a face and hands and ticked. The room felt a bit homelike—better than an airport lounge until an ambulance's wailing siren hit a crescendo outside and then abruptly cut off.

Laurel sat up straight. "You crying, Claire?" she asked.

"No." Claire's nose was running, so the word sounded more like *Doh*. She groped for a box of tissues on a table next to the couch.

"Did you get Arnie?" she asked.

"Uh-huh." Claire scrubbed at her nose.

"Was Charles there?" Laurel asked.

They were talking quietly, trying to not disturb the man, who, now that he had eaten, had walked over to the window and was staring out over the parking lot. His hands were clasped behind his back, and his back was to them.

"Mm-hmm," Claire answered.

"How'd they sound?" Laurel asked.

"Really glad to hear from us. Charles asked about, you know, fluid in the lungs."

"And Arnie took his head off, I bet," Laurel said. She put her head in her hands.

"No. No, he didn't," Claire said. "They—they sounded OK. Worried, you know, but not about to turn on each other."

"Oh," Laurel said. "That's good. That's really good. Because, I'm not going to be able to type up notes for a while. I'm going to just help Jen. We don't need them arguing—" She gave Claire a stricken look.

Claire stared back at her. "You slept with Arnie," she said. "You said he was a hairy, bullnecked cretin, and then you slept with him."

"He's not," Laurel said. "He does have hair on his back. But he's not a cretin."

"Arnie's *married*," Claire said.

"So I heard. Why didn't you tell me?"

"Laurel. Why would I think you'd need to know?" Claire asked. "Why did he do it? He's Chinese Food and Movies. Not Mr. I Need Sex."

"I asked him to." Laurel looked woebegone. "I've never—never approached anyone. I don't think it will happen again."

Claire's expression softened. "We were both wrong," she said. "Our intentions and predictions. Remember, we talked about them at the motel?"

"I forgot," Laurel said. "What did I predict?"

"No empathy."

"I don't think I'm good at that. Even reading, for long-term learning, we need empathy."

"Only you, Laurel, would relate sex to reading."

That's not true, Laurel thought. Arnie did.

"And I said I wouldn't get involved until I figure out who I'm turning into. But Charles seems to like me for who I am, right now. It's confusing."

"I wish I could see Jen."

"I wish I'd brought a flask," Claire said.

20

THERAPY

Jen continued to make progress in the days that followed. Once she was moved from intensive care into a private room, Laurel was given a strange, uncomfortable reclining chair in the room with Jen.

"I think this chair was designed for a tall man," Laurel said.

But if she lined the chair with pillows, she could sleep in it comfortably, and if she cramped up, she put the hospital pillows on the floor and slept next to Jen's bed. Sometimes, one of Jen's hands would dangle off the narrow mattress, and Laurel could reach up and touch her daughter's fingers. When Jen slept on her back, her hands drifted to the position they'd found when she was a little girl—her right hand near her face, her left above her head, clutching strands of her own dark hair. Laurel found herself thinking that the right hand could help guide a breast or bottle into an infant's mouth; the other hand, with its tendrils of hair, could fend off the instinctive fear of falling, of being dropped. Laurel felt as though she had dropped her child. Like an atheist in a foxhole, she did a lot of praying, along the lines of, "Take me, God. Goddess." She often ended with, "Shit. I suck at this."

Jen, still taking opiates, lagged at conversations and slept a great deal, but was glad to have Laurel there. Jen's doctor came in after five days, cut back on her pain medication, and told her she could start, with her physical therapist's supervision, some gentle leg lifts while lying in bed. "If that doesn't hurt or slow healing," he said, "we'll start getting you up and around."

Claire had gone back to her house, under Arnie's duress. The two of them stopped by Everything Michigan, both to stock up on food and so Arnie could talk to Ann.

"George's family." Ann paused in thought. "Salt of the earth people. Grandparents, I was told, were farmers who rented land to other farmers. Not rich, but stable. His parents—you know they lived near us—had a printing business in Grayling and owned but didn't manage a small restaurant where the farmer's market is now. They probably had a couple bad years when local printing went south, but George always had better clothes than the rest of us did. He had a blazer that he wore to church, and we girls all thought it was the epitome of cool. He wanted to be, and he was, someone special. He held his head up and his shoulders back. When he went to away to college, his parents sold property. Zoe Weathers bought one of the parcels, the one that's next to your house now," Ann said.

Claire bought everything she could think of to buy, except salmon. Koeze peanut butter. Bread. Smoked ham, which she hadn't bought once since meeting the Marshes' pigs. Apples, dried apricots, nut-studded brownies, a pear pie complete with cream and rum. Comfort food.

People helped themselves to food when they were hungry. Laurel simply ignored the security cameras. She slept in George's white V-neck T-shirts, which seemed to keep getting longer on her. Either they were stretching or she was losing weight. Or both.

When she came out to the kitchen, Arnie said, "That's a new look. Don't wear it to the office."

"We were going to give these to Tansy. She said some residents could use them."

"As Patsy says," Arnie quoted, "And yet…"

Claire was more self-conscious with the security cameras. She wore her own nightgowns and caftans, but the shoulder she'd hurt falling down the stairs made it hard to brush her hair. It fell, full of tangles, down her back. She had stopped drinking, as she had when George was dying.

"I think at some point," she said to Laurel, "my dopamine receptors decide 'rewards' are bullshit. When enough goes wrong, I don't get anything out of alcohol, or candy, or even ice cream, and it's been decades since I tried drugs. If I'm not getting anything out of my bad habits, why suck down extra calories?"

Instead, she cleaned kitchen cupboards as a penance for Jen's suffering. It was possible there were important papers hidden in a pie safe or in between chipped Blue Onion plates someone had pushed to the back. When she looked into the cupboards, she saw someone had left her tall stems of chicory, and in another one, she found half a black walnut with little stick feet glued on so it looked like an owl.

She held the trinket in her hands, the way a child holds an insect, and trekked down to the basement, opening her hands and showing it to Charles. "Of course you wouldn't know anything about this."

He smiled and shook his head. "Looks bafflingly like a token from an admirer. Haven't a clue."

"I love it," she said. "But it confuses me, too, because from the first minute I saw it, it has reminded me of Laurel, but Laurel isn't dark-skinned, wrinkly, or twice as wide as she is tall."

Charles's smile widened, and the expression reached his eyes, which in turn, made Claire smile.

"Now that you mention it, Laurel reminds me of a saw-whet owl. Saw-whets are small and like solitude, and even when they're adult, their heads look big for their bodies, which makes them undeniably cute. When the temperature is freezing, a saw-whet stores extra food in trees and then comes back when it's hungry to sit on the cache and thaw out its dinner, looking as though it's sitting on a clutch of eggs."

"Laurel never does that with food. At least, I hope not."

"She caches what she reads, though. She tucks things away in her brain, and when she's bored, she incubates, devours, and digests."

"Um. Yeah. How did you happen to think of Laurel as an owl?"

"I don't know. Watching her read, I guess, as she takes off her glasses and gazes into the distance for a minute before going back to a computer or her book. You spend enough time in the woods, and you start getting intuitions. Something is moving toward you. Or something—familiar, not familiar—is pacing along by your side. E.O. Wilson, an extraordinary bug guy, calls it 'the naturalist's trance.' There was a naturalist over by Ludington who kept feeling she was being watched; she was thinking bobcat, maybe, and it took her a while to realize there was a young cougar moving silently along with her, keeping just uphill from her. Not stalking her, she thought, just curious. We've still got the instincts that tell us when someone is watching us."

Claire fidgeted, remembering the first night Laurel had spent at her house.

"Everyone has multiple aspects," Charles muttered. "I've been thinking there was a marten near here. Martens are small, gold-brown weasels that weigh about two pounds, generate massive rage when threatened, and can take down bigger prey. I thought I might be getting impressions of Arnie. Martens almost always den away from their mate and kits. Arnie doesn't live with his family, which could produce tension. He used to feel like a big ball of frustration, unfocused anger, and defensiveness. But now Arnie's—well, focused on problems here. He reminds me of a goshawk. They zigzag through dense forest on the wing or even run after lizards or small mammals on foot. Ferocious defending a nest site. Squawking, dive bombing attacks."

Claire thought privately that Arnie, descending squawking from above, would rout the most determined predator. "What about you?"

"I've decided I'm a snipe. Shy, secretive. Eyes in the back of my head. However, I make daring, dazzling, headfirst dive courtship displays in spring. That had a lot of D words, didn't it? Which reminds me," he continued, "I know David's bird type. The dickcissel looks like a bit like a meadowlark. Its call is its own name, trilled, and it's polygynous, mating with up to eight females every spring, which means it does not help females when they're nesting or brooding."

"David Dickcissel? Jen wouldn't like that."

"I wouldn't say it to Jen. Though you could say it to Laurel. I picture him striding down corridors, seeing a likely female and trilling, 'Dickcissel, dickcissel, dickcissel!'"

"Did you see the way Arnie lit into him?" Claire asked.

"I didn't see it, but that somehow doesn't surprise me."

THERE WERE MOMENTS for socializing, but time stretched like runny taffy. Like Claire, people chose odd tasks.

Elaine Santana collected all the framed pictures and mirrors she could find and took them out of old-fashioned frames, checking for messages between cardboard and photographs. Not discovering anything, she laboriously reassembled the lot, using Windex on the glass and dusting the picture frames. She ran her hands over wallpaper in the upstairs bedrooms, trying to see if there were telltale bulges to explore, and unscrewed the light switch plates to make sure nothing hid behind their blank, snub-nosed faces and that no one had tampered with the wiring.

When Charles wasn't with Jen or pottering in the basement, he washed dishes at the sink that was too low for him, so he stood stooped, like an Ichabod Crane caricature. He wiped his wet hands on khaki pants and peered through spattered glasses, muttering about dirty teacups and custard hardened onto Pyrex, but he shooed away anyone else who tried to take over the task.

Twice, Pearl brought him voles he'd carried up from the basement, but he never presented them to him when he could be seen entering the house.

"He's onto me," he told Arnie.

"Work harder," Arnie said.

21

WATER LIKE BEER

"It looks like beer," Claire said. "I had to show it to you."

The water pouring over the small dam in the river had the faint gold hint of tannin, and it splashed and burbled down to the base of the rocks with so much force, bubbles rose to the surface.

Laurel raised her half of the sub she was eating and then frowned. "Don't say 'It don't get no better than this.'"

"I don't even like Old Milwaukee," Claire reassured her. "That was the most annoying commercial ever made."

"I'm glad you talked me into meeting for lunch." Laurel chewed and swallowed bread, cheese, lettuce, and salami. "Why are school and hospital walls beige?"

"Sometimes mint green, but mostly beige," Claire agreed. "That's where someone with decorating smarts could knock the ball out of the ballpark. How's my decorator doing?"

"Jen confounds the doctors. She's young, so she's healing fast. They're keeping new skin from forming over the punctures so the wounds heal from the inside out. Her doctor says the cold water might have slowed bacterial growth, which was his first concern, so she's full of antibiotics, but her stomach does better with them than mine. It was great of Zoe to insist on staying with her. She didn't take any guff from me when I said I should be there. She reminded me that she's a doctor, even if she is retired, and pushed me out of the door."

They were both dressed to visit Jen at the hospital later—Laurel in a straight, knee-length gold dress and sandals, Claire wearing white slacks, a navy tank top, and white tennis shoes.

"Isn't this the park where Zoe rescued those puppies?" Laurel asked.

"Sure is," Claire responded. "Right across the road is the starting place for the Au Sable River Canoe Marathon, but this is the site where Zoe Weathers chastised the man who wanted to drown what he thought were his puppies, only to find they belonged to Zoe. I bet he had one of those bumper stickers: 'My dog, my wife, my gun. You can take my wife.'"

Laurel grimaced. She was thinking of Jen, held underwater by the trap and fighting for air.

"If Zoe ever needs anything—"

"Doubtful," Claire responded.

"Tell me."

The day was cool, but the sun was bright. Arnie dozed in the shade near them. A couple of high school students wandered through the park holding hands. On the other side of the river, a mother with her toddler on a leash was doing yoga exercises. A white-haired woman with her glasses down on her nose sat on a bench, reading an issue of *Smithsonian* magazine.

"Is Arnie asleep?" Claire whispered.

"I think so," Laurel said. "Do you know what this bit of the river reminds me of? The time I went camping with your family. I had a crush on Doyle, but your brothers ditched us so fast, you'd think we had leprosy."

"I didn't know you liked Doyle! Ugh. He's fine now, but they were all obnoxious then."

"We were packed into your parents' station wagon like sardines in a tin. I thought his sweat smelled sexy."

"Laurel! You have the worst taste in men! My sweaty brother?"

"Yup," Laurel said. "I hadn't been physically close to many boys. I kept trying to time my breathing to rise and fall in counterpoint to his, but he didn't notice."

"That one park—near the mouth of the Platte—did have a fall like this." Claire closed her eyes, remembering. "The river pours out into Lake Michigan, with warm shallows and cool incoming waves. There were places where we stood on sandbars and places where we could swim."

"Do you miss Lake Michigan?"

"I guess not," Claire said, rubbing her nose in thought. "The beach kept getting more and more crowded. The last time George and I went, I forgot my sandals, and we had to park on the drive. I got blisters the size of silver dollars on my heels and the balls of my feet. At least the DNR roped off piping plover breeding areas."

"What's Doyle doing now?" Laurel asked. "Is he still an outdoorsman?"

"He is. But he's in Oregon, working for their DNR. He does fish counts, like swim-underwater fish counts. Fish census work."

"The rest of your sibs?"

"Jan's in California. She taught for a while, but now she's got kid complications and is a stay-at-home mother. My parents live with Mark and his wife in North Carolina; he manages their condominium complex and turns a blind eye to my dad's eccentricity. Brian is an assistant recruiting director for the Chicago Bears. Big money, but he's on the road a lot. Matt's an air traffic controller with the Navy, stationed in Germany, up for twenty-and-out soon. Jimmy—we never know, with Jimmy. Last I knew, he piloted a whale sighting charter boat off the coast of Washington. He's a wanderer. I think he's been in every state."

"We went on our own adventure that summer. You remember."

"God, yes," Claire replied. "I have never had such a prolonged encounter with saw grass. One side of a dune all sandy and friendly, and the next side, burrs and thorns."

"Bathing suits—not the right attire to hike the dunes."

"It didn't seem as though we walked that far, when we were walking and talking," Claire said. "We walked the dunes because the beaches were covered with dead alewives and flies."

Laurel added. "I still loathe flies. Thank God planting salmon solved the alewife problem."

"Back in the dunes, there was a little breeze. But if the rain hadn't started," Claire recalled "we would've been a lot more sunburned."

"If it hadn't rained, we would have melted."

"And when we were exhausted, walking north, there were those dogs playing on the beach by a river. We could swim in the rain and frolic with somebody's pets, because dogs were allowed on that section of the beach. Remember the couple that walked their black labs most mornings, three seasons of the year, to look for Petoskey stones? Anyway, the dogs were shouldering each other in and out of the water. One of them almost did a dog somersault. "

"Too bad we got halfway down the hill before we figured out we were seeing bear cubs." Laurel sighed. "I nearly had a heart attack trying to run back up that hill, with sand sliding out from under our feet every step we took."

"It worked better turning our feet sort of sideways," Claire recalled.

Arnie sat up. "How close did you get?" he asked.

"You've been listening," Claire exclaimed. "We thought you were sleeping."

"I slept through the part about Doyle's sweat," he said.

"We were probably seventy yards away," Claire said. "We ran back over a ripple in the dunes, closer to the trees and farther away from all that tasty, rotting salmon. That's why we got so scratched. There were more burrs and even wild roses."

"We saw a fox," Laurel said.

"But you never saw the mother bear?"

"No, thank God," Laurel answered him.

"The lampreys are controlled now," Claire said. "So not many dead fish. Fewer chances to meet Br'er Bear."

"I wish we could have gone down to that river," Laurel said. "It would have been a great place for an Indian village. I think there are whole villages buried under some dunes, especially where rivers cut through the forests. Families could fish, hunt, and follow the river back to farming plots and berry bushes, and willow and ash for basket making."

"I think we've missed our chance. We walked seven miles north," Claire said, "and going back was harder. I don't think either of us could do that now. Could you, Arnie?"

He rubbed his stubbly jaw. "I could if I had to, but I would not consider it an adventure. By the way, 'the worst taste in men,' Claire?"

"*Have* might've been the wrong verb tense for me to use, Arnie. We got you a sub. Mayo, lettuce, and mustard?"

"You get napkins?"

"Sorry, we used them." Laurel was watching a family of ducks on the far side of the park. "Wait, this one's not too bad."

"Your brothers must have been jealous of you," Arnie said, taking the mustard-stained napkin.

"My brothers didn't believe us. They were moving out of the 'Claire is our buddy' stage and into one of their 'Guys rule, girls drool' stages. That was the last summer that I wasn't self-conscious about how my bathing suit fit, or how my hair looked, or if bits of me bounced when I ran."

"My mother would've had a fit if she'd seen what we looked like," Laurel said. "That was our last summer of scorching hot dogs, spitting watermelon seeds, eating your mom's lard crust pies, and never looking at a mirror."

"After that—summer jobs," Claire said. "I worked at a mom-and-pop restaurant."

"I sold lingerie in an upscale store," Laurel said. "My mother got me the job. I had a 15 percent discount, and she encouraged me to shop."

"I drove a mowing machine," Arnie said. "Bet I made more money."

Both women favored him with a withering look.

Claire was chewing on a grass stem.

"Working at the restaurant helped me get a job at the Embers when I was at Central," Claire said. "Not much salary, but great tips, especially from bourbon drinkers."

"I didn't work in college," Laurel said. "There weren't many jobs around Albion. My parents didn't want me to work. They wanted a hothouse flower."

Arnie snorted the last of his sub up his nose.

"Ow," he protested. "Ow. Salambi in sinduses 'urdts."

"Drive me back to the hospital," Laurel suggested. "A doctor with long, sharp-tipped tweezers can reach right up your nose and tweak that salami out."

Arnie drove them both back to the hospital and dropped them off.

"If I go home to snag some clean clothes, will both of you promise to go straight to Jen's room? I'll be back in twenty minutes."

He peered at both of them. "No walking the dunes, and no bears that look like dogs."

"No dune walking," Claire said. "I can't wait to see Jen."

His truck pulled away, bumping over ruts in the parking lot. They stood side by side, watching him go, and then Claire turned to Laurel. "What if," she suggested, "we went on a very *small* adventure. Let's steal five minutes and visit the Dominican Sisters' labyrinth."

"You're weird," Laurel said.

"What can happen? It's right behind the hospital. Maybe on hospital grounds. The last time I was there, I was with George. I swore I'd keep George from dying, but that promise didn't work well. Let me try again. Let's renew our ninth-grade pledge we'll always stay friends."

"Sounds good," Laurel said. "In the face of ghosties, ghoulies, and things that go bump in the night—"

"We'll trust each other," Claire said.

The labyrinth was a simple brick path winding in diminishing circles to a center where once, a statue or plant had been raised on a plinth. Perhaps the small garden had once been more grandiose, because there was a marble cherub's head, missing one ear and its nose, lying on its side in a clump of scraggly asters. A pair of cement doves lay on the ground near a bench. Clusters of ragged cedar trees shaded one side.

Claire reached down and adjusted one of the doves so that its winged side leaned against its mate. The day she was here with George, there had been a twig wreath holding the doves in position, but the wreath now lay outside the circle. Someone—a girl, she guessed—had woven in a clover chain.

Outside the path, order—the wreath, the statues, the wilting flowers—changed to long grass and nearby swamp-loving shrubs she was sure led to the river.

Claire wasn't particularly religious. Exposure to church had inoculated her when she was young, and left her heart open to people without expecting good and bad points would be kept by God on a tab behind a bar. At that moment, though, cloud shadows and sunlight flickered like a procession across the brick path, and she shivered in recognition of everyday miracles.

"We gotta keep looking for portents," she said. "It's easy to overlook them."

"Oh my gosh," Laurel said, pointing, then dropping her hand and walking with a fixed gaze toward the opposite shrub line. "I found a sign," she called back to Claire. "Look what I found, Claire! Over there in the grass, the book I use! The text for my creative writing class. It's not my copy, either."

Claire followed after her. Stepping over the bricks wasn't easy in sandals. Laurel turned an ankle and stumbled on.

"What are the chances someone else in Grayling, Michigan, would love this book?" she asked Claire. "Maybe it's a sign that I should stick around."

"So instead of a burning bush, a soggy textbook?"

The trade paperback lay near scrubby bushes. Now that neither Claire nor Laurel was talking, they could hear the river flowing nearby.

"*Steering the Craft*," Laurel murmured, waiting for Claire to catch up before she picked up the book. "It's by Ursula K. Le Guin. You know, dragons and much more. We both read her. She's an actual, real writer who wrote a textbook. Most textbooks read as though robots shat them out. Wow!" she exclaimed. "This is like being ten years old and finding someone else believes in magic."

"See if there's a name in the front," Claire said. "Maybe you can find the owner."

"It's been out in the rain, maybe? The front edge is discolored. There's a bookmark, I think," Laurel said. "It's got a bulge in the middle." She bent and scooped up the book, walking back toward Claire and holding it for a moment to show her the cover was still mostly white, the sailboat—"the craft"—outlined in black ink.

She was standing near the center of the labyrinth when she opened the book at the bookmark. A stinking, wet ooze splattered over her. At the same time, the small massasauga inside writhed onto her hands. As she shrieked and flung the book away, it dropped loose and clung to her feet.

Laurel kicked out and stumbled back, flailing. The limp, black-and-gray sinuous form flopped from her feet but landed only inches away. The elegant diamond pattern on the rattlesnake's back and sides was alarmingly clear. She could feel her heart beating hard in her chest, hear her own inhalation. Twisting to one side to run, she lost her balance and fell, hitting her head on the stone path.

Arnie's arm was around her shoulders when she came to.

Claire knelt beside her, clasping one of her hands. "It's dead, Laurel," Claire kept repeating. "It was dead. The snake was dead when you found it. Dead."

"Don't try to get up yet," Arnie said. "You've got a great fat lump on the back of your head. The emergency room found you a cup of sugary tea."

"How did you get here? You left," Laurel said.

"I drove from my house when Claire called me. She said you'd been bitten by a rattlesnake. I pictured something three feet long, but thank God, this one was a baby, and long past biting anything."

Laurel's eyes filled with tears. "I'm an idiot," she said. "Of course it had to have been dead to be stuck in that textbook. But it—it seemed to lunge out. And it f-f-fell on my ankles. And I'm not that scared of snakes, but I panicked. Ugh." She shuddered with revulsion.

"You got some distance between you and the snake. That was a healthy reaction." Arnie rubbed her back. "I don't know if your snake was glued in or just stuck on with its own dried visceral juices, but it must have dropped out when you opened that book. Whoa. Don't throw up on me. Is that tea cool enough? If it is, take a sip."

Claire scrubbed tear tracks from her face with muddy hands.

"What's that smell?" Laurel asked. "I think it's me."

"That snake had been dead a while," Claire admitted. "And it was full of—full of rotty little frog parts."

"The rotty little frog parts had been in the snake for a while," Laurel guessed.

Claire pulled off her tank top and used it to gently wipe Laurel's hands and face and the front of her dress.

"Hospital windows, indecent exposure, Claire." Laurel looked worried.

"Blinds are closed to keep out the sun," Arnie reassured them.

"I'm wearing a sports bra. Have you seen what teenagers wear now? And anyway, I don't give a damn," Claire said.

"I'm covered with frog and snake guts," Laurel said.

"I wiped off most of the bits," Claire told her.

"How did the snake's innards and its food get outside of the snake?"

"Sip more tea. You're pale."

"How, Claire? Had someone run over it with a mower?"

"And then put it in the book? No, sweetheart," Arnie said. "I don't know what killed the snake. But after it died, someone slit its ventral side from right under the head down to its two little rattles, and left it for you to find when you were visiting Jen. Claire says that's a text you use?"

Laurel sat up straight and craned her neck around. "Ow. Where is that book now? Where is the snake?"

"Arnie picked the snake and the textbook up with barbeque tongs and put them in a cooler. He just called you *sweetheart*," Claire noted absently.

"Cut me some slack, Claire," Arnie said. "I thought she might have been poisoned. Only two people have died, on record, in Michigan from eastern massasauga bites, but one of you two could have managed it. They're shy snakes, mind you, either threatened or endangered. I don't even know if this hospital has antivenom."

"How did someone get that book?" Laurel clutched Claire's hand.

"All they'd have to do is look up the textbook you use online," Arnie said.

Laurel leaned back into the support of his arm, reassured, though Arnie didn't seem look all that happy about the thought.

"Don't tell Charles about this," she said. "He'll have a fit about the snake."

"I don't care a frog's left foot about Charles's feelings."

"Neither do I, in this case," Claire said.

"I want to get up," Laurel said.

"Do you need me to carry you?"

"I think I can walk, Arnie."

"Let me help." He put a hand under her elbow to help her balance.

"There probably wasn't much venom," she said. "Even if I had gotten bit."

"There was venom, all right," he told her. "The kind of venom people spew. And from now on, you, as well as Claire, are grounded. Claire, call Jen and tell her that Laurel is indisposed and will no longer be on her visiting list."

Laurel pulled away from him.

He said, "Do you want to bring your attacker into the hospital and closer to Jen?"

"No." She bit her lower lip.

"I'll call now," Claire said.

Arnie put his arm around Laurel's waist. "Threatened. Endangered. When I find out who did this, I'll slit him ventrally."

22

DEPARTURES AND DISCOVERIES

Charles said little about the snake, except to reassure Laurel that much as he admired snakes, if one fell out of a book he picked up, he would have hysterics.

"No rants about endangered species?" Arnie asked.

"No. I feel sorry for snakes, that's all. Can you imagine what gigantic monsters we must seem to them, like walking electrical conduit towers, making the ground vibrate and waving huge arms and hands?"

"Not really." Arnie scratched his head. He hadn't been surprised when no prints had been found on the snake or the textbook. He moved about the house if he was on duty or sat at the kitchen table playing security videos on his laptop. Elaine and Bertram Allarbee bedded down somewhere upstairs if they were too tired to drive home after being on duty, but no one ever expressed curiosity about where they slept.

At some point, George's T-shirts got mixed in with a tank top Elaine had dyed a vivid green.

"Nice," Arnie said. "What would Jen call that color—pistachio?"

"No one else has noticed the T-shirt color change but you," Laurel said. "I keep thinking I smell like snake, and then I take another shower. I burned the dress and sandals I was wearing, so I'm short on clothes. Oh, Arnie, Claire and I were so stupid."

"You were," he said. "But whoever left the textbook would have found another place where you would have found it. I don't think you could have avoided it."

"Thanks for not yelling at us," she said.

"God, Laurel. You don't have that terrible taste in men. Hey, look, I got the ring cleaned for you. I thought you could use some bling to go with the T-shirts." He pulled the citrine in its newly shining setting out of his uniform shirt pocket, minus the box but displayed on a new, white handkerchief.

Laurel took it, staring at Arnie. He saw tears glisten in her eyes and looked away. She tried to stuff it down her cleavage, realized that would work only if she were wearing a bra, and went back to Jen's room, where she hid it in the toe of a jogging shoe.

Hours later, Charles found Arnie sitting on the steps that led to the kitchen. Arnie held a cup of coffee; Charles had a cup of herbal tea.

"Don't sit down next to me with fermented onion crap." Arnie's voice was angry, his scowl ferocious.

Charles sat down and gave Arnie a quizzical look. "Who drinks fermented onions?" he asked. "Why are you in a mood? I thought I heard you chatting up Laurel. I'll swear you walked away whistling."

"Fuck off," Arnie said. "I don't want to talk about it."

Pearl slid around his ankles, and he shoved him aside.

Charles moved his cup closer to Arnie, so that the steam floated into Arnie's face.

"Laurel dump you? Out with it."

"I'll slug you," Arnie threatened.

"Don't go berserker on me." Charles set the cup down on the far side of the steps. The two sat in silence that, if not companionable, became less strained.

"Murphy's gone," Arnie said. "I walked over to see him. There's almost no trace he was ever there. *Walden*. A Bible. A manual of military training. A blanket on a cot."

"Any signs of a fight?" Charles asked.

"Not that I could see. Those walking sticks in the corner. An old aluminum coffee pot hanging over the fireplace. Not even a change of clothes. We'll check for fingerprints, but I think he left. Departed. Skedaddled."

"Did you get anywhere when you went to talk to the Marshes?"

"Not really. One of their kittens died in its sleep."

"Any chance of poison?"

"Guess not," Arnie said. "They had Sanjay check it. He said it had a heart murmur when he'd first seen it, but he hadn't thought it was significant and hadn't wanted to worry them with it."

"In other words, he fucked up," Charles said, looking indignant.

"As do we all," Arnie said. "Anyway, they'd just finished burying it under lilac bushes, in a plot that is their animal cemetery. Every critter they've ever owned is buried there but the horses, which take a backhoe and a lot of space to inter. All in all, it was a gloomy conversation. They agreed George's parents and grandparents had gone through some financial struggles but came out squeaky clean. The only thing they could suggest about Murphy's disappearance was that we check out farms that just had a horse put down. Said more than one farm wife disappeared under a nag."

"I'll bet they didn't say it that way."

"You're right. They didn't."

"Hey, Arn."

Arnie gave him a mulish look. "No one calls me Arn."

"Maybe they should. Sounds like a Viking name. Arn Sweener Swaggerson, son of Scyld, great among the Geats."

Arnie didn't say anything. Charles looked concerned.

"You look banefully burdened."

"I am that," Arnie said.

"Something besides Murphy being gone."

Arnie stretched his legs out and leaned his arms back on the step behind him. The wood held the day's warmth.

"I didn't save a kid's life."

"What kid?" Charles sat up, startled.

"By any chance did Claire tell you a Sanjay story? About Sanjay and Zoe rescuing a lamb?"

"The black lamb video maker. She did," Charles said. "We were sorting coins and comic books in the basement. I think she told me because telling the story cheered her up."

"Claire would like an 'everything ends happily ever after' story."

"But it didn't, did it?"

"He's not dead, but he's in a world of trouble. Heading for prison, I suspect. It's a long story. You sure you're up for this?"

"Sure. You need more coffee?"

"I need a good stiff drink," Arnie said. "No. Don't get it. I'm on duty."

"Seems like you're always on duty."

"Seems like," Arnie said. "So, I stopped in at the department when Elaine and Bertram were here. An elderly man—elderly being anyone older than I am—was bitching about his neighbor's barking dog. Normally, we'd think, *turn down your hearing aid, Grampa*, but this guy didn't seem like the grampa type. He said he was worried about the dog, said he had never heard it do that. So I said I'd stop by, and once I asked headquarters to check the address, I realized the people who live there are the parents of the video perp. This wasn't good.

"When I got to the house, I asked Gramps to go home. I didn't want him standing on the sidewalk and getting in my way, maybe drawing a crowd. I didn't want to tell him he could get hurt, but I was thinking that could happen.

"Front door, back door were all locked up. The dog was growling and howling. There weren't any lights on. No one answered the phone. No one answered the door. There were packages piled on the porch, and the mailbox was overflowing."

"That sounds like, what? Someone was dead in there?" Charles asked.

"I didn't know. I had dog biscuits in my pocket, but I pulled my gun out just in case and used a lockpick to get in. It was a nice door; why bust it? 'Good dog, good dog, good boy,' I said, thinking I was going to get my knee chewed off.

"By the time I was in the entry way, the dog was groveling for attention. It was a white mutt of some kind, only it wasn't white anymore."

"Blood?" Charles's eyes were wide.

"Dog shit. No one was home. I went through every room—you know, the routine. The dog stuck to my leg, whining and slobbering on my feet and shaking, as though I was the only friend it had in the world. I rubbed its ears and its stomach. It didn't want the biscuits I'd brought. No wonder. I found an empty bag of dog food on the kitchen floor and an almost full bag, torn open, right next to it. There were kibbles all over the place and there were five pails of water set out near it—two almost empty and the others pretty much full. The dog had shit all over the house and then walked through its own feces.

"I definitely did not find any sign of the 'I'll get him into counseling' father. I called Dannie Christie, Elaine's partner, and in less than fifteen minutes, a couple of guys pulled up to take the dog away, telling 'Snookums' he could sleep in their bed after many ablutions with their shampoo and conditioner. LGBT people take in strays in. That's one thing you can count on, Charles."

"That's it?" Charles's furrowed his brow at Arnie. "That's the story? What about the kid?"

"We put out an all-points bulletin. A Roscommon officer named Bob Duncan found him in a closed-up summer home, so drunk and high—who knows on what, now that fentanyl's around—that when he resisted arrest, he shot his girlfriend, who was trying to defend him. She turned toward him when he shot, and he just nicked the jugular, but that was all it took. When she bled out all over him, the kid went catatonic."

Charles said nothing.

"Fuck," Arnie summed up. "I should have checked up on the kid. Seems like he and his girlfriend enjoyed a vandalism spree every time the boy's parents went to Vegas. Maybe before, he and Dead Girl had taken the dog with them, fed it pizza. I don't know.

All I know is, I could have followed up. Or put two and two together. Screwed up kid, video maker, he and Dead Girl shooting porn, only it wasn't even real porn, Duncan said, just pathetic—nothing most kids haven't seen—except for the fact that he and D.G. had a lot of piercings in places most people wouldn't want pierced."

"Christ," Charles said.

"The kid's screwed," Arnie agreed. "He's no longer catatonic, but he might be better off if he was. Not that we know fuck-all about mental disorders. He's gonna get crucified. By police, by his parents. I don't know if he ever had a chance. But he's really, truly screwed."

"You sure you can't have a drink?" Charles said.

"I might not stop drinking."

"Nothing that happened, or will happen, to that boy is your fault."

"I'm not sure," Arnie said. "God, I wish I could get a break in Claire's situation. I just sit here, a fat fart, getting nothing done."

Charles said, "I know how Pearl gets in."

"Christ on a crutch. Tell me."

"I can do better than tell you. Get up. I can show you, but we have to let Pearl out."

While they were outside, Charles opened a can of cat food and waved it tantalizingly in front of Pearl. He then shut the screen door in Pearl's face. Pearl, attracted by the fishy smell, backed away, his feelings hurt. Charles and Arnie made a deliberate racket when they descended the cellar stairs. Five minutes later, they were sitting on the basement floor near the Ping-Pong table that still held a few comic books.

"Shhh," Charles said. "Look straight ahead. Keep quiet."

The basement was mostly empty. Looking straight ahead focused their attention on the old oak cabinet. As Arnie watched, a small, black, weasel-like head began to squeeze itself, inch by furry inch, from the back of the cabinet. The space was so small, Pearl's ears and whiskers were pinned back.

"Gawd," Arnie whispered. "Looks like a bat in a stocking cap."

"Pearl shouldn't be able to do what he's doing. Cats use their whiskers to see if they'll fit through narrow spaces," Charles said. "According to his whisker length, Pearl can't fit through the space between the basement wall and the cabinet."

Pearl's body was now oozing up through the space.

"*Mreow*?" Pearl commented. Having popped free of his confinement, like a bubble emerging from the puckered mouth of a child, he looked regally down at them. Charles expected him to throw kisses. He licked his bushy tail with fastidious care before descending to the floor to rub against their shoes before starting in on the food.

"How the hell did you figure that out?" Arnie was flabbergasted.

"Patience," Charles said.

They waited while the cat ate its food before looking at the oak cabinet. Then Charles fussed with the wooden peg he'd found on the back of the cupboard. "I don't want to break it," he said. Eventually, he managed to press in on the peg, which worked as a swivel, and the whole closet-like structure swung out.

Pearl gave him a look that said, "*You cheat. I did it without hands.*"

The men were facing a rough-set doorway to an older part of the basement.

Charles pulled out a flashlight.

There was nothing to be seen. The dirt floor stretched before them. In one corner, an old dressmaker's frame had been abandoned; in another, a wooden frame tennis racket without strings tilted against a wall. A barred door to the outside was slightly off kilter.

"Got mead?" Arnie asked.

23

CLOSING THE STORE

Jen came home after ten days in the hospital. She was installed in the first-floor bedroom. Laurel was given the recliner, which was moved just outside of Jen's room. Claire slept on the couch. Charles continued to sleep on the book room floor.

Soon Jen was being helped by an occupational therapist, and the bedside commode became a thing of the past. A physical therapist made her lift arm weights, work on core strength, and flex her right foot, its arch, and empurpled toes. Bill and Barbara Marsh came by almost daily, sometimes bringing broth—beef, not from their chickens. They often brought at least one kitten with them. Black Pearl generally ignored their presence, following Claire most of the time, but sometimes, during the day, he would sleep with Jen. Pearl would insinuate himself next to Jen in one smooth pour, like the pour of sun-melted chocolate squares.

Charles sketched, wrote a little, and sometimes took over for Laurel, who often read to Jen from one of the children's books Jen had loved as a child. Right now, they were reading Elinor Lyon's *Run Away Home*. Charles had gotten to the point in the book when the lorry driver knows Cathie is behind him because he can smell peppermint bull's-eye candies. Jen's room, of course, did not smell like peppermints; it held the slight fragrance of butterfly bush blossoms. The flowers did not last overnight, so each day, Laurel looked for heather, cosmos, or whatever was blooming, and recreated a purple bouquet. Life had taken on a new daily pattern.

Then, out of nowhere, David stood in Claire's kitchen, introducing his new love, Bethanie. Bethanie was pert and bleached blond, and held a vase of eight pink, short-stemmed roses. Claire, who'd been on a ladder finishing the last cupboard, descended grudgingly. Her shoulder ached. She focused on David. They hadn't heard one word from him since Jen had nearly died.

"I want to see Jen," David said, as though he'd been prevented from coming.

"We both do! Poor girl!" Bethanie's lipstick was the same shade as the roses. She was wearing a white, lace smock top over pink-and-black patterned stretch pants. Her black, chunk-heeled sandals brought her close to Claire's height.

"We came as soon as we knew!" Bethanie said. "We were visiting my parents, and David had left his cell at home so we could all just chill out, with no worries. We had the nicest Labor Day weekend. Then we got back home, and there was the ring you sent so David could give it to me! Doesn't it look pretty with this nail polish?" She extended her left hand in a gesture that at one point in time would have signaled the hand could be kissed. "Of course, then we found news about Jen. What a terrible thing! David was absolutely devastated!"

"You'll have to wait a couple of minutes. Jen's with a physical therapist. Do you want to sit down?" Claire asked. "Laurel's ring looks great on you."

It did look great. Laurel had always chewed her nails, and right now, her knuckles were swollen, maybe with a little arthritis. Claire could picture her friend's hands and felt a great surge of hate, mostly at David.

She swallowed hard. "How did you two meet?"

"I do marketing for the college," Bethanie said. "I do campus tours for high school kids!"

"You're supposed to say 'young adults,'" David chided her.

Bethanie brought her left hand to her mouth and looked as though she was going to chew her nails.

"Ah-ah-ah," said David.

Ohhhh. She's still a baby, Claire thought, and sent a glare at David that made him back up a step.

The therapist exited Jen's room and grinned at the group in the kitchen.

"My God, Jen's a worker!" he said. "I'll be back next week to check her, but until then, she can practice with the soft walking cast. Not just in her room. Young orthopedic patients are like puppies. Once they heal, you can't keep them down."

"I'm her father," David said, extending his hand.

The therapist gave him a blank look and a perfunctory handshake. "Didn't know you were in the picture at all," he said. "I met Laurel shortly after Jen got hurt, of course. One of you must have good genes. Ma'am," he nodded to Bethanie, "you can take those flowers in."

Claire went to the refrigerator, opened a bottle of beer she didn't like, and drank out of the bottle. She sat back down at the table and eavesdropped shamelessly. The house was reasonably small, and the now bare floors made conversations reverberate.

"How wonderful to meet you!" That would be Bethanie.

Then Jen's voice: "Careful hugs! Don't step on my foot, Dad! What pretty flowers. Where can we put this vase?"

Mumble, mumble. Jen's room was already filled with books, a breakfast tray, cards and letters, a pile of clothes and towels left within easy reach, and a carving of a quail Charles had bought at Everything Michigan, leaving little room for a vase of flowers.

Mumble, mumble, mumble.

"Don't move the quail," Jen said. "Put the vase on the windowsill. It's narrow, but the vase should fit there."

Claire could hear David's voice very clearly.

"Thought you might want to come home with us," he said. "This house isn't safe. I'm sure our insurance company will sue Claire."

The river is a public waterway, you dipshit, Claire thought.

"The house is safe enough for Mom, but not for me?" Jen asked.

"Your mother is old enough to make up her own mind."

Jen will love that, Claire thought.

"Dad, my physical therapist is coming back next week. And I have to go to the hospital here, have X-rays, and be checked by my orthopedic surgeon."

"I guess we could come back for you next week." David sounded magnanimous. "Or, well, whenever. Bethanie would like some company when I have to work at night."

Oh, David, Claire thought. The kind of night work you were doing when your foot got broken?

"We could have fun," Bethanie said. "We could go clubbing!"

"Not dancing much just now," Jen said.

"You must be Bethanie." Laurel's voice. Claire didn't know where she'd been. Out on the patio with Arnie?

"Hi, Mom. Bethanie, this is my mother, Laurel."

"It's a pleasure to meet you," Laurel said to Bethanie. "After all, we have a lot in common."

David said, "That wasn't funny, Laurel. Have you been drinking?"

"When did you get so stuffy, David?" Laurel asked. "Quite the father figure, aren't you?"

"Mom! Take your sarcasm out of my sickroom. Dad, you and Bethanie should leave too. I'm supposed to lie down and deep breathe, or something."

"Oh, my God!" Bethanie's voice. "That's such a gorgeous ring! David, did you see it? Where did you get it, Laurel? Can I try it on?"

Mumble, mumble, mumble.

Claire got a second beer and fled to the basement.

Charles was there, looking worried.

"Jen can be up and practice walking by herself in that cast." Claire waved the beer at him. "I'm celebrating. Want some?"

He waved away the beer and gave her a profound kiss. It was the first time they'd touched since Jen got hurt, and she found herself weak in the knees.

"We can't use the Ping-Pong table," she said. "It would collapse."

"Actually," he said, "I thought I'd regale you by retelling my story of how I tracked Pearl."

They could just barely hear conversation upstairs.

"What's Laurel going on about?" he asked.

"I'll tell you later," she said. She kissed him and then suffered through what would obviously become the saga of Black Pearl and the Mysterious Cabinet. Today, she thought, I am happy again.

BILL MARSH FOUND Patsy lying sprawled and dead, face-up in their front garden, where she'd gone to collect the kittens. If it hadn't been for the fact that Patsy had driven Ann's car, Bill wouldn't have recognized the woman at all. She was lying about ten feet from the porch, her face swollen to the size of a large pumpkin, her tongue purplish-blue and protruding from attempts to gasp for air. Her eyes were swollen shut. Her scarlet face and thinning hair were still crawling with honeybees that had killed her. As Bill watched, a bee crawled into one of Patsy's nostrils, which, from his angle, displayed a few graying hairs.

He wasn't repelled. He lived on a farm and saw death often—death, bloat, insects, and a great deal worse. Usually, he and Barbara knew when a horse was going to die, called the vet, and got on with the process, but it wasn't always possible to predict when a horse would go down. He'd mourned those more than he would mourn for Patsy. He knelt and took her pulse, though he knew better, and covered her face with a pocket handkerchief.

He looked around and frowned, then saw the cat carrier, which had been knocked across the driveway. He checked on the kittens, who were curled next to each other each other, unharmed and packed into the peaked top of the upside-down carrier. He took them back into the house and loosed them on Colby. He called Crawford County's emergency dispatch service and stood on the back porch. As he went back to the barn to tell Barbara what had happened, he recalled that they'd been happy the set of hives they rented from a neighbor had thrived this year.

He thought about calling Ann. Instead, he called Tansy at Best to Be. Tansy would call Ann.

Ann closed her store.

There was no autopsy. The death was ruled to be the result of natural causes. Few attended the funeral, which was closed casket at Immaculate Medal of Mary, except for neighbors. Tansy sent perishable food to a community pantry, whose recipients gorged on triple crème cheeses. Frustrated drive-up customers made jokes about Ann's store closing. Everything *in* Michigan, they said, is shutting down.

Barbara Marsh said she would keep any abandoned kittens. When asked about it, she shrugged. "I'll figure out a way to place them," she said.

Three days after Patsy's death, Tansy called Zoe Weathers, who had retired from practice but agreed to come by.

"I'm worried about my mother," she said. "She doesn't cry, but she doesn't sleep or eat, either. She wants me to look at pictures of me as a baby, when she and Patsy both took care of me. I could do that with her for a few days, but eventually, I have to get back to work."

Zoe visited Ann, who let her in reluctantly. "Don't tell me to take pills," Ann told the doctor. "Except for Tansy, who has her own life to lead, Patsy was my only friend that counted. I sat by myself when Monty died," she added. "I sat by myself in the evenings, for most of a year. When you're old enough, you know sometimes you have to sit through grief."

Something about the phrase "sit through grief" resonated with Zoe.

"Don't you sit Shiva?" she asked Sanjay.

"Not me," he responded. "I'm half Hindu, which would mean a trip to the Ganges, but neither of my parents were observant."

"Dad's parents were Notre Dame Catholic," she said. "Isn't sitting Shiva like a Catholic wake? Ideally, for a wake, you still have the body."

"Shiva," he said, "is seven days, I think."

Zoe looked thoughtful. "A wake is one night, or, with a lot of heavy drinking, as many days as the food and liquor hold out. The old people get drunk, and the younger people toke. I think a wake is a good idea, but we should limit it to one afternoon."

24

GOD GIVE US SKUNK SPRAY

"Come," Claire pleaded with Ann on the phone. "I'm going to have people over. I think, since Patsy was Catholic, it would matter to her to be remembered, and mourned, and celebrated. I don't think you should have to do it. You have been through enough."

"I won't come," Ann said.

But she came anyway. She came late, bringing hot cinnamon apples in a copper kettle, which she banged down on the stove and stirred. "Go save us a seat, Tansy," she said, as though the handful of neighbors might conspire to keep her on her feet the whole time she was there. Tansy slunk through the kitchen, aware her mother was irritated with her.

The priest of Medal of Mary, Father Cleary, arrived while Ann was still stirring. He'd been distant, even aloof at the funeral service.

"Go on by me, Father," Ann said in a tone that could grate lemons. "Got to keep syrup from crystallizing."

"Annie Campbell," he said, slipping an arm around her shoulders. "Walk me into the next room. I'm that weak on my feet." He reached past her, turning the burner down to simmer.

"It's a drink I'm needing," he said. "The Lord blessed the Irish with little enough, but he gave us souls and a good ear for stories. Sit down with me, and I'll tell you a story of Patty you don't know."

Ann let him steer her away from the stove and out to the living room, where they both joined Tansy on Claire's new couch.

Father Cleary kept his promise over a tumbler of Jameson, drinking enough to slap his thigh and say that, as a girl, Patty Cluny had twice escaped boarding school by slipping through a restroom window, which the school had then boarded up.

"You mean *Patsy*. Patsy Cluny," Ann said.

"Right through the rose bushes Patty would go." He chuckled. "Scratched and scabby as a heathen. She was a good girl at heart. Just wanted to be out in the sun, jump rope, and bicycle through puddles, splashing her mother's hanging laundry. Her mother would have her kneeling on the kitchen floor all night. She and her mother both were stubborn. Remember, we Catholics weren't always accepted in those days. We didn't really mind girls with some spirit and stubbornness."

"That was a good thing," Ann agreed. "Her name was Patsy, not Patty."

"Have a drink with me, Annie," he said. "Give some of your grief to Mary; you know she's stretching her hands to you. Patty loved you, and she wouldn't want you grieving. Here's your daughter, Tansy; she doesn't want you grieving. You're a good woman, Annie Campbell. You helped with the roof of our church. You've paid for poor, faithful women who couldn't put a dime in the collection plate, and you helped Best to Be put that chapel in. Though that now welcomes all kinds, it was a good thing to do."

Ann's lower lip quavered. The priest held out his glass to her, and she took a sip.

"Drink that, Ann," Sanjay said, handing the priest a second full glass.

Ann glared at Sanjay.

"They call it a reflection room now," she said. "All Faiths Welcome." Capital letters could be heard in her speech.

"Not my fault!" protested Sanjay.

Claire got up to get the priest and Ann plates of food. She and Laurel had kept it simple—escalloped potatoes, relishes, and a spiral sliced ham—so everything could be set out on the table. Zoe had brought Zingerman's Magic Brownies, which they had placed on the piano.

"I swear, piggies," she said under her breath. "From now on, new resolution: I will drink, but eschew pork." She didn't get either Ann or the priest the cream of chicken soup the Marshes had contributed. Nor did she try ladling up cinnamon apples. She tried each, but they were bubbling hot. She turned down the burners a bit more.

In the meantime, Father Cleary was still weaving his spell, recalling the day Patty (he continued to ignore Ann's corrections) let a dog, covered with soapsuds so it looked rabid, into the chapel. And the day she told Sister Mary Agnes that all nuns have bad breath. Ann, seated between Tansy and Father Cleary, visibly relaxed, possibly because of the Jameson, which she was now drinking slowly but steadily from her own glass. The rest of what Charles called "the potluck club" began to talk about Patsy. How she carried heavy purchases from Ann's store out to the car. How she'd been a rescue wagon for forlorn kittens. Bill Marsh told a story no one but Ann had heard about how Patsy used to demonstrate swing steps using six-year-old Tansy as her partner.

Ann began to look rosy-cheeked and a bit tipsy. When she peeled off her cardigan sweater and dropped it on the floor, Tansy brought her mother a bowl of soup.

Light faded. Booze bottles emptied. The soup, escalloped potatoes, ham, and the cinnamon apples all vanished. Brownie crumbs littered the floor. Sanjay was singing "Amazing Grace," harmonizing with Jen, who had joined the company and been promptly seated in the recliner.

"She was so beautiful." Ann started sobbing. "None of you remember her as I do. You think of her as a woman with fat around her midriff and stringy hair. I remember Patsy when she was young and blond, and didn't want to get married. You wouldn't have either, if you'd known her father. She was that desperate to be out of her parents' house. Moving in with me and Tansy gave her a second family. Bill Marsh, I bet you were one of those kids who watched her slide Tansy under her legs, spin, and pick her up again, and never miss a beat."

She took a long drink of her whiskey, then put down her empty glass.

"I killed Patsy," she said, and collapsed sobbing into Tansy's lap. "I told her," she said. "I told her. I told her. Her EpiPen was way past date. They cost $700, once that awful man got the patent. I told her I'd buy one for her. She was so goddamn stubborn; she wouldn't listen. She said, 'And yet, if people bought at that price, poor folk that couldn't afford it would be out of luck.' I should have just bought it for her. Now she's dead, and it's my fault."

"My dear child!" Father Cleary said. "My dear child. Of course you're not to blame." He waved his tumbler at Ann, making the sign of the cross, and then extended both arms to include all seated there. "God is kind. God is merciful. He will protect this house. May you dwell in the house of the Lord."

It wasn't a traditional benediction, but the priest seemed genuinely moved by Ann's misery.

Each person there reassured Ann. Zoe, more than anyone, besides Tansy, looked deeply concerned. "I'm sorry," she said. "Medicine changes so fast. It's things like this—drug prices—that made me retire. Well, that and the fact that I had money without my practice. Patsy made a mistake, but she wasn't entirely wrong."

Sanjay muttered, "The same medications often cost less for animals."

Barbara added, sotto voce, "And prices for animals, God knows, are high enough."

Laurel was holding an arm around Jen, aware that her medical insurance had eased Jen's transition from being maimed to being on her feet. Everyone had a story to tell about medical prices, insurance rates, and disabilities. Ann joined in, citing her share of a bill for a hip replacement as a self-employed patient. She didn't mention the sum, but implied the amount would have gilded Medal of Mary's roof.

"Tis a sin, what they charge," Father Cleary blurted loudly. "If you must blame someone, Annie, blame scoundrels who get rich off the suffering of the poor."

Ann seemed at least partially absolved for Patsy's death. "I'll drink to all of you here," she said. "Good health, long life, and may you be in heaven before the devil knows you're dead!"

Neither Arnie nor Charles was there to join in the toast. Charles stayed in the basement sorting through the last of the comics. He said he would rather try to solve problems for Claire and let Father Cleary try to console Ann. Arnie had gone back to the sheriff's department to update his records.

Bertram didn't join in the toast because he was on duty. He and Elaine had filled plates with food and tried to be invisible. Elaine was enjoying herself but also observing the company, and Bertram was sitting stolidly near the kitchen door.

The first inkling that something was wrong came with Bertram's mad dash for the bushes.

Father Cleary said, "That boy's odd. He didn't join Annie's toast, either."

Then Bill said, "Excuse me. What's that smell?"

"Did someone accidentally turn up the heat under an empty pan?" Zoe asked. "Whatever it is, it smells a bit like burned chicken soup."

A sudden fizzling noise sounded, as though someone had shaken a mammoth bottle of soda, uncapped it, and turned it upside down on the floor.

"Oh!" Laurel's face had gone pale. "Oh! Oh, I'm sorry, but I'm going to be sick. Don't, Jen, don't," she said. "Stay away!"

Claire, realizing Laurel's concern, conscripted Zoe. "Don't let Jen try to help," she told her. Laurel half rose from the chair she'd been sitting in. An incredibly awful-smelling fart resounded, and a pool of beige froth appeared under her.

Tansy shoved Ann's sweater under Laurel and eased her back on top of the sweater.

"Sit down," she warned. "You're white as a communion wafer. You're going to faint."

"Tansy, that's my good wool sweater," Ann complained.

"Get a grip!" Tansy retorted.

Barbara reached to comfort Laurel, but collapsed on the floor, writhing. Bill knelt by his wife's side, his face ashen. Jen, still a little drugged out, leaned toward Laurel and tugged, in a futile effort, at Zoe's restraining arm.

Charles's steps could be heard pounding up the stairs from the basement. The small group of friends stared at each other, caught in a scene from *The Exorcist*.

"Avaunt!" Father Cleary pronounced. He spilled his recently topped up drink, stepping away from the couch.

Ann's face took on a green color that was obvious even in faint light. She began to gasp and vomit in regular expulsions that spewed from her mouth and sounded like whooping cough.

"Flatulence. Projectile vomiting!" Sanjay exclaimed, sounding like Hercule Poirot, then covered a leg of the grand piano in a torrent of undigested food.

"This is poisoning," Zoe said. "Nobody leave this room!" She was virtually the last person standing.

Elaine ignored her and bolted for Jen's bathroom.

Through the window, Allarbee's bare buttocks could be seen, his head still occupied in the bushes. Claire felt nauseated but stood, wobbling and indecisive. She could hear Charles in the kitchen. He was summoning 911.

"What the bejesus fuckin' sort of travesty is this?" Father Cleary roared. "This stench would shame a hoor's pudendum. Never have I seen such indignity at a wake!" He vomited whiskey.

"I need the bathroom!" he yelled at Elaine, who ignored him, and then, crouched in terror, he ran into the kitchen, drooling Jameson.

The miasma filling Claire's remodeled room made eyes water and everyone think, "God give us skunk spray!" Even those who felt well—Tansy, Bill, Zoe, Jen, and Claire—though she didn't feel spectacular—didn't know where to walk. Oscar's salmon had been infinitely better. The floor and everyone's shoes were splattered with curds of acid vomit and runny feces.

"Charles?" Claire said.

Then his arms were around her.

"Hang on," he said. "I've got you."

"Laurel?" she asked.

"Just hang on," he said.

25

OPEN UP THE HOUSE

Bertram Allarbee hid behind his clump of bushes until the ambulance left, partly out of shame and partly out of stubbornness. Ann, Laurel, Barbara, and Father Cleary went to emergency. Father Cleary had protested that he felt quite clearheaded and should get back to his congregation. One of the ambulance attendants was overheard saying, "Father, with respect, these people could die unshriven." And the priest had straightened his clerical collar and allowed himself to be helped to the ambulance.

"Unshriven?" another worker asked as the old man was bundled in.

"Hook up the old guy's fluids," the other said.

Bill Marsh followed the ambulance, crumpled in the driver's seat. Tears ran down his face as he pictured the day he'd first shown Barbara the farm. He'd wondered then what woman would like such a quiet life, and he still marveled that they were beatifically in love.

Over her angry protestations, Sanjay staggered off to walk toward Zoe's house.

"I'm the doctor, you stupid man. I'm *your* doctor."

"I'm a doctor and your lover. And I'm not throwing up in your car."

"I'm going home," Zoe told Charles. "I'm not helping or holding barf basins. Not here, not at the hospital. I'll look after Sanjay, and I'll look after myself, but I saw enough vomit when I was getting paid for it. And if Arnie wants to talk to me, he can come to my house."

Elaine called Dannie to come get her.

"Want a ride to the hospital, Tansy?" Dannie asked.

They had shooed Jen, who was exhausted and limping, back to bed, assuring her and Claire that they would stay with Laurel.

"I'd better drive," Tansy said. "I might have to go back to work."

"I want to go," Claire wailed. "Laurel came to help me, and now she's dying!"

"No one is going to die," Charles said.

"You are not leaving without me," Arnie said to Claire, his face contorting with frustration. "I have to be here, so you have to be here."

Claire sat on the kitchen steps with the door open and her knees hugged to her chest. "Everyone who knows me gets hurt or sick."

Charles sat down next to her. "Not everyone who knows you gets hurt or sick," he reassured her. "And your friends aren't feeling well, but they will be all right."

The muscle tic in Arnie's jaw stopped pulsing, but he still stood with his head lowered and shoulders bunched, like a bull about to charge.

Pearl appeared from the basement, tufted ears back and gold eyes wide, then ducked back down the stairs.

Charles looked at Arnie's clenched hands. "Arnie, would you open some windows? Downstairs and upstairs too? It'll help, I promise."

"Got it," Arnie said.

Charles could hear him moving about the house, opening windows and yelling at Elaine to retrieve Bertram Allarbee.

The phone rang.

"Claire," he said. "Just stay here and breathe while I get this."

"I promise," she said.

"Charles." Ed's voice broke like a teenager's.

"Yeah. Right here. Oscar OK?"

"Oscar's OK, but there's bad news. Jeez, I don't know how to tell you."

Now what, Charles thought. "Did my cabin burn down?"

"Uh. No."

"Power out?"

"No."

"Deeter's burn down? Your chickens die?"

"No, no. Wait a minute, Charles. Someone's been in your cabin, and they messed up the place."

"There's not that much to mess up," Charles said.

"That leather thing you showed me? That 'keep to the right' thing your dad had?"

Charles was silent.

"Someone burned it," Ed said.

"It was in a glass case. Framed."

"Someone built a fire on your fold-up bed. Blankets, your books. That book you wrote about feathers."

His collection of Jean-Henri Fabre, then, with descriptions of those wonderful, lumbering dung beetles. Mantises that colored plates showed green as green spring leaves. The books that, more than any other, had led him to be a naturalist, led him to be an observer and to wander creeks and woods, wanting, even as a child, to step as lightly as Fabre had stepped. Fabre had used dead insects when he found them but never killed what he studied. Because of those books, Charles aspired to let small, woodsy creatures influence him more than he influenced them.

"Your computer, too. Boy Howdy, what a mess. I could see the smoke from my place."

Karma, Charles thought. But he doubted his ex-girlfriend whose computer he'd drowned had tracked him down after years had passed.

"The books under the bed?"

"They're OK. Seems like the mattress didn't burn good. Just a big black hole in it like God Almighty stubbed out one big cigar. Didn't get the fire department. Burn permits are on, and your place sure smelled like burning garbage. I came down in time to see someone just getting into a car. Black T-shirt, black jeans, black baseball cap. Ha!"

"Ha?"

"That bird of yours sure didn't like him! That's what had him leaving so quick. Didn't get the license. Black car, though. Some kind of Honda?"

"Tell me about Oscar."

"Oh, yeah. That bird comes diving down, wing healed, pecking—hell, Oscar's got a mouth like channel locks, pecking's not the right word—swooping, slashing, stabbing with that beak of his, making a hell of a racket, and this guy's startled and fumbling with the keys, and then three *more* ravens come out of the trees like Spitfires—oh, man, I cracked up. But I'm sorry about your bed."

"Uh." Good thing he never bought an early edition Audubon. And maybe a good thing he hadn't been closer to his grandfather, because as it was, the loss of the "Maintiens le Droit" leatherwork hurt his heart. He took off his glasses and set them on the kitchen table, pinching the bridge of his nose between the fingers of his left hand.

"So, Oscar's the boss raven, huh," said Ed.

"Ravens recognize faces. They'll stick together, mob people."

"Me?"

"Not you, Ed. Ravens have been hanging out with people, especially hunters, and some predator animals to eat their scraps for thousands of years. The Inuit believe they'll even lead predators to potential prey. Usually people and ravens have a working relationship. But bad people, ravens will go after. Say one raven says, 'Enemy of ravens!' Other ravens want their DNA to go on, so they pile on whoever is hurting the first raven."

"Awesome," Ed said.

"Listen, I gotta get off the phone. I owe you one, buddy."

"Naw, you don't. Seeing the raven attack was worth it. You still seeing the blond lady?"

"Maybe," he said. "I'll talk to you when I get there. Put some eggs out for Oscar and his friends if you think of it."

He ended the call and sat down, thinking that Claire was close to right. He had just joined the list of people whose lives had been damaged.

Claire.

Oscar, who counted as a person.

Elaine Santana.

Zoe Weathers, through targeting Whitsuntide Whirlwind.

Jen. And even if Jen's injury was a mistake, it had deflated Laurel as though her lungs had blown out.

Patsy, her life taken.

And now everyone who had been at Patsy's wake.

Arnie came downstairs, retrieved Claire, and seated her in the recliner. "Jen is asleep," he told Charles. "You look flummoxed. Was the call bad news?"

"Not as bad as it could have been." Charles shrugged.

"Talk to me about what happened here," Arnie said. "I'd like to not sound ignorant when I write up this report."

Charles didn't respond. He was trying to remember if he had backed up his work on his external hard drive.

"Come on, Professor. Get your head out of the clouds."

"That's an asinine thing to say," Charles at last responded, his tone acidic. "Do you know what happens if you go around with your head in the clouds?"

"You trip?" Arnie hazarded.

"You're electrocuted," Charles said.

Arnie sat down on the steps that led out to the patio. Charles leaned against the trunk of a tree.

"You have something to say?" Arnie asked Charles.

Charles said, "What made people sick? I'd bet every cent I have that they ate vomiter mushrooms, and I'll bet the mushrooms were in the cream of chicken soup. Some people eat them and get sick; other people don't react. Anyone who has spent any time picking mushrooms knows the rule is: If you don't know it, don't pick it. If someone else picks it, don't eat it. What I don't understand is how Barbara Marsh, who's had a place here for years, could have made such an egregious mistake."

"They'll be all right?" Arnie said.

"No one's been known yet to die from eating them. But as you can see, they make some people hellaciously miserable and don't bother others at all."

"They'll *all* be all right?" Arnie said. "Laurel will be all right?"

Charles gave Arnie a thoughtful look. "They'll all be fine. Squirrels and deer eat vomiter mushrooms all the time. If your wake participants had eaten death angel, they'd already be dead."

Arnie rubbed his eyes, thinking. "Could someone have added vomitous mushrooms to the soup? Sounded to me like everyone but the priest was in the kitchen."

"That would have worked. Everyone but the priest and Jen were in the kitchen, I think. And you're going to want to talk about *green-spored parasol mushrooms* if you want to sound scientific."

"Aren't there some Latin words I can use?" Arnie asked.

"There are. But do you really want to keep saying *Chlorophyllum molybdites*?"

"Right. Green-spored vomiters. I think, with this many people, the state police will at least check this."

"It's not always easy to confirm what happened," Charles said. "Irritants break down when exposed to gastric juices. Some break down with time, some with heat, some even with alcohol. Get a sample from the piano leg," he added.

"How long before they're better?"

"Maybe a few hours. With older people, like the priest, sometimes longer. He wasn't what I expected at all."

"He's a disgusting old reprobate." Arnie added, "You're not what I thought you were either. Any more bright ideas?"

"Did anyone check Patsy's body for honey?"

"What? Like smell her hair for honey butter?"

"Just curious. People have used honey for a lot of things. Cosmetics. Embalming."

"She was cremated," Arnie said. "I think it's too late to sniff her."

"I'm wondering if she might have been snuffed," Charles said.

"We'll check out her room," Arnie said. "Give me a hand here."

"Am I doing dishes again?"

"Nope. We're going to label pots and pans and booze bottles, and whose drink glasses were whose. We're not cleaning, and we're not moving things."

"That will be a pleasant change," Charles said.

26

BEST LAID PLANS

As Charles predicted, all of the poisoned participants recovered completely. Jen began to venture outside the house, with Laurel's blessing and Bertram Allarbee's company.

The pans and plates and other paraphernalia were labeled as evidence, sealed in plastic containers, and stored in the basement of the sheriff's department. Arnie let Claire clean and keep the piano leg.

Barbara Marsh explained that she had not made the soup.

"I run a farm," she said. "I don't know who made it. It was in the freezer at church, and I left money for it. Bill and I had some before we came!"

The Unitarian Universalist Church helped return Claire's house to order, and in this case, to breathable air.

When Arnie checked Ann's house, over Ann's objections, he found—in a shared downstairs bathroom, way at the back of a cluttered drawer—a small jar proclaiming to be beeswax. "*Good for the hands, good for the scalp*," the label on the glass jar read. "*Almond Milk and Beeswax Paste*." Someone should have sniffed her hair, Arnie thought. Would a commercial product using something bees make have made Patsy more attractive to bees? He pictured a few bees innocently exploring Patsy's delicious-to-bees smelling skin and hair, and Patsy tossing the kitten carrier aside and flailing in panic.

THEY HAD MOVED into the days when sun sluices through the trees and bathes the world in slanted light. The morning was cool and smelled like fall and adventure. Dannie threw back the quilt and prodded Elaine.

"Cold," Elaine said. "You left the window open."

"I got used to the polar elements while fetching your ice."

"My butt cheek looks much better now. But cold." Elaine struggled for the quilt.

"I'll check out your butt cheek later," Dannie said. "Come on, get up! You promised me last night you'd see if Bertram will take the shift."

"I just said that to get you to stop bothering me," Elaine told her.

"I want to see a movie! I want popcorn with extra butter. I want a root beer, dammit. If we never relax together, we'll never get old together, and we'll never join OLAA!"

"What the fuck is OLAA?" Elaine said. She dug around under the quilt and found and put on a cotton shirt.

"You remember. Old Lesbians Against Ageism. My mom sent me one of their shirts. Seriously, Elaine, my pet, my cranky darling, you know Bertram will work tonight. And Arnie wouldn't leave that house if you dragged him behind a tank."

"I dunno," Elaine said. "I'm worried about Jen. If she'd gotten sick that night, and then fallen…"

"Don't be morbid. She's crutching around, designing things. Oh, hey! I've got a great idea. We should take Jen!"

"You think she'd get a doctor's OK?"

"She can't stay under her mom's wing forever. Let's get her out of there. Make her laugh."

"Technically speaking, we'd be seeing if Margaret Cho would make her laugh. And Jen's not gay."

Dannie shot Elaine a vamping look. "But how does one—*know*?"

"One usually knows by Jen's age," Elaine said. "Sometimes, one knows by seventh grade."

"You were precocious. Think *Fun Home*. Everyone has a choice. If nothing else, we'd boost the attendance for Arnie's film club. How many people from Grayling are going to attend stuff like *Moonlight*? *Moonlight* doesn't have Jackie Chan or The Rock."

"More people than will come to see *I'm the One That I Want*." Elaine sounded derisive.

"Huh. Maybe Arnie should invite the ladies from Best to Be."

"That's not a bad idea," Elaine said. "Maybe hard to do tonight, but—what's next month's film?"

"*Get Out*," Dannie said.

"Tell you what," Elaine said. "We'll try this little by little. You ask Jen, and I'll ask Tansy Campbell."

"That's ridiculous," Dannie said. "But deal. You're on."

Jen and Tansy were both willing to have their horizons expanded. Tansy gave a wide grin, so wide it showed she had a dimple.

"Sure," Tansy said. "I can get the night off. I do watch Amazon and Netflix. People think I've been lobotomized because I like older people."

Jen had Laurel put some highlights in her hair and asked Bertram to stuff the Bentley with pillows so she could support her foot and leg. They learned on the drive to the theater that Bertram had already seen *I'm the One That I Want*.

"My mom's gay," he said. "She and Dad split years ago."

Elaine texted Arnie, "If you knew Bertram's mom is gay, you should have told me."

"I couldn't," Arnie texted back. "You had no need to know."

"But Bertram's so quiet, I've been treating him like a dildo. Bad choice of words. But you know what I mean."

Arnie's text came back. "Your problem. You fix it."

"Maybe Arnie's right," Elaine said. "Maybe finding out what kind of movies people watch would give us insight."

"Maybe," Dannie said darkly. "But I am never watching *Noah*."

IF OSCAR HADN'T hung around, Charles asked himself, would his cabin have gone up in flames?

He'd never get permission to rebuild anywhere on his property that ran along the stream. The Wild and Scenic Rivers Acts would have left him living in a tent or in the apple tree with Oscar.

Had he put Ed's life at risk?

What if he had talked Claire into going back to the cottage? Would someone have tossed a Molotov cocktail into bed with them?

Someone wanted Claire out of her house. That much seemed clear. *Widow. Woman. Witch. Cunt. Get Out.* This house was like the center of a shock wave. The damage rippled outward, hurting more people at greater distances.

They had searched the house top to bottom. Taken feathers out of pillows, then restuffed them. Looked under mattresses. Peered in toilet tanks.

He tried to think of even a small place they should still be looking.

A dark place, he thought, rubbing a hand through his hair so it stood on end. Not a place like the beach in *Run Away Home*, known for seashells and golden sand.

A place where people were not expected to go.

A shrew's house, a mouse's house, a place where bats flew.

He thought of the bit of bone Pearl had brought him, the bone Zoe had helped him identify. Small, fragile, and shaped like half a pistachio. He thought about the basement. Who knew what it had seen? Bathtub gin? Sugar water and baker's yeast?

But the fact was, he and Arnie had already done a quick perusal, sneezing in unison as they did. There was nothing to see but dirt floors and dry mouse turds. No wardrobes, no broken toys, no sleds that said *Rosebud*. The floor had some uneven levels, but that wasn't unusual in houses this old. He knew people who'd dug trenches in cellars just so they could bury trash without hauling it up the stairs. He knew one family who'd dug up the old basement, reinforced a wall, and propped up their house, leaving it yawning cavernously over unsupported space.

He thought about the cabinet again, the pivot peg that would open the earthy-smelling world he could explore.

He liked bats. Caves didn't faze him.

Doves nested in open areas that fronted spectacular caves.

He should wait for Arnie before he went exploring, but Arnie was engrossed in a different project.

Charles knew he wasn't an action hero.

But someone had tried to burn his house and hurt—with the single exception of his sister—all of the people he loved.

ARNIE STOOD OUTSIDE the patio doors. The new cedar chairs were inviting, but he didn't plan to sleep. It was a cool night. Supposed to go down to the forties. He'd added logs, ready to light, in the fire pit Jen had designed and Zoe had paid for.

Zoe had explained that she and Sanjay could use it from time to time. She'd asked Sanjay to move in with her and had bought him two cases of Mawby Blanc de Noir as a welcoming present. The first bottle, Arnie suspected, was already chilling, because Zoe and Sanjay would want to uncork it while there was a little daylight. They'd have the first glass by Whit's stall, probably sharing some with him. Horses that had won races could develop a taste for champagne.

Jen would soon come home with friends, after seeing the movie, and enjoy her own bit of triumph at the design feat everyone would enjoy.

The kit Zoe sent had been easy to assemble, the concrete veneer of the wall set with polished river stones. He hadn't seen

Charles recently, but remembered him saying he might go out to look for hollow trees that held nests of flying squirrels. The Adirondack chairs Tansy purchased sat a little low. Claire might want to set them on a platform, to make it easier to see the fire while sitting in the chairs, but for now, people could perch on the wall's generous corners. Maybe, in time, people would celebrate here, see the flames reflect from the patio window and entertain thoughts of new beginnings. Weird phrase, that one. Though beginnings, he guessed, could get old.

Arnie waved to Bertram Allarbee, who had moved a chair to sit outside of the kitchen door. The man just sat, stolid as a stalagmite. Solid as a brick outhouse, boys used to say when he was a kid. *She's built like a brick outhouse.*

"Hey, Bertram," he called.

Bertram Allarbee didn't respond.

Arnie looked at Bertram again. There was no reason for the tension creeping up his own back. No reason his ears should feel as though he'd just come out of the water, the eardrums aching as though someone had shoved Q-tips into them.

Shit, he thought. He hadn't heard a thing while he was moving logs around. And he hadn't noticed when the last of the crickets stopped chirping. Except for the river, the night was silent. He drew his Glock as he lurched for cover, cursing.

A shot near the heart took him down in an explosion of pain. The shot that creased his forehead knocked him back and threw him into blackness even the river's murmur couldn't penetrate.

27

CHARLES ENTOMBED

Charles woke slowly, his head pounding and the sound of his own heart loud in his ears. Every bone in his body ached in a way it hadn't since long ago. As a boy in high school, he'd briefly tried being a quarterback. He hadn't been fast enough then, and obviously, he hadn't been fast enough when someone standing in shadow had smashed him on the head. He guessed he was lying in the excavated area of the Michigan basement he'd been about to explore when the world had gone dark.

His feet were roped together, and his hands were roped together behind him. A rope ran from his ankle tethers to the rope imprisoning his hands, pulling his shoulders and arms back uncomfortably and making it impossible for him to lurch from his back to his feet.

A gag, smelling faintly of chloroform, and much more strongly of lavender perfume, had been stuffed into his mouth and was held in place by duct tape wrapped around his head. There were also slight scents of putrescence, old wood furniture, and dust.

There wasn't much light, but being nearsighted without his glasses, he could at least see he was lying in a trench about three feet deep.

How long had he been out? An hour? Two hours? Sunset's light glowed like a blurred spider web through cracks in the far wall. He listened hard and could just barely hear the high-pitched *chip* of a cardinal's warning call. Or was it the squeak of a mouse? Or a brown rat. Charles was quite fond of the docile, even affectionate, laboratory-bred hooded rats. He'd kept a pair as pets in college. They had taken balls of cream cheese from him in their small fingered hands and—though they'd made holes in his socks—had never nipped, let alone bitten him. That did not mean he wanted to become supper for a common Norway rat descendent cousin. As a child, he'd read his father's terrifying and amazingly racist Fu Manchu books, which had left him with a phobia—of sorts—of being tortuously, slowly eaten alive.

Maybe not a phobia, he thought. Fuck this.

He arched his back, which resulted in a pulling wrench in his shoulders. He dropped his weight back and felt the bottom of the trench give the way branches give if you throw a tarp over them. He rocked his weight from side to side. This time, the bottom of the trench crackled, and the stench of death penetrated through the drenching lavender scent. His scrabbling fingers found cloth—the felted wool of old blankets.

He was in the top bunk of a grave.

He closed his eyes and made himself take deep, dust-filled breaths, filling his chest and forcing air down past the diaphragm. Three—he would take at least three, mentally cleansing inhalations before he let his body spasm in mindless, self-punishing panic—

He lay there, trying to relax from his clenched toes to his forehead, acknowledging aching shoulders, admitting he was cold.

I apologize, he told his body. I put you at risk too often. We are one, but my mind lets you down. Rest a bit, he thought. Calm body, calm mind.

Will someone find me?

What has happened to the others?

Will the person who finds me hurt me?

Where is Claire? Has someone hurt her?

How will Lane feel when I'm dead?

After each unbidden question, he tried to calm his conscious mind, which wanted to spin at top speed like a hamster in a wheel. He had relaxed his cramping feet, slowed his heartbeat, steadied his breathing. Then whiskers touched his left eyelid. His eyes flew open, and his sudden inhalations resulted in him pulling the gag deeper into his mouth.

Pearl's round eyes gazed down at him. He smelled of dry cat food. He patted Charles's face with one soft paw and purred with affection. Or was it curiosity?

Some affection, anyway, Charles decided, knowing he would never be able to say again, "I'm not a cat person."

True, the cat might not lead rescuers to him, but his friends knew Pearl patrolled the basement. Sooner or later, they would look for Pearl and find him, and Charles was much less likely to be rodent fodder.

Find us both soon, he thought. Before the night gets any darker.

Pearl appeared perplexed but pleased. He leaned down and sniffed at Charles's face, then jumped down beside his hips.

If Charles turned on one side, he could see down the length of his body. Pearl strummed the rope that held his feet together. Next, Pearl scent-marked the rope by rubbing against it. Then, Pearl sharpened his claws on the blanket—the blanket that divided Charles from...*Murphy*?

His brain rushed back into his skull with a virtual popping sensation, filling the vacuum that had occupied his head once he'd forced the fear out.

Who else's body would be so thin?

Laurel? Jen?

But he'd seen each of them that morning over coffee.

Murphy. A gristly little man alive. A gristly corpse dead.

Somehow, Charles would have to flex in these ropes. He would have to bend stiff knees until he was in a supine kneeling position. He would have to wriggle numb fingers and tear at the felting that kept his feet from Murphy's feet.

There was at least a chance Murphy had been buried with his boots on. Or, like Charles, left fully clothed, to be buried later. With his boots on.

And according to Jen, there was a sheath knife in his right boot.

Charles had the arms, hands, and fingers of a man who had spent years climbing up and down trees looking for owl nests, and scrabbling about on rock faces looking for swallows. The occasions when he'd fallen and hung also stood him in good stead. Over time, he'd developed the sometimes critically important, sometimes disastrous ability to ignore pain when he set his mind to it.

Inch by sweaty inch, shoulders, calf, and bum muscles aching, he moved around until he could rip at the matted wool. He was afraid Murphy might have been double-wrapped, like high-end cold cuts in cellophane *and* butcher's paper—only in this case, Charles was afraid he'd find the blanket and a tarp.

Pearl had spent a blissful twenty minutes chewing the plastic tips off Charles's shoelaces, and Charles had broken off most of his fingernails by the time he maneuvered into position. The broken nails snagged on the wool, splitting and ripping off. As the last light disappeared, he touched and recoiled from the hair on Murphy's ankles, which suddenly made the man's body and death unpleasantly real.

He flexed his fingers. Murphy's sock had scrunched down at some point and puddled in the heel of his boot. Charles touched cold skin, then an edge of leather. More maneuvering, then leg cramps so sharp and sudden they made him convulse, but he remained impervious to the pain in his hands.

Breathe. Breathe. Breathe. He'd cried out, which brought Pearl back to peer down at him. The small black cat was all but invisible now, the wide-open yellow eyes all Charles could see.

Slow, now, he told himself. If he jerked and shoved the knife, he might lose any chance to—

Don't think. Mind blank. He wriggled his fingertips as gently as if he were scratching Pearl under the chin.

The metal, when he touched it, was smooth, and his hands were slippery with blood. Pearl was now curious and jumped down on top of him, bumping at his wrist, trying to help his excavation. He swore through his gag at the cat, making enough noise that Pearl walked up his body, sniffed at the gag, and rubbed against his cheek, purring.

Goddamn it, he thought. Goddamn cat. Get your ass out of my face! To keep Pearl from rolling against his nose, he moved his neck and eased his head back, realizing his leg cramps had eased. When he cut through the first rope that held him, he realized how much his hands were bleeding. Gobbets of blood. Chicken-gut-sized globs of blood.

By the time he managed to roll up and out from the excavation, his arms were smeared with blood up to his elbows. His fingers oozed blood. He swayed on hands and knees.

He no longer functioned coherently.

He remembered losing the first of his molars when he was a child: the salt-blood taste in his mouth, the tooth tottering when his tongue pushed against it, one root still holding, a tap root linking his childhood to an adult world.

In this case, the tap root linked an adult world to his future existence. Pull yourself together, he told himself. Push yourself up or die here.

Goddamn it, you bastard, push.

28

KINDLING

When Charles pulled himself up the basement stairs to the kitchen, he remembered Claire's plunge down them. He'd thought, when he gained the kitchen, he would have some respite, but after glancing out the windows, he lowered himself to the floor and crawled to the outside door. He let himself tumble to the driveway, sick with horror. Shit, he thought. Holy God. Shit, shit, shit.

He didn't think anyone on the patio had seen him. Certainly Bertram Allarbee—upright in a kitchen chair with a hole in his forehead—would not see or hear anything ever again.

His best chance of helping Claire and Laurel would take him around the kitchen corner, past the cedar trees. If he was seen, he could at least provide a distraction. If he was shot, Arnie might hear. He crawled, keeping his head low, gravel embedding in cuts in his hands, forearms, and knees. When he turned the corner, he saw the only cover he had was Arnie's body.

He had always thought of Arnie as a big man, but he knew that in death, until bloat set in, all things collapse, ribs sinking inward once lungs are deprived of breath. His only reaction was cowardly and plaintive. Why couldn't the man have been bigger? A half-ton of a man, a bulwark he could hide behind?

Beyond Arnie, what he saw seemed surreal. Burning branches spat and cracked. Heat made the air above the fire pit waver. Smoke and sparks stank of beeswax and lavender.

Ann Campbell, wearing a black shirt, tennis shoes, and slacks, stood with her back to him, silhouetted in the light of the fire pit. She looked like a small, pudgy version of Modesty Blaise, the heroine of British books and comic strips once worshipped by his adolescent self.

Ann had pulled her hair back from her forehead with a black scarf that tied in back and swayed with her body's movements. Her right wrist dangled, supporting the slight weight of a woman's mother-of-pearl-handled pepper-box revolver that took small caliber bullets. His dad hadn't taught him to drink, but he knew his guns.

Ann was facing the fire pit. Claire sat in an Adirondack chair, her legs dangling to either side, her shift falling back above her knees. She looked drugged. Her head lolled on one bare shoulder, her hair half in her face, half blending with what she was wearing.

Laurel, wearing a man's T-shirt and a pair of women's boxer shorts, sat on the ground next to Claire's chair. Her arms and legs were crossed, and her chin was tipped up, her mouth set in a disdainful look.

Was there a way he could let Laurel, and only Laurel, know he was there? Throw pebbles? Try an owl call?

"Hello, Charles," Ann said.

"She's got two pistols. Bertram's dead, and Arnie might be— two shots, one in the chest, one in the head. She says she's got six bullets," Laurel rattled off.

"What's wrong with Claire?" he asked Ann, scooting toward her.

"Rohypnol. Not a lot."

Charles looked blank.

"Date rape drug," Ann said. "I brought some samples of cheese-cake and doctored apple jack. Bertram wouldn't drink on duty, but he let me in. If he'd taken a drink, I wouldn't have had to kill him. Miss Priss here," she nodded at Laurel, "must have just pretended to drink."

"Where did you get the drug?" Charles asked—not that it mattered, but the longer he could keep Ann talking, the more chance he had to think.

"None of your business. Don't come any closer, or I'll put a bullet in Laurel's stomach," Ann warned him. "I didn't want Claire comatose. Just a little woozy. I needn't have bothered. Neither of them could get away from me. I told Laurel I'd shoot Claire, and Claire I'd shoot Laurel. They're soppy as newborn kittens. Think the world is all milk, milk, milk."

"Bitch," Claire said, her words slurred.

"There won't be any more kittens," Ann said. "Patsy took care of kittens. Claire has a lot to answer for, Charles, but it's your fault Patsy's dead."

Claire moved in the chair, twisting her head and torso, eyes still closed, face still blank. Drool ran down her chin, following the line of her neck into her cleavage. She made a visible effort to swallow and adjust her jaw so her lips closed. She swallowed hard again.

Charles looked more closely at the way she was sitting and realized her feet were tied—one on each side of the chair, splaying her legs and immobilizing the lower half of her body. Her wrists were tied to the armrests. Jesus God.

"Laurel. Are you tied up?"

"No. But I can't get up fast. Why is it Charles's fault Patsy is dead?" she asked Ann.

"Patsy Cluny had a code, a leftover Catholic thing," Ann said. "She was willing to help me get Claire out of this house, but it turned out she was using a rationalization: we could set the stage for accidents if good could prevail. Claire and the basement stairs? Zoe Weathers's horse? No one got *really* hurt. We made that sign to try to scare Claire out, but it didn't hurt anyone.

"When it came to setting that trap in the river, Patsy wouldn't help me. I paid Murphy a lot of money, but I didn't trust him much."

"You thought Claire, not Jen, would be the first to swim after the path was cleared," Charles said.

"I damn well did," Ann told him. "We all heard about your beautiful stream, Charles, and how energized Claire was from being there with you. But it was Jen who nearly drowned. And then Murphy and Patsy both went soft on me. I don't see why people are so sentimental about younger people dying. Just because they're young doesn't mean they're worth much. Murphy was angry. Of course, he had to go. And Patsy started *looking* at me. She started using rosary beads and crossing herself in the store, as though Jen was my fault."

"And Jen wasn't your fault?" Charles asked.

"Jen was in the wrong place at the wrong time. Laurel and the snake—just my little joke."

"Then you poisoned everyone at the wake, including yourself. You spread suspicion and distracted us all from Patsy's death. How did you come to know about green-spored parasol mushrooms?"

"Patsy and I picked some by accident once, a long time ago, so I knew I would react to them. More important, I buy for the store. You think I can't look up mushrooms? Do you think I'm stupid, Charles?"

Charles saw Laurel flex her legs as though preparing to lurch forward.

"Not stupid, but mean. The way Patsy's father was mean, Ann. You offered her a refuge, and then you killed her."

"I was never mean to Patsy! She was my best friend! She had the best food, the best medical care. She never knew pain and suffering, once she moved in with me."

"Bee stings?" Charles asked her.

"Don't bait me. I knocked her out before I dropped the branch with the hive on her. And then, I had to walk home and leave the car there." She narrowed her eyes. "What I want to know, Charles, is why you suspected me. You weren't surprised to see me just now. It could have been Sanjay who spooked Whit. Zoe's always liked him, but now, she's crazy about him. And I bet he made a pile of money taking care of that horse. It could have been Bill Marsh. Did you think of him? Maybe Barbara's insured, and he needs money for the farm."

"I notice fibs," he said. "You said everything you sold was made in Michigan. But the citrus hand lotion? Really? And you told everyone Murphy hand carved those 'lucky sticks.' Claire asked me if I thought one of those would be helpful for Jen. They're just small trees that honeysuckle vines snake around, so they grow in grooved spirals that take a little smoothing out. It didn't seem very important, but I wondered why you would stretch the truth about something so banal. And why would Murphy go along with it? You couldn't have been paying him much. His underwear looked like he'd been discharged in it.

"I started to think about Murphy and you. Both of you with an angry edge—him from his time in the service, you from thinking people dismissed you as a shopkeeper. And neither Sanjay nor Bill could have tried to burn my cabin. Bill's taller than the man Ed described, and Sanjay has the shoulders of a big animal vet. So I thought—Murphy. But now I've seen Murphy, and I know it couldn't have been him."

"I wanted the bitch out of here! If she hadn't been stubborn, if the neighbors hadn't been soft, she could have just sold this place. But no—rally around the bereaved."

She leaned forward and pulled Claire's chair closer to the fire. There were embers in the fire pit. Ann, keeping hold of a gun with her right hand, scooped some coals with what looked like a metal soup ladle, stared at them a long minute, and threw them over Claire. Tendrils of Claire's hair caught fire, and Claire jerked her head back and struggled. Laurel lunged to put out the flames.

Ann snickered. "Sit down, bone ass. Save some energy to use when your lardy friend catches fire. I don't intent to kill you. I may not even kill Claire." She drew Claire's name out. "I want to know, before I leave—and I am leaving—what kind of magic *Claire* has in her cunt."

She slowly used the ladle—oh God, Charles thought, it was sterling silver—to catch the hem of Claire's slip and push it up her thighs.

"Did you read *Johnny Tremain*?" Ann asked.

Claire threw up, covering her rounded, silk-clad stomach with alcohol and bile.

"Actually, it was *Johnny Tremain: A Story of Boston in Revolt*," Laurel said. "She could tell you that herself, if you hadn't drugged her. She worked in a children's bookstore."

"I read. Libraries." Claire's head came up a little. Her voice was less slurry. She hit the R hard, because a teacher had shamed her once for saying "libary."

"I know that," Ann said. "I know all about you. The main thing I know is, we were a lot alike, you and me. My family Irish and Polish, yours Irish and German. Both of us growing up fast, our parents not liking it. Boys always after me, wanting to rub against me. Me, staying a good girl. But that's not what you did." She swayed like a cobra, swinging the ladle hypnotically from her right to her left and back.

"This is…about Georsh," Claire said. She straightened in the chair, eyes focused on Ann. "You slept with *George*."

"I slept with George when I was fourteen," Ann said. "Fourteen. In the hay field. It hurt, the first time."

"He was years older than you," Laurel exclaimed.

"He tried to be gentle. He was nicer than other boys. He said I was his innocent. We were in an innocent place."

"The beeswax. The lavender," Charles said.

"He said he'd come back. We made love so often, those first days. The sun moving over us, wild flowers around us. Then he said he had to go away—first, to college, then to get a business started. I waited for him. And he did come back. Once a month.

"Then his business was going great. And he couldn't come back so often. But he still came, and we still made love, only we went to hotels then. Once, there was a band, and we danced.

"And then he didn't come for six months. He told me he loved me, but that he needed to be married, married to someone more like him. He needed to marry someone who'd been to school, because I didn't go on past high school, you know. I had to look after my mother. He said he was marrying this woman who was smart, but cold, and that he'd always love me, and as soon as he had enough money, he'd retire and we would travel the world. And then, I didn't see him, and I waited and waited...until I couldn't wait any longer."

"Were you pregnant?" Laurel asked.

"Aren't you the schoolmarm smart one! You should learn to keep your mouth shut!" Ann slapped Laurel with the ladle, which stuck momentarily. When Ann pulled it off, a red, raw weal crossed Laurel's cheek.

Charles said nothing. He had held George's picture in his hands—the one in a silver frame, the only picture Claire kept on her dresser. He recalled the broad forehead, the wide set eyes, the open smile. He'd thought what it might mean to be as handsome as George had been.

"But he didn't come back," Ann said. "And I almost forgot him. I had Tansy, and I had Patsy to help me, and I had the store, and I found out I was good at something. Tansy grew up, and George had cancer when he retired. I knew then that we wouldn't travel the world."

Claire stared at her, blistered lips parted. "I'm sorry."

"How dare you be sorry for me! What did you ever do? You never ran a business. You never raised a child. George didn't want a child with you! You had dribs and drabs of jobs and threw artsy-fartsy parties." Ann scowled. "We even look alike. Did you notice that? We both freckle, and we both have good breasts. But you got fatter than I did, and your hair started turning white before mine did! So why did he love *you*?"

Claire stared, unable to answer.

Laurel looked as though holding back words would choke her. Charles shook his head at Laurel, trying, without words, to tell her not to piss Ann off.

He interjected, trying to stall before Laurel could answer, "You two did have a lot in common. You running a store. Claire being a corporate wife. To do either you need to empathize with customers, send flowers, throw parties. But she could handle small talk more easily than you, because college gives you a little gloss of the world. Her parents expected she would go to college; I am guessing yours didn't.

"Laurel helped too, because when Claire doubted herself, she could call and ask Laurel, 'What's an *unreliable narrator*?' and Laurel would tell her."

"She already knew the idea," Laurel said. "She just didn't know the word."

"David," Claire said. "And George." She had no trouble pronouncing either name. In fact, her tone was venomous.

They heard a car pull up the driveway and saw car lights play across the yard. The Bentley. Tansy got out from the driver's side door.

29
IMMOLATION

"You're saying," Ann asked, "that George didn't love me because I didn't have the right *background*?"

"Mom." Tansy inserted herself, quiet and sounding worried.

"What are you doing here, baby?" Ann said.

"We came home early. Jen's foot hurt. She took some codeine tablets, and she's out cold in the car. I wanted some help getting her into the house." She paused. "I heard what you said, Mom. Is that a gun? I don't get it. You have a lot of friends. The neighbors all love you. And we've always been friends, more than most mothers and daughters. And Patsy loved you. For gosh sake, give me the gun. Don't shoot yourself," Tansy said.

"You're giving me too much credit," Ann said. She'd moved to put her back to the river, able to see Tansy while still keeping an eye on Charles.

"You always helped me, Mom. When Simon left, and I gave up the baby, you helped me get my job before I finished school."

Ann looked trapped between the fire she'd fed and the daughter she had nourished.

"You've had some kind of a breakdown," Tansy said, moving closer. "But I can help. Let's just go, before you hurt someone." She clearly hadn't seen Arnie or Bertram Allarbee's body.

"Your mother's gone bat shit crazy," Laurel said.

"I'm teaching Claire." Ann's voice was surly.

Seething anger raced through Claire. Maybe George *had* loved Ann. Maybe Ann had symbolized a time when life had been simple, and maybe he ached for that. Maybe, when he'd traveled, he'd found ways to see her. Maybe he had been fulfilling a promise when they'd moved back to his hometown. In fact, why had she believed his "I just happened to find this house" shit?

Why couldn't he just have said he wanted out, once he'd retired and didn't need her to throw cocktail parties for him? Once he wasn't depending on her to order peeled jumbo shrimp and a seasonal floral display? Divorce couldn't be that hard. Millions of people all over the world did it. His bread had been Michigan-buttered on both sides, and he'd seen no reason to cut back, because, to George Monroe, only George Monroe mattered.

She mattered, goddamn it! Laurel and Charles mattered, and George's cowardice had set them all up to die. Even Patsy had mattered. How had she, Claire—street hockey player—spent all those years married to a greedy little prick?

Tansy continued to step toward her mother, using the careful movements and tones she'd use on a hurt animal. "Let's go home," Tansy soothed. "I'll make cocoa."

"We could go abroad," Ann said. "We could travel. You could meet the most wonderful men and go dancing. I've got airline tickets to Brazil."

"I just want to ask you one thing," Tansy said, sliding something out of a skirt pocket. "I don't understand where this came from." She stepped slowly, carefully, toward her mother.

"Beats me," Ann said. "Looks like some kind of bone."

"It's a toe bone from a polydactyl foot," Charles said. "I mailed it to you, Tansy. Pearl found it in the basement of this house."

"So you said in your note." Tansy was quiet.

Charles could hear the river. Near the fire pit, a few crickets had ventured out.

"Simon's feet hurt," Tansy said. "Sometimes he'd limp."

Ann waved the ladle. "Simon said he loved you, but he left without saying goodbye. What kind of boy does that? He left when you got pregnant. What kind of child would you get with DNA like that?"

"The funny thing is," Tansy said, "you told me not to do an open adoption, but I did it anyway. Right at the last minute, when you'd gone down to start the car, I asked how to reverse closed adoption records. How to get in touch."

Ann stilled. Laurel crouched, and Charles scooted.

"I've got pictures, Mom," Tansy said. "The doctors operated on my baby's feet when he was six weeks old. They say the surgery's simpler now, and then no one calls your kid Troll Toes."

"Well, good," Ann said. She put down the ladle and tucked a gun in her belt.

"Mom." Tansy reached forward and touched her mother's shoulder. "Charles says this toe bone came from the basement here."

"'Charles says,'" Ann said, jerking away from Tansy. "*Charles says. Charles says.*"

"Mom, is Simon's body in the basement? I'll love you, and I'll take care of you, no matter what you say."

Ann turned to Charles.

"You fucking dipshit," she said. "Claire, if we had time, I'd heat this ladle to molten metal and ram it up your cunt." She leaned toward Tansy and touched her cheek. Then she pulled on Claire's binding, and the ropes came off with that single tug. "Guess I'll have to let you go," she said.

Then, in a single fluid motion, she jerked Claire toward her and lifted Claire across her chest, as easily as she'd lifted heavy boxes in the store.

Charles tried to get to his feet, but his body failed him. His haunches collapsed, and he slid the rest of the way down the slight embankment. Closer to the fire pit, the lavender smell filled the air.

Ann stood poised as though preparing to toss a caber, supporting and finding the balance for Claire's weight. Ann was a strong woman, but Claire was no longer limp. She was thrashing furiously, more muscled than Ann had probably expected. The air stirred, and sparks flew around the three women, fused in a triptych that shimmered in the heat.

Laurel was on her feet for a second before Tansy pushed her backward. "Stay down!" she said, her eyes focused on Ann. "Let me help," Tansy told her mother. "I love you, Mom." She leaned in to kiss her.

Then she pulled Claire from her mother, swiveled, and dropped her. Claire's head hit and bumped down the outside of the fire pit.

Ann was thrown off balance and wobbled, knees bent, body tilted backward. Then Tansy hip checked her, and Ann landed in the fire pit, thrashing and screaming, scrabbling on her hands and knees in the coals. Her elbows thrust out. She was keeping her face out of the fire, but they could smell her burning—the terrible smell of rare, scorching meat.

Tansy turned away from her mother—away from them all—and walking fast, took the path down to the river. Charles could hear her splash across to the opposite bank.

Laurel stared stupefied.

Small, flickering tendrils of fire, like the flames atop birthday candles, raced up the scarf that trailed down Ann's neck, and dripped beneath her rib cage.

Laurel bent and picked up the pistol that Ann had dropped. Holding it by the barrel, she slammed it into Ann's head repeatedly until there was an audible crack. She kept slamming the gun into Ann's skull until Ann's whole body collapsed in the flames that now roared higher. The night sky filled with sparks and smoke.

30
COLD COMFORT

Outside the farmhouse windows, Laurel could see Bill and Barbara hooking down hay bales from the loft in the barn. Every now and then, the couple would stop their work, put their arms around each other, and talk and laugh.

Charles, who looked as though he'd been dragged through nails and gravel, had gotten up early and set the coffee pot and mugs on the round table in the farmhouse kitchen.

"Chicken mugs," Claire said. "Why am I not surprised Barbara has mugs with chickens on them?"

She had cut her own hair off, unevenly, just below her cheekbones, and was wearing a high-necked smocked dress that had long sleeves and a skirt that covered her knees. She had seen the advertisements and knew she looked like Eleven in *Stranger Things*. Most of the blackened burn scabs were gone, but antibiotic cream made healing spots show like dots of mercury.

"I thought you were a tough guy," Charles said to Arnie. "Now that I know you are going to survive I am going to ask. How did you know to wear a vest?"

"You think I don't have one iota of sense?" Arnie asked. "After your vomitous mushrooms, Bertram and I both wore vests. Ah, fuck," he said. "I hate cracked ribs."

"You're going to have a scar on your forehead."

"That's an understatement," Laurel said.

One of Arnie's eyes was patched, and his head had been shaved. The bullet that had careened around the right of his skull, plowing up the scalp, had lost momentum and stalled four inches back of his left ear. The bandages had been removed, but stitches ran around his head like railroad tracks.

"At least I have a forehead. I'll be prettier than Bertram Allarbee."

"Prettier than Ann Campbell," Charles added judiciously.

"Do you remember that game we played as kids?" Laurel asked. "Cootie. You had to assemble them. They looked a little like big crickets. When she was in that fire pit, she made me think of a burning, plastic cootie, and I kept thinking she could fly at my face, like a grasshopper in a field."

Charles said, "She reminded me of a fossa, up on the bones of her toes, trying to lift herself out of the flames."

"I'm not asking you what a goddamn fossa is," Arnie growled.

"Civet. Sort of," Charles said.

"Arnie, even I'm prettier than you," Claire said.

"Debatable. You look like you've had smallpox. Or sand flea bites could look like that," Charles told her. "I like the hair, though. It's not quite as short as Zoe's."

"At least I don't walk as if I've been stretched on a rack," Claire retorted.

"Thank God for the Marshes' spare bedrooms and warm, cushy beds," Laurel said. "It took me days to stop feeling as though I'd been put through basic training, and most of what I did was just sit on hard ground. I have my new idea of heaven. Down pillows and comforters are free if anyone wants them. What are your thought about the afterlife, Arnie?"

"A place where people don't kill each other," Arnie said.

"In my very non-theological heaven," Charles said, "all the species on earth but humans exist."

"Mine," Claire said glumly, "is going to take some revising." She flushed red around her burn pocks, but no one looked at her. Instead, heads turned as Jen walked through the door, followed by Tansy.

"Sit down, you two. You want tea or coffee?" Usually, Charles made this offer, but in this case, Arnie spoke.

"I'd love coffee," Jen said, pulling out a chair and sitting down heavily.

Tansy sat down. She was wearing blue jeans and a plain black T-shirt. Her expression was, well, expressionless.

"I burned my mother alive." She looked straight at Arnie. "Will there be an inquest?"

"You didn't kill her," Arnie said.

"I killed your mother," Laurel confessed. "She was trying to get up. I hit her on the head with her gun. Hard. A number of times."

Tansy just looked at Laurel. No reaction.

"How did Jen find you?" Arnie asked.

"I stayed with friends above the flower shop," Tansy said. "I could ignore you and Elaine, but Jen limping from store to store, looking for me, made me feel guilty. I knew I'd have to go back to work, anyway."

Claire reached one burn-pocked hand out to her. "You saved my life, Tansy. And I don't know what was wrong with your mom, but people sometimes change with age, or illness, or tension."

Tansy shook her head. "She killed Simon," she said. "Isn't that what happened, Charles?"

Arnie answered. "We did find bones in the basement of Claire's house. Under Murphy's body."

"Like New Orleans stacked poverty burials," Charles mused. Laurel kicked one of his shins as hard as she could. "Jesus Christ," he muttered. "My mind wanders when I'm tense."

"*Shut up*, Charles," Jen said. "Tansy, we're sorry."

"Shutting up," Charles said.

"Some of the hurt's worn off," Tansy said. "I didn't think Simon would just leave me, especially after I told him I was pregnant. He seemed happy. So all these years, I've wondered what happened to him. When you lose someone like that, you think about them all the time. Did he drown? Did he have amnesia? Did he break a leg, roll down into a hollow, and die slowly because no one could hear him?"

"He died because someone put a bullet through his skull," Arnie said. "His death was fast and painless, but I'm sorry all this time has passed without you knowing that."

"It's what she tried to do to you," Tansy said, "and—what was his name?—Bertram Wannabee."

"Bertram Allarbee," Arnie said. "I always thought that was a Charlie Brown kind of name. You know, the kind you have to say the first *and* last half? But he was a brave kid. A brave man, actually. When there's a bridge named after him, it can just be Allarbee Bridge."

Now Tansy was tearing up.

"I don't think we'll know exactly what killed Ann," Arnie said. "A seizure, maybe, followed by burns and brain trauma. Somehow, her pepper-box gun discharged several times. Who knows why? Could be she had a hallucination, an after-effect caused by those mushrooms." They all knew he was prevaricating. "I don't think she could have or would have wanted to live."

Arnie was blocking out dreams he had of Ann, leaping, charred and burning, over the wall of the fire pit and running after Claire. When he dreamed about this, the woods caught on fire, and flames roiled around Claire and her house, leaving all of them on the ground like apocalyptic skeletons. Some part of his mind knew he was drawing on *Terminator 3: Rise of the Machines*. Humans alone could destroy enough.

"What happens now?" Tansy asked.

"We keep digging up Claire's basement," Arnie said. "There will have to be an inquest, but we'll try to keep publicity toned down. And you'll be busy, involved in other things by then. You should try to find Simon's family. We can help."

Tansy left hand clenched, and she put it to her mouth, staring hard at the daylight to stop herself from crying.

"We can get in touch with them. They might want to see their grandchild, if the adoptive parents will let them."

"They'll know my mother killed him. Why would they talk to me?" She sounded dubious.

"They might want to see their grandchild," Arnie repeated. "And they'll know your mother helped many people, with the exception of two periods in her life when some kind of disastrous compulsion drove her to act in ways that no one understands."

"How will they know that?" Tansy said.

"We'll tell them," Claire told her. "We'll tell them you tried to prevent her from hurting herself or from hurting anyone else."

"What about what I did? Aren't I guilty of something?" Laurel said.

"Not to my mind," Arnie said.

Black Pearl ran into the kitchen and jumped on Arnie's shoulders, sniffing at his eye patch. Colby, fat and fascinated, followed him into the room.

"Off! Off!" Arnie waved his arms.

Black Pearl jumped down and rubbed against Claire's ankles, spreading black hair on her antibiotic cream. Then he smacked Colby and turned, belly up, on the floor.

"He and Colby will miss each other," Jen said.

"He may stay here," Claire said. "He loves being a barn cat— Orra to rub against in the barn, Colby to pester, mice to chase, and straw to roll in."

"Are you going to stay here" Jen asked. "As in, here on the North Branch?"

"I don't think I can," Claire said. "George and Ann. Ann burning. Police excavating my cellar. It's a lot to process. You should take videos of the way you redesigned my house. Get them up on YouTube. I'll take the quilt Zoe gave me wherever I go, Jen."

"Back to your condominium in Grand Rapids," Jen predicted.

"I might sell the place in Grand Rapids. I've been looking at condo associations on the Main Branch, closer to Grayling. I might be somewhere else during summer, when tubes and canoes go by. Sanjay will rent or buy my house here. He and Zoe love each other passionately, but they can't seem to spend nights together. He likes rooms warm; she likes them cold. He likes to read before bed; she hates even computer light. He likes to go down for a snack at midnight, but then she hogs the bed, according to him, and strenuously resists his attempts to repossess it. She says she wakes up with crumbs of his food in the blankets. He could sleep at my house and be at Zoe's in time for breakfast. And he says he'll put in a hot tub where the fire pit was."

Charles asked, "Do they like the same breakfast food?"

"They both like eggs Benedict, orange juice, and granola. They differ on kippers, though. Zoe likes them," Claire said.

"Can my mom's ashes be buried in a Catholic cemetery? It's what she would have wanted." Tansy rubbed her eyes.

"Father Cleary will know," Charles predicted. "I would guess Ann had a will and left everything to you. So, offer Father Cleary a bequest, and I think he will bury your mother wherever you want her. Where was Patsy buried? Do we know?"

"Medal of Mary," Tansy answered. "Monty, too, though he was Presbyterian."

"If there's room nearby one or both of them, ask if Ann can be buried there," Laurel said, then voiced second thoughts. "Unless you mind, Claire?"

Claire looked at her. "Why would I care? *I'm* not going to be buried in Medal of Mary's graveyard. Being with Father Cleary at the wake was hard enough."

Jen and Tansy walked out together.

"You could stay here, with the Marshes," Jen said to Tansy. "I've never known kinder, less judgmental people."

"I'm going to go back to Best to Be," Tansy said. "I do like my job. I've been thinking. One reason I feel safe there is probably because Patsy, who was older than my mother, took care of me when I was young."

"What happens to Everything Michigan?"

"Someone from Chicago buys it? I haven't decided for sure yet, but I can't picture going back there. Every item of food I ordered or sold, I'd picture my mother. I can't imagine there will be a time when I don't think of her."

Jen looked at her. "Some people get better as they get older."

"Some people don't," Tansy told her. "But I am going to try."

"I'm going to stay at the Marshes for a while," Jen said. "I walked out on their horse track today, and it was level. Right now, I can handle up to a 5 percent grade, but anything uneven or hillier hurts my ankle. I talked to Barbara about staying. She said I could feed and help take care of some of the animals. Sanjay says he'll help find homes for stray kittens."

"Pearl would like having you around," Tansy said. She sounded wistful.

"I might take classes online from Parsons School of Design."

"Come over and walk at Best to Be when it's raining," Tansy said. "There are carpeted halls and handrails, and ramps you can use instead of stairs."

"Thank you," Jen said warmly. "That would help. I hurt in cold, wet weather."

"There's a little snack bar there, besides the restaurant. You could stop and get coffee or a cup of soup if you're tired."

"I'll do that."

"Maybe I'll see you then," Tansy told her. "And sometime, maybe in the spring, you, Dannie, Elaine, and I could see another movie."

"I'll ask Arnie what will be playing," Jen said.

31

SWEET FERN

"I wanted to stay up until I saw you," Arnie said to Laurel. He had gone back to his bedroom, but was lying on top of the comforter.

Laurel froze in the doorway. She was still wearing blue jeans and a plain white blouse, but sported Arnie's citrine ring on her right hand.

"I called Neddie." He sat up halfway and leaned toward her.

"She must be relieved. A garbled version of our story made the Detroit papers."

"Charles called her once he knew I wasn't taking the low road to Scotland and told her to wait to see me until I was recovering."

"So she'll be here soon," Laurel said. "With Sawyer."

"She wasn't sure how to tell me, but she and the man she's been seeing want to get married. Sawyer likes him," Arnie said, "and she has insurance now."

Laurel sat next to him on the bed.

"When I'm better, I thought you and I might meet them in Ann Arbor," said Arnie. "Maybe see Sawyer in a soccer game? And sometime, if Jen moves back to New York, you and I could take a train to see her and check out the movie museum. That is, if you want to."

"I'd love to," Laurel said. "I've been thinking. There are a couple of community colleges and four-year schools near Grayling. I don't really want to keep running into Bethanie. I could retire early, take a smaller pension, and maybe teach part-time. I love working with students, but teaching writing is burn-out work, and that's what the college board wants now—each of us working in our own specialty. I'd like to teach a literature class again or a reading class. Not that those are easy."

"I bet you could find places to teach here. But it gets colder in Grayling than you're used to," Arnie warned her. At the same time, he took the citrine off her right hand and with a bit of a struggle, slid it on a finger of her left hand.

"We'll buy comforters," Laurel said. She lay next to him, careful not to crowd his ribs. "I can watch *Guardians of the Galaxy Vol. 2*, and you can read Michael Connelly novels."

"Or," he said, "I could peruse *The Collected Works of Justice Holmes*." He was rewarded when she sat up in the bed and stared at him. Arnie said, "I'd feel better if we were married. I know marriage doesn't statistically matter. I know a lot of married people cheat. But I'd like some kind of everyone-knows-it commitment."

"Um…are you Catholic?" Laurel asked.

"I'm Go See Our Local Judge," Arnie said.

A wave of affection swept over Laurel.

"I've lost weight, so I shouldn't squash you," Arnie continued. "Hospital food."

"Good," Laurel said. "I'll start eating more."

AT ABOUT THE same time Laurel was promising a change in diet, Charles was sharing a similar conversation with Claire.

"What do you think, long term?" he asked. They had a space heater in the room, so she wouldn't need covers. She was wearing the kind of slip she had worn the night Ann Campbell tried to burn her alive. He'd pulled the sheet up to his chin and was wearing only his glasses.

He touched her lips with his fingers. Her cracked lips hurt, and she moved his hand away.

"I'd like to see your stream again."

"Ah. Picture us beatific—you in a caftan and me splendidly nude. You strip, and we skinny-dip."

She didn't find it easy to meet Charles's eyes. The skin on her face felt stretched when she smiled, and the corners of her mouth were peeling. It helped to remember he was black-and-blue from his chin to his toes, with one large bruise across his abdomen shaped, as he said, like an enormous pickle. So she shouldn't have felt self-conscious, but she did.

She'd said she'd been too out of it to remember Ann's smoldering hatred, but, in fact, she remembered most of that night. She remembered Ann's threats, and sweating with terror, wondering if scar tissue could be reconstructed.

"Claire, look at me. I should be ashamed to face you. I didn't know Laurel or you well enough to blather about animal aspects. Annie Dillard says you can't know something's reality unless you love it, or have spent the time and energy to be knowledgeable about it. I'd like to know and love you. But you and Laurel—both of you complex human beings—saved each other, while I did a snipe dive and ended on my butt."

She did look at him. "You could have gotten free and left me when you first got out of the basement. You could have hitchhiked on down the road. You distracted her—Ann. You and Laurel kept her mouthing off until Tansy showed up."

Charles pulled himself together and managed to look indignant. "Don't be ridiculous," he told her. "I'd have to be gormless to think I could replace you. It took me twenty years after Lane to find another woman I loved. Do you think at my advanced age I can afford to waste decades? And what if, with my magnetic charm, I attract another romance writer? Do you want to see me shuffle into the future, an aging, heartbroken man wearing pointy-toed shoes?"

"I'm sorry about your cabin and your work," Claire said. "That's your pure passion."

He took his glasses off and looked at her. He did look older—not just the scrapes and the bruises and the cuts, but the bruise-like circles under his eyes that had come from not sleeping. The skin there looked thinner, too, almost translucent.

"I want to go on learning, not to nest on what I've learned, like it's a pile of—a pile of—I don't know."

"Fungus sticks?"

"Claire, I'm trying to say I won't leave you to follow Arctic terns. You are my pure passion. We can trundle about during the day and learn together, and at night, we can learn each other's love."

"How about Oscar? If we trundle around together, will I see Oscar?"

"Ed says Oscar flew off with a gang of young ravens. He may have flown north. Ravens can find good hunting even in the Arctic. But he'll most likely be back here, cruising this area, and to be honest, he'd recognize you with or without me. He might even say hello."

Claire struggled to sit up. "He'd be more likely to recognize me if you were with me."

"I suppose," Charles said. "If I forgive you for suggesting I could have run away, we could winter on the Main Branch. We'd see the river swing out wide under snow-laden white cedars. We could watch the northern night sky when light from the Aurora Borealis shimmers like emerald rivers. We could regale each other over micro-brews at Spike's Keg 'O' Nails."

She lay back in the bed. "It'll be nice to drink again," Claire said. "The doctor said blah, blah, blah, burns and the immune system; stay hydrated. Blah, blah don't drink for two months, blah, blah. Blah."

"We'll celebrate by chilling champagne in snow or wrapping up in a quilt and having Irish coffee the way it ought to be made—with cognac in plain white cups. Or hot chocolate, made with squares of baking chocolate and cream. We'd need vanilla beans."

"Many choices," she mused. "I could do fundraising parties for Trout Unlimited."

"Or install a wall for rock climbing," he suggested, frowning at his scarred hands.

"A revised heaven." Claire looked thoughtful.

"What happened to your old one?"

"George and Ann Campbell are in the brick house I thought I'd move into," she said. "Maybe she was the gold-brown marten you thought of. She cared so desperately that twice in her life, she tore other lives apart. Maybe he loved her but was afraid to lose the life he and I had—the life he'd planned for, the life he'd built over time. He wasn't so physically passionate by the time he'd moved 'home.' At least not with me. He'd moved to the place he remembered and found he had friends, status, and two compensations of aging—money and stability. I still feel sorry for Ann. She ended up bringing him custards after she'd waited a lifetime for him. She's stuck with George now, and the brick house, but she can't have the black cat."

"Claire?" Charles sounded worried. "What, ah, *shape* is Ann in, in that view of an afterlife?"

"I don't think I'll ever know that for sure."

He wondered if he'd awakened her most traumatic memories, which would surely be those of the fire.

"I'm going to miss Laurel!" Claire wailed. "I hate it that she's leaving. How can she go back and see David at work every day? We've barely had a chance to *reminisce.*" She'd taken pain pills, and her voice was drowsy.

"Have Laurel come visit," Charles said. "Have her move in, if you want. I like Laurel. We'll find out what her plans are. You can ask her when you both wake up."

"This last time she came," Claire said, "her visit went all wrong. She might not want to come back here, Charles. Awful things happened."

Charles smoothed her hair back. He said, "Some bad things did happen."

"And yet," she said, "some good things happened too."

After she fell asleep, he slid out of bed and cracked open a window. Barbara had tacked a branch of drying sweet fern to the window frame, and the breeze blowing into their room smelled of balsam trees.

32

AU SABLE REUNION

"To old friends and new friends," Charles proposed, raising his glass. The blast of wind and snow outside Claire's condominium swirled through the pine trees by the Au Sable, scoured the window glass with bits of ice and spruce needles, and tried to push the river current back.

Claire and Laurel sat together on a gold sofa.

"To spring," Claire added to the toast. "Warmer weather must be coming."

"Good insurance," Arnie suggested.

"Healing," Laurel said.

They clinked glasses and each drank at least a few swallows of champagne. Arnie left most of his drink. Claire eyed it but reached for an orange slice dipped in dark chocolate. Food rested on an antique immigrant's chest she and Charles had found at a community garage sale under a pile of frayed cotton rugs. The letters on it read, "*Christian Braun, uber Liverpool nacht New York.*" The boards on the top had separated, leaving a few wide cracks, but it still made a good serving table for drinks and desserts, in this case, from Zingerman's in Ann Arbor. There were—besides the oranges in chocolate—figs and a plate of strangely addictive white and dark chocolate covered marshmallows.

Nine months had passed since Ann died in flames. Arnie had lost weight; Laurel had gained weight. Claire's skin no longer sported multiple pox-like silver scars. Charles had a bum knee, but got cortisone injections.

Arnie had been off work with full pay. He'd tried to return to work but still had some problems with loss of balance. He was now on half pay. By the end of the summer, if he didn't meet department standards, he'd have decisions to make.

Laurel and Arnie would be the first of Claire and Charles's friends to spend the night. They'd had Reuben sandwiches, also from Zingerman's, which made for an easy supper, and had planned to put on boots and coats and snow pants and walk down to the river's edge. The wind whipping up had convinced them discretion was the better part of valor, so they put on night clothes instead and moved to softer chairs.

Charles, wearing sweatpants, long-sleeved thermal under-wear, and heavy wool socks, had stretched out on the floor, where he could eye a stack of oversized books. Arnie, seated in the rocker where he could lean his head back, was nattily attired in the maroon pajamas and matching robe he'd bought for Sawyer and Nellie's visit. New, black wool slippers completed the outfit. His hair had grown out and pretty much covered the scar, so that when Laurel looked at him, she was tempted to say, "Who are you, and what have you done with my husband?"

Claire had changed into a long, straight, hooded red robe that she'd chosen because it could cover her hair, and Laurel was wearing a pair of ankle-high, cream-colored slippers and pajamas printed with black cats. They shared the couch, bodies turned sideways and feet meeting in the middle, so they could eye Charles and Arnie or look out at the boughs of wind-tossed cedar trees and snow clouds swallowing stars.

Laurel had just gotten back from visiting Jen in New York. Neddie and Sawyer had visited Arnie in Grayling, since his driving was limited to checking in at work and getting to and from phys-ical therapy. Charles and Claire had overseen the reconstruction of his cabin that fall, but as the weather had gotten colder, they'd spent more and more time at the condominium she'd bought on the Main Branch. He'd joined her, lugging in piles of books, by the time

Christmas came. The rooms were sparsely furnished, with a small cherry table and four oak chairs in the living room, along with the couch, the immigrant's chest, and a red plaid platform rocker.

The two bedrooms had queen-sized beds, with flannel sheets that were lightweight but held warmth and piles of quilts, and pillows, and wool blankets. The pine dressers in each bedroom were new and serviceable. The lined drapes, like those in the rest of the house, were white, and when they were open, they showcased the snow. The silk quilt Zoe had given them hung above the bed Claire slept in. Usually Charles slept there with her, but there were nights when his knee hurt, and he slept in the platform rocker, or he read in the chair, or looked at the stars.

"I like the cat pajamas," Claire said to Laurel.

"Thanks. Sawyer got them for me after we took him to see Pearl."

"I take it my buddy's OK?" Charles sat up, crossing his legs, to attend to the conversation.

"*Your* buddy? I like that!" Claire objected.

"Oh, yeah. Black Pearl is fine," Arnie assured them. "He's lord of the barnyard. He and a big red rooster had it out this fall. Pearl took on this sidewinding, caterwauling swagger and then charged at the rooster, who flew back to the coop. Nights, Pearl either snuggles with Colby or sleeps on Bill's stomach, kneading it like Bill's his mama. Days, he sometimes sleeps on Braytoven the donkey's back."

"How's Sawyer?" Claire asked.

"Seems good. He has a girlfriend." Arnie shook his head. "He sure isn't as shy as I was at that age. Neddie seems happy."

Charles snagged another marshmallow. "Does Jen like design school?" He looked skeptical.

"The verdict's still out," Laurel said. "But then, she just started. She's hardly limping at all. Bill and Barbara have a new project. With Orra's help, they're wet nursing a calf that turned up starving in January. It's a female. They're thinking of keeping it for milk."

"Sanjay and Zoe?" Claire looked away when she posed the question.

"Sanjay plays the piano—with lots of arpeggios—and Zoe loves the hot tub," Laurel said.

"Tansy?" Charles asked so Claire wouldn't have to. Sometimes, Claire would still have nightmares, and it seemed easier if he brought the question up. "Is she doing all right, considering?"

"I think so," Laurel said. "She hasn't heard back from Simon's parents or whether they want to know the name of the people who adopted their grandchild. But she might still hear," she added. "Decisions that important take time. She and Jen keep in touch."

"Are Dannie and Elaine still looking for a sperm donor?" Claire asked.

"They are," Arnie answered. "There's a doula service of sorts that matches a donor to parents, kind of like matchmaking adults. The woman they're using has worked with a gynecologist they trust, so they should avoid anyone like that slimeball in California who donated thousands of units of sperm at clinics all over the state. It might be Elaine who gets pregnant," Arnie said, with a trace of annoyance. "Turns out Dannie has serious varicose veins."

"You have a problem with that?" Laurel asked.

"Elaine is a bit like my godchild," Arnie admitted. "There are risks in pregnancy. And she's my source of information, damn it. Anything happening in the force, I know she'll fill me in. For instance, the video perp I should have followed up with, before he hurt anyone? He's in a minimum security prison. Not ideal, but it could have been worse."

"Could have been worse," Charles said, "sums a lot up."

Momentary silence descended. Charles thought about his cabin—the progress made, the things he still should do. Laurel remembered the shock of hitting Ann traveling up her arm. The hair on her arm had grown back. She tried not to dwell and was, for the most, part successful. Claire had a pang of contrition. Good Old George—or "Gog," as she spitefully called him—could have left his money to Ann in his will.

"House sparrows in New Zealand—but only in New Zealand—hover near magnetic gizmos that open doors to cafeterias," Charles offered. "I could teach Oscar that, but I'd end up with store owners gunning for ravens."

"Did you see him this fall?" Arnie asked. He'd gotten more interested in Oscar after he heard about the bird leading an attack on Ann.

"Nope," Charles said. "He may be heading farther north, where deer that don't make it through winter, brought down by age or predators, provide ravens free pickings."

"Ugh." Laurel groaned. "Claire, how do you stand him?"

"I'm doing penance for sins I will commit later in life."

"All right, I'll do guy talk," Charles said patiently. "Hey, Arnie. How's the Explorer? You get a good deal on it?"

Arnie stretched out his legs, looking pleased. "I did. Bought it from a friend who drove it for two years, so it was just coming off lease. Four-wheel drive. Enough room for Laurel to sleep in back, if she wants to curl up. I'm not crazy about pushing through when we're tired, anyway. Hey, want to see it? Go kick the tires?"

Charles put on boots, and he and Arnie threw on coats before heading through the kitchen and out to the garage.

Laurel took a meditative bite from a fig and leaned forward to talk to Claire.

"How's married love life?" Claire asked.

Laurel choked on the fig.

"Good," she answered. "Arnie's concussion still gives him blinding headaches when we least expect it. We wouldn't win a sexual Olympics competition, but I never feel as if I have to perform, the way I did with David. I never thought I'd be one of those women who says this, but when we're going to sleep and Arnie puts his arm around me, I sometimes think, 'Trust is the ultimate intimacy.' Are you and Charles OK?"

"Charles is. I think I still have trust issues, after what happened with George. I find myself trying to not count on Charles being there."

"His brain changes channels so fast, sometimes I can't follow him," Laurel said. "Does it ever hurt your feelings, if you say something to him and he answers you with migratory counts?"

"It startled me the first hundred or so times it happened. But when I reel Charles back to the conversation, he's completely aware of what's being discussed, and he does answer, right on target, empathy and all. George's was more of an "If you say so, dear," responder. We didn't converse, really. We talked about his work or talked about the house. I never knew what he felt."

She seemed to veer off topic, adding, "I feel weird about this condo. You notice there's a dearth of personality here?"

"I noticed there's not much clutter. Not much that looks like you here, to be honest."

"I bought new dishes," Claire said.

"Nice. I like the blueberry pattern."

"I just can't seem to get going, house-decoration wise. Maybe I always did it to please George? I just sort of don't want to get all domestic here. What if Charles gets sick of me, and I don't want to stay on this hauntingly beautiful river by myself?"

CHARLES AND ARNIE were sitting in Arnie's Explorer—Arnie in the driver's seat, and Charles in the passenger seat. They looked at the dials, but their conversation had moved beyond the car's mileage.

"I can't picture Claire wanting to be with me forever," Charles said. "She has a place in Grand Rapids. She had a life and friends in Grand Rapids.

"All I know is, for now, I'm a lucky man. I loved Lane from afar most of my life, but I'm realizing that as getting-older adults, we aren't much alike. She's serious about her children's success. Fair enough, really. She's invested in her music. She's a competitive runner. But when we talked, she didn't sound like she takes time to laugh much or go for walks anymore. Her life is packed to the gills with self-improvement projects, and Claire and I are still looking for new bends in the road."

Arnie nodded. "I know what you're saying. I worry Laurel is going to miss her full-time job and be too kind to tell me. She's smart, and she's helped me understand myself. She says I've got something called 'visual literacy.' Sometimes, she reads when we're together, but we've watched some terrific movies since my headaches have gotten better: *The Florida Project, Three Billboards Outside Ebbing, Missouri, The Shape of Water, Icarus.*

"Before I met Laurel, I never felt like anyone really got me. I can work through print; I understand written instructions, and I can draft what Laurel calls 'cogent' memos. But I feel like an ox trying to write. When we watch movies together, I can feel connections, make comparisons, empathize. We go out for breakfast and talk about what we've seen, and I can keep up with her, even see things she's missed.

"*Icarus* terrified me. Laurel cried—though she laughed, too— watching kids in *The Florida Project.* She said if she were still teaching, she'd have those kids in her classes when they grew up."

"Even newly hatched songbirds need good nutrition and low stress levels to sing right when they've fledged," Charles commiserated.

"I didn't know people could bond over movies," Arnie mused.

Charles said, "Maybe Claire and I should watch more."

"Try *The Shape of Water,*" Arnie suggested. "You're the ecology guy. The harbor in the movie could use some help."

"God, it's cold out here. Let's go back in," Charles said.

Claire and Laurel looked up when the back door slammed open as Charles and Arnie came in, their coats wafting cold air.

"Still cold," Arnie reported. "The wind's dying down, or at least it seemed quieter to me."

"You two have a chance to catch up?" Claire asked.

"We talked about warranties," Charles answered, looking down to peel off his boots. "Arnie's car-truck thing has got a lot of room to pick up things you find along the road. I found a railway lantern once. I think it fell off a truck, and I gave it to my sister for her rec room. Did Claire show you her sketches?" he asked Laurel.

"What sketches?" Laurel asked, eyeing Claire curiously.

"I did some sketches last fall," Claire admitted. "Southern iris— the little ones. I had to learn to do it, which was hard…but I liked it."

"Colored pencil," Charles said. "Looked like book illustrations. Hey! You two finished the marshmallows."

"Can we see them?" Arnie asked. And when Claire spread them out, he and Laurel both looked serious.

"These are good, Claire," Laurel said.

Arnie nodded. "I've never liked prints of plants much. They seem forced to me, somehow. But these look kind of warm. Familiar."

"I think it's because I left in tattered leaves and discolored flowers," Claire said. "I wanted them to look fragile."

Conversation came to a sudden, sober halt. Each was remembering something from the North Branch. Arnie thought of raspberry canes. Laurel pictured deliquescing oranges in the blue bowl on the piano, and Claire thought of snowdrops she and George had found in the spring.

"I know what we need," Charles said abruptly. "We need to take a road trip. We need to make new memories. All of us. Well, me less than you three, maybe, but you all need new pictures in your heads. Not just wildflowers. New rivers. Pileated woodpeckers. Birch groves. Bittersweet."

They stared at him like children. Arnie pushed his hair back from the scar on his forehead. Laurel's jaw dropped, and Claire suddenly looked goggle-eyed with fatigue.

"Tahquamenon Falls. You've been there?"

All three shook their heads.

"You've lived in Michigan all your lives, and one of the Michigan attractions that pulls Japanese and Swedes and Sudanese doesn't get your time of day? It has wood-chipped, 5 percent graded walking paths, benches, boats to rent. A shady island. I've been there three times. I'll be your tour guide."

"That will be safe," Arnie muttered. "And I hate the Mackinac Bridge."

Laurel elbowed him gently. Getting Arnie to stop obsessing about his job would be a relief to her, and maybe that change alone would help heal his concussion.

"We'll talk about it at breakfast. We'll need maps. Plans. Places to eat! But you all look tired. Go to sleep and dream," Charles said, and shooed them to bed. "No griping," he said. "Wait until morning, when the sun is out."

33
DREAMS

Claire dreamed that she was edging between the car, and the house and the small patch of dirt that held lilies of the valley, their scent rising for her, the essence of childhood. She bent down, inhaling, and carefully pulled a few of the stems so that each stem came complete from the ground, tender at the tip, each bell swaying in her hand, opaque white with a breath of green. She raised them to her face so she could look into the flowers. She picked two leaves, and babying them in her hand, pulled open the screen door and ran up the stairs, dropping her coat and books as she went. Ma would be in the dining room, surrounded by piles of ironing, the boys' shirts hanging from a door jam, that crisp cotton smell filling the house.

She walked through the small kitchen. There was the sink where Ma washed their hair using the sink sprayer attachment, and the one long counter, where last year, struggling with a turkey that spun out of control and shot across the kitchen, Ma had cussed, using words her brothers used. The ironing board was up; piles of laundry lay folded—jeans and shirts and Dad's work clothes.

"Hey! Hey, I'm home! Is anyone here? Jan, Mark, Brian? Ma?"

Where were they all? No *As the World Turns* playing from the living room, though the drapes Ma had laboriously made were pulled against the west sun.

She reached to a shadow box, fingers wrapping around the perfume vase with the heart-shaped stopper for the lilies of the valley. The vase was small. You had to run the water just right or it filled the neck of the tiny vase but didn't trickle in. She eased the stems in, one by one, so she wouldn't smush them, and only got a little water up her sweater sleeves. She pushed her sleeves up, knowing the wrists would stretch out and the rash that never quite left the insides of her forearms would prickle. Still, it was an achievement to have gotten down the tiny vase without knocking over any of the other glass bottles there—one green crackle glass, a small, tall, slender perfume bottle that had been her gramma's, and a purple-swirled vase that would hold lilacs, later in the year. Some of her friend's mothers had Avon perfume bottles, but her mother's bottles were antiques, from Germany, though Claire wasn't sure what that meant.

The house was so quiet. Her dad was at work, making sure the tire production line ran smoothly. Kind of funny Ma wasn't there. She could hear the kitchen clock tick. Almost four o'clock— she should start her homework. The sun, moving west, slid behind a neighbor's box elder tree. Ma hated box elder bugs. The room seemed to slide into shadow, the way a globe rotates on its stand...

Suddenly, for no reason, she was terrified. Goose bumps broke out on her arms, and hair prickled on the back of her neck. Maybe Ma was already dead, spread-eagle on a bed, the way the Horst twins said women in movies died, only the women in movies had on nightgowns with lace cut low around their boobies, not the pajamas Ma wore.

A ticking sound from behind her. Not the clock. The iron. Jesus and Mary, the iron was still on. Ma would never do that unless she'd been dragged away. Maybe was being gnawed on right then, or something like that; the Horst twins had never been clear about that part. In the corner of the dining room was the roll-away bed that Gramma used when she came to visit.

There was a cover on it now to hide the fact, Claire guessed, that they had a bed in the dining room. When she was small, she could slide between the folded metal legs, under the mattress folded upward, in half like butterfly wings. Some would call it spying, but she was simply *learning* things, observing adult quarrels and watching her brothers coming down to water liquor bottles.

She found herself on the floor, struggling though the familiar process, but this time, her shoes stuck on an angled bit of metal. She doubled up her leg, but the shoe popped off her foot. She couldn't stay hidden and reach past the foot to recover her shoe. A blast of cold struck the room. The iron ticked louder now, seeming to say, "Claire's hiding, Claire's hiding, Claire's hiding." She felt squashed and smothered, and dust made her want to sneeze. She put her face down on the hardwood floor, trying not to breathe, knowing that any minute, a hard, knobby hand would grab her. The worst thing wasn't knowing she was going to die—probably stabbed through the heart—but that the whole world had gone *wrong*, and nothing she had ever believed in had been true.

She jerked upright in Charles's arms.

ARNIE RUBBED HIS blurring eyes. His room was filled with fog, or at least his eyes were. This was, obviously, a dream. If he pulled up the covers and slept a little more, he'd get rid of the intruding fog. What was it Scrooge had said? A bit of indigestion from eating tacos?

Well, not tacos. He tugged the light wool blanket up to his chin and settled in. The luxury of that few more minutes of sleep. God, what a good thing that his cell phone alarm wasn't ringing.

Well, it wouldn't be ringing, would it, if this was a dream? What time was it, anyway? Somehow, it seemed as if he had slept past noon. He opened one eye to peer at his watch, which he'd worn to bed. He'd taken off his belt, but otherwise, he was wearing his uniform.

He sat up in bed, suddenly wide awake. His vision *was* blurry. Worse than before. It was like being in a plane flying through clouds that are static and solid, as though flying through corridors of white-painted hospital walls.

That was when he heard Sawyer crying in the next room. He swung his feet out of bed, lurching out of the covers and holding up his pants, which were too loose, with one hand.

"Sawyer? Sawyer, what's wrong, kiddo? Don't worry, Dad'll be there. Dad'll be right there."

Goddamn it, where was the doorframe? Surely he'd walked in a straight line from the bed, and the door—the door should be right *there*. Whatever was wrong with his eyes, he could get it fixed later—if it could be fixed later. He had a friend who'd lost vision in one eye—a torn retina—but not both eyes. But so what? It didn't matter. Where was the fucking door?

He tripped over his dragging pant cuffs and struggled to free his legs and step out of the damn pants, but then he lost his balance and went crashing to the floor.

"Dad? Dad? Where are you?" Sawyer's voice was higher in pitch now. Arnie got to his feet and felt for the edge of the bookcase that should be right next to him, but he was disoriented. He felt for the wall and nearly tumbled forward again when he didn't find it.

Arnie struggled to not fall. He was sweating now, in panic, his uniform shirt clammy. He thrashed with his arms to maintain his balance, and to his horror, hit his hand against what had to be his bed. He'd gotten completely turned around. What if Sawyer really needed him? Maybe he had appendicitis, or even had just wet the bed, because if the kid was really sleeping hard, that was a possibility, maybe once or twice a year.

Damn it! Damn it! And now the phone was ringing, but that was good, because he could ask for help, if he could find his damn cell phone.

Five rings. It started up again. Five rings. Elaine.

Wait. No.

Elaine wouldn't be calling.

He struggled to sit up in bed but was weighed down by a pile of covers. His pajamas had twisted and had a choke hold around his neck.

Light from the moon reflected off snow that had piled up near the window.

He rubbed his hands over his face. Goddamn it, what good was he to anyone?

THE WILLOW CATKINS were yellow with pollen. In the park, ducks paired off and slid into the water, which was higher now than it had been last fall. The last time Laurel had left school a little late and crossed the two-lane road to jog over to the small stand of red pines, she'd seem a heron standing in the shallows. She stood still, watching it, inhaling the scent of new grass and old, decaying vegetation.

Only now she wasn't in the park. She was in, of all things, a study hall, looking through big glass windows that faced the road and the park. This room once had been a cafeteria, but now that an addition had created a quite nice lunchroom, this long, window-lined room had been converted into an all-purpose area. Parent-teacher conferences were held here. Science fair projects were set up on the tables. Speakers came in for small group meetings. And today, with three teachers out with the flu and only one substitute available, two last-hour classes had been sent there en masse to wait out the hour.

In spite of the rule against sleeping, a number of students had propped books up on their desk and slouched down behind them, napping. The substitute, at a table near the doors that faced the hall, was grading papers and doing her best to ignore rule infringements. Periodically, one of the coaches who was running track in the gym across the hall would peer in to make sure no one got too rowdy.

Near the back, a small group of girls that hung out with Claire were writing notes. Some of the notes got passed to boys at the next table, who mostly ignored them or flicked them into the trash. They were playing cards and elaborately ignoring the girls. People who opened these notes might find anything from "*Daryl, I love you. Can you take me for a ride?*" to "*Daryl, you have a boner, and your face is turning red.*"

One of the girls who had befriended Laurel on Claire's behalf, and had turned out to be a reasonably good friend, raised her eyes at Laurel and tipped her head toward an empty seat at their table.

Laurel shook her head, mouthing, "*Thank you,*" and ducked behind her book. Going over there would leave her feeling more alone than she was now. Claire was home sick and holding a conversation seemed impossible without her.

She wouldn't be ignored, but Claire protected her from the endless questions. Why didn't Laurel have a boyfriend? Who did she think was cute? Did she have a crush on someone? Maybe Laurel likes girls? Soft, just-a-joke shoves against her shoulder. Sticks of gum broken into pieces and passed around. If the gum ran out, a note was sent to the boys' table, which sometimes elicited gum, tossed overhand, and sometimes a note saying, "*69, foxes.*" Shrieks and giggles. Gossip about a girl who was—don't tell—pregnant.

Laurel had known about sex since her mother, while buying Laurel her first training bra, had told her stuff she shouldn't do, starting with French kissing and expanding from there, ending with, "Lord, Laurel, comb your hair and pull up your bra straps." But some of the things her mother had talked about just seemed private. She'd had a couple of crushes and could talk about them to Claire, but mostly, she told everyone she'd met an older boy, a friend of her parents, whose family had moved to Scotland. They wrote each other long letters. She brought stationery and envelopes to school, and now pulled out the heather blue paper and retired behind a stack of books.

But the sun had come around the south side of the school and was beaming through the windows. Some bees had come into the school and were now buzzing against the glass. When everyone left, she and the science teacher might open the far doors to the ball field and shoo them out, but for now, they weren't hurting anything, and their escape attempts and buzzing didn't bother her. In fact, they were kind of soothing, because they seemed to have some kind of purpose in life. She let her head rest on her folded arms for a minute, trying to think of some things to write to her friend, and suddenly, she found herself—what's the word? Transported?

She was outside the school and over in the park, by the water. She began to run along the pond, delighted with her cool freedom, and it seemed as if she were wearing tennis shoes instead of her school loafers, which flapped at her heels. She'd never run with such ease. Maybe she would be a runner! Her feet squished in a bit where snow had left wet patches, but she pulled her skirt above her knees and pushed up her sweater sleeves. The wind was cool, but the sun was warm, and she was perfectly relaxed. Her pace was so smooth, the grass and tree roots seemed to flow beneath her.

And then she was aware of a young man running along beside her—well, almost beside her. His legs were longer than hers, but he was slowing his pace—she was sure of it—so that he didn't catch up with her, or frighten her, or pass her.

"May I join you?" he asked.

"You may," she said, "since you asked so nicely." She glanced briefly over her shoulder. He was wearing a white dress shirt and blue trousers and had dark hair.

Then they ran on for a while, and little by little, he caught up with her, matching her pace. And then, when she was finally out of breath, he put his hands on her shoulders, and they sank down on a sunny patch of grass, hidden by a huge red pine tree from the school and road. She was in his arms, perfectly safe, and knew it didn't matter to him that that she had pine needles in her hair.

Laurel woke and saw Arnie, sitting on the end of the bed, facing away from her with his shoulders slumped.

"Hey," she said. "Can you lie down a minute and hold me? I had a dream, and then I just woke up."

"Good dream, or bad dream?" he asked.

"A good dream," she answered decisively. If the boy in the dream was younger and thinner than Arnie, she had been younger then too.

"You were in my dream," she said. "And you held me in your arms."

CHARLES SAT IN a yoga position in the middle of a small island, surrounded by last year's grass, branches that had broken off aspen bushes under snow and ice, and the thundering spring-level stream. He'd brought a rubber raincoat out and had folded it in a square. Sitting on it had initially protected his rump and legs, but as his weight and warmth encouraged ground thawing, his jeans had soaked through.

He was cold but happy. He could see a mallard and his mate making a nest on the next small island. Looking upstream, he saw the path the sun made, turning the water diamond bright. A muskrat passed him, moving downstream with the current.

He didn't see the otter until it pulled itself out of the water and sat down like a cat, less than a foot from him, splaying its legs to fastidiously groom.

"Hello," he said.

The otter ignored him.

"Didn't I see you before?" Charles ventured. "Two years ago, you and your pups made a snow slide just upstream from my cabin. They slid down it on their tummies and splashed into the water, then got out, ran around, and did the whole thing again for twenty minutes before your mate, and then you, joined in. Looked like fun. I wish I could have joined you."

"Well, you couldn't have," the otter said. "It's rude to even think of it."

"Sorry," Charles said. "Since you've joined me today, I wonder if I'm in your way. It's really your stream, not mine."

"Did you get rid of that bird?" the otter asked. "Visiting is one thing, but I don't want ravens here as a regular thing. They eat a lot of the same things we weasels eat—ground-nesting birds and chipmunks. You know that perfectly well."

"Oscar stops by," Charles said. "He isn't staying. He's a young bird, not mated, restless. We're friends, but he has places to go."

After a minute or so of deliberation, the otter looked out at the stream and said in a low voice, "There's something else you could do for me."

"Anything," Charles said.

"I know you," the otter said. "You watched otters on the big river this past winter. We otters do attend council. We heard you and your mate were seen lying on your backs in the snow, waving your arms and legs and making those snow things that look like birds with flared tail feathers. You're both too big. Don't do that. Or don't do it near rivers. It packs the snow down so it's harder for the food to make tunnels. Do you never think?"

"Sorry," Charles said again. "You seem ill-tempered."

"You would be too, if humans who eat corn, and humans who put water in plastic bottles, and humans who make seeds all alike, which makes it harder to find grasshoppers—wait, I'm getting off track." The otter swiped a paw across its face, and Charles suddenly had the terrible feeling that the animal was crying.

"Here's the thing," the otter said. "We know there are humans who do want to be outdoors and want their children to be, too. There's a sandpiper group and a fish group, there are squirrel groups and maybe a raccoon group. I don't know if there's an otter group. I don't even know if we'd want one. But I can tell you, all humans need to take care of the water. The stream was low last year. And hot, too. Trout don't like it. We don't like it. God doesn't like it."

"How do you know that last bit?" Charles asked.

"God is a river otter. Pteronura brasiliensis. I thought you knew that. There were people here a long time ago who used to know."

"I wasn't thinking," Charles admitted.

"Hah! Hah," the animal said, baring his teeth slightly. "Take your mate on a trip, if you want. She looks mangy. Take her to the Big Lakes, the ones that connect to the Waters of the World. But when you're back, find some way to hawk up cash for the cause. Write another book. Prattle about that raven. Tell about the owl—nasty creatures, owls—that was hit by a car and would have frozen if you hadn't let it warm up in your cabin."

"I don't want to write another book." Charles had put his hands down now. He looked crestfallen but stubborn. "I hate writing books. And no one pays attention to books unless you go around touting them. I have had ideas for books, but I hate touting."

The otter whuffled its mustache. "There you go! Another book! Get your mate to tout."

"I can't do it!" Charles said.

"No?" The otter whistled. And then something happened that Charles would remember all his life, though he never told anyone, not even Claire, about it. The otter turned its back on him, and when it turned around, it had somehow transformed itself into a six-foot-long giant river otter. He braced himself on his tail and crunched through a fish he held in one paw, the way Charles held an ice cream cone. The otter grunted with annoyance. It pointed the now headless fish at him.

"Here's the thing we need help with: Humans don't understand there is no such thing as private water. All the water flows together, and it's *mine*. It's my blood. Humans take my blood that I give for communion, just as I share with the rest of my creatures. But that's not enough for you." He hissed, breathing harder.

"Oh, no. My blood in plastic bottles with artificial flavors. My heart's blood pumped through shale. You spray pig shit, which is fine in small quantities, to poison my litters. You pour filth from tourist ships into salt heavens where bat-winged angels fly. Even your kind can't swim off the great coasts without getting sick. South African children wait in line for my bounty while Indian nouveau riche bathe daily in vast pools of my blood that cannot return to my veins. Lands freeze, fall in mudslides, or burn.

"You don't respect the holy or the consecrated. Do you know what happens when a god is ignored, you amateur anthropologist?"

Charles whispered, "The god, uh, disappears."

"*The god disappears.* You're right about that, babycakes. And sometimes, when the god disappears, *the people disappear with it.* Look it up."

The giant river otter turned its back on Charles and slid into the creek, where the ripples were so bright he could no longer see.

WHEN CHARLES SLID out of his moment of meditation, which he had been practicing on his back, he stretched his legs, waiting for his muscles to twang in rebellion against the classic yoga stance he hadn't tried in years. Given the fact that he was still in bed—and the seat of his pants dry—he had to assume the visitation had been a dream. But it had seemed so real! The "fish group"? Trout Unlimited, he thought. Audubon. Sierra Club. Raccoons Unlimited?

Damn, he thought. Claire had joked about fundraisers for Trout Unlimited, and he'd chimed in suggesting a rock-climbing wall. How did you make a dent in this administration? If, like a protesting Buddhist or the gay activist who had received no attention in the press, he poured gasoline over himself and set himself on fire, would Trump pee on him?

Claire came into the bedroom wrapped in a white towel, with another white towel turban wrapped around her hair. "I had the worst dream last night," she said. "I dreamt nothing was true. But then the dream wasn't true, so I decided I would just get up and take a shower."

"My dream may have been true, but it wasn't good, either."

"Sketchy results from you telling us to 'go to sleep and dream.'" She sat next to him.

"Interesting choice of words," Charles said, "from a woman who sketches."

"Tries to, yes. Wildflowers."

"We have to start somewhere," he said. "I'll make pancakes with maple syrup when Arnie and Laurel get up. We can talk about our dreams."

"I don't think Arnie will like that," Claire said.

"And yet," Charles said, "we're all going to have to keep sharing our lives when we take this trip."

ABOUT THE AUTHOR

Deb Davies enjoys writing mysteries about her favorite place: Michigan. She is passionate about rescued ani- mals and nature, and also enjoys classical music. She resides with her husband, Rick, in an old farmhouse and they summer in a cabin on a trout stream near Luzerne, Michigan. *Northern Light* is the debut novel in her Coast-to-Coast Michigan Mystery series.